THE PLAINSWALKER

M.A. ROTHMAN

Primordial Press

Cover Art by Allen Morris
Interior Art by Allen Morris

Paperback ISBN: 978-0-9976793-3-5

ALSO BY M.A. ROTHMAN

Technothrillers: (Thrillers with science / Hard-Science Fiction)

- Primordial Threat
- Freedom's Last Gasp

- Darwin's Cipher

Levi Yoder Thrillers:

- Perimeter
- The Inside Man
- Never Again

Epic Fantasy / Dystopian:

- Agent of Prophecy
- Heirs of Prophecy
- Tools of Prophecy
- Lords of Prophecy

- Running From Destiny
- The Code Breaker
- Dispocalypse

- The Plainswalker
- The Sage's Tower

This work was inspired by two people who never met each other, and couldn't have more different backgrounds.

Jerry Pournelle and Gary Gygax, thank you for entertaining and inspiring the next generations.

CONTENTS

Prologue	1
Chapter 1	5
Chapter 2	19
Chapter 3	31
Chapter 4	46
Chapter 5	57
Chapter 6	80
Chapter 7	96
Chapter 8	111
Chapter 9	132
Chapter 10	149
Chapter 11	167
Chapter 12	180
Chapter 13	203
Chapter 14	220
Chapter 15	231
Chapter 16	248
Chapter 17	262
Chapter 18	275
Chapter 19	287
Chapter 20	304
Preview of The Sage's Tower	318
Author's Note	331
Addendum	341
About the Author	365

Any sufficiently advanced technology is indistinguishable from magic.

—Arthur C. Clarke

INTERNATIONAL SCIENCE FOUNDATION
ISF 24/7: Computer Scientist-Cyber Division
Posting Type: Current Permanent Employee or Referral
Posting ID: PERME-A15293-1
Recruiting Location: WASHINGTON, DC
Department: D16-TECHNICAL OPERATIONS UNIT

Key Requirements:

- Must be a current permanent employee or referred by a current senior (GS-14+) member of the Cyber Division.
- Must be able to obtain a Top Secret security clearance.
- Must be between the ages of 23 and 36 years of age.
- Must meet all physical requirements.
- If currently active duty in the military, must be within 15 months of completing your service before submitting your application.

Major Duties:

The specific details will be discussed once hired, however the ideal candidate will have the following background:

- Familiarity with both black and white box testing.
- A self-starter with strong organizational skills and the ability to memorize complex instructions.

- Q-Course qualified, MCMAP black belt, or equivalent CQC experience, which can include civilian martial arts background at second dan or better.

PROLOGUE

In an isolated room fifty feet under Marine Base Quantico, Jolie lay back in what looked like a dentist's chair with an IV hooked up to her right arm and a rat's nest of wires trailing off of her. The monitoring devices beeped incessantly as a pair of nurses checked and double-checked the equipment's settings.

"Miss Lachance, your heart's racing at almost 130 beats per minute. Can you please try to relax?"

Jolie rolled her eyes. "You can't exactly blame me for being excited about this."

The nurse was covered from head to toe with sterile garb, but behind her face shield, Jolie saw the hints of a smile. "Honey, I understand. Under other circumstances, I'd give you a sedative—but I can't give you anything that might interfere with the serum's effectiveness. Just do me a favor and breathe deeply and slowly. I don't want you having a heart attack before we even start."

"Fine, I'll do what I can," Jolie said. But there was only so much she could do to calm herself. After all, she was about to make history.

A speaker in the ceiling crackled and a man's voice broadcast through the room. *"Launch Room Alpha, report in."*

The nurse picked up a red phone attached to the wall. "I've hung the serum and we're a go for launch."

The second nurse lowered a device from the ceiling that looked vaguely like a submarine's periscope. She eased the viewfinder against Jolie's forehead. "Focus on the flashing lights. It'll help the scanners synchronize with your brain signals and turn whatever you see over there into a coherent datagram for the computers to interpret."

Jolie looked into the viewfinder and heard a click. Soon a warm sensation was creeping up her arm and up into her neck. That must be the serum wending its way into her. As she watched the flashing green and red lights, the nurse's voice slowly faded, and then, so did the lights. Jolie lost all sense of her surroundings.

It was almost like… no, it was *exactly* like she was a disembodied mind in a dark room.

A faint voice echoed from somewhere around her. *"Lachance launched."*

The Watcher's sacred duty is to keep the secret of the Nameless One, keep watch over the plains, and when a plainswalker comes north, seek them out and lend whatever assistance they need.

Ivan was a Watcher. For thirty years he'd watched over the arid plains that bordered the great central forest, but only twice had he seen a plainswalker. Each time, it wasn't a true plainswalker, but a semi-transparent image of one. He'd followed each of the ghost-like apparitions as they headed north, away from their hidden home rumored to be somewhere on the southern coast of the island. Each plainswalker made a complete circuit of the island and returned to the south. Ivan had no idea why these apparitions had begun to show themselves in his grandfather's generation, but his place was not to ask such things. Only to follow and report on their whereabouts.

It had been at least ten years since his last plainswalker sighting.

A loud rumbling erupted from somewhere high above, and Ivan craned his neck to look up.

"What in the—"

A blinding bolt of white-hot light pierced the clouds and slammed into the grassy plains less than a mile away. The pillar of light released a keening wail, and the very ground began to tremble beneath his feet.

Then a billowing shimmer raced outward from the light, moving across the plains in all directions. The searing wind hit Ivan and blew him head over heels like he was a fallen leaf. He felt his hair curling up in the heat as the nonstop torrent blasted against him.

The world was on fire.

And then it stopped.

The light. The heat. The shrieking sound. They all vanished.

Leaving destruction in their wake, the plains were now a steaming expanse of sand, glass, and devastation.

All that had been… was now gone.

Ivan pushed himself to his feet, amazed that he hadn't broken anything. And as he looked across the desolate and burnt countryside, he spotted someone.

By some miracle, despite the devastation that had just occurred, there was someone walking north.

Ivan's mouth fell open with shock.

A plainswalker was heading straight for him. And this one was no apparition.

CHAPTER ONE

"Hey, Bo, how goes it?"

Peabo Smith rolled off the sofa and onto the floor, groaning and blinking the sleep from his eyes. "Um, who is this?"

"It's Nolan from the dojo. Is it too early to call?"

Peabo sat up, fumbling with his cell phone as he squinted at the digital clock on the cable box. It was eight a.m. and he'd gotten a whole two hours of sleep. "No, it's fine. I'm awake. What's up?"

"Well, I'm at work and just found out about an opportunity that might be up your alley. You still looking for a job?"

Peabo wracked his brain trying to remember what this guy did for a living, but came up with nothing. All he knew for sure was that he was another of the senior students at the dojo, like him.

"I've got some feelers out there, but I'm kind of up for anything at this point. Why, where do you work?"

"Well, it's a government position. You said you're ex-Special Forces?"

"Yup, and I'd probably still be in the Army if I hadn't gotten into a car accident and busted up my ankle."

"Yes, but that's obviously all healed now. You're degreed, right? You mentioned something about a dissertation. Do you have a master's?"

"Yes. After I got medically discharged from the Army I went back to Georgetown, got my master's in chemical engineering, and just finished up the research for my dissertation. Hopefully land the PhD in a couple months."

"Awesome. Well, I can't really say too much about what the job entails, but if you're okay with it, I'd like to file this referral with HR, which should generate an invite for you. This isn't something that anyone can just apply for. What's your email address?"

Peabo got a sense of wrongness about this kind gesture from a guy he barely knew, but he was also hungry to start up the income stream again. So he spelled out his email.

"Okay, sent. You should get something any second now. Hopefully it'll be self-explanatory."

"Nolan, I don't mean to sound ungrateful, but I'm wondering why—"

"Why I suddenly looked your name up on the dojo roster and called you out of the blue? What's my angle?"

Peabo chuckled and ran his fingers through his unruly mop of hair. "Well… yeah."

"Truthfully, I get five hundred bucks for a referral if you take the job. So I figured it couldn't hurt to poke you and see if

you're in the market. You mind just checking to see if you got an email yet?"

"Hang on." Peabo grabbed his laptop, set it on his lap, and pulled up his email. "Yep, just got something. You work for the International Science Foundation?"

"Give or take," Nolan said with an airy tone. *"Do you live in Arlington?"*

"Yeah, why?"

"That'll give you a pretty good bump in locality pay. I'm telling you, this is a pretty sweet offering for someone just finishing out their degree, if you can get it."

Peabo scanned the email. It looked like a job application for a computer scientist, but some of the requirements were… unexpected.

"Nolan, why does a computer job need someone with martial arts or Special Forces experience?"

"Oh, they always list stuff on these things that's meaningless. Like I said, I can't say much about what I do, but I can tell you that the biggest fight I got into in the last three years working here was with the copy machine. Don't worry about it. You're a third dan black belt and I figure you're testing for your fourth stripe soon enough. That, plus your Special Forces background will be more than enough to impress these pasty-faced types I work with."

Nolan laughed, but to Peabo it sounded fake, and his Spidey senses tingled. Then again, he couldn't exactly afford to be picky. Everything was so damned expensive around here, even for a guy living in a crappy one-bedroom apartment. The

GI Bill and his savings would only last so long before he'd have to make some drastic life decisions.

"Okay, I guess I'll fill this out and send it off today."

"Cool. Well, I've got to catch a meeting. I hope things work out, I really do. Talk at you later."

Peabo shook his head as Nolan hung up. "Yup, you have five hundred reasons to hope it works out."

Still, a job was a job.

His mind drifted back to the odd requirements. Martial arts. Special Forces. After his medical discharge, he knew he'd never get to be on an A-team again. But who knew—maybe this was a sneak path into a position that could get him back into some kind of action.

That would be too good to be true.

Nothing ventured, nothing gained. Peabo pulled up the online application and began filling it out.

In a location nearly one hundred feet directly beneath the White House, a man shook his head. "She's dead?"

"I'm afraid so," said Jerry, the lab director, though the furrow between his eyebrows was the only outward sign of frustration at the experiment having gone awry.

The man didn't care for Jerry's seeming lack of concern. "Jerry, I've *promised* headway on this during the current administration's tenure. And I don't need to remind you that STAG's black bag operations cannot stay hidden without the cooperation of the Executive Branch. You were all giddy during the operation—so what happened?"

Jerry raked his fingers through his thick, graying hair. "Honestly, we're not yet sure. She had a normal medical screening before we started, and there weren't any signs of heart problems—"

The man cut him off. "And yet she's dead." He slid the photo of the dead engineer across the table toward Jerry. Feeling his impatience rising, he growled. "Did we get anything? Anything at all?"

"We got confirmation of arrival," the lab director said eagerly. "The serum worked just fine, we got some images of the target, though none of the memories stuck where they should. And since she coded on the way back, we couldn't get much out of her other than what was transmitted. Turned out she had the memory retention of a gnat."

"I don't understand. What difference does that make?"

"The serum works on certain parts of the brain, like the prefrontal cortex. It allows us to get a working stream of data out of the subject, pulling key memories and visual-spatial awareness out of various parts of the brain. Basically, as our gal sees the stuff, we can pick up the signals in a way that we can interpret. But if your memory is somehow impaired, or, as in this case, if it just generally sucks, the serum's effectiveness is reduced."

"So what's your plan for round two?"

"We have another test engineer currently being put through memory training. But we're also doubling up for this round. I want to stagger two test subjects, one after the other, so I've already put feelers out for another test engineer while we make more of the serum."

"And how long before the new tests start?"

"Um... two months," Jerry said sheepishly. "We're trying to speed up the process up for creating the serum, but... that's where we're at."

The man took a deep breath and let it out slowly, trying hard not to let his anger take over. Throwing Jerry to the wolves would be premature. So much had been invested in this, and none of them would get another chance if this failed. Round two *had* to work.

"You've got two months," he said at last. "But make sure these test subjects have working tickers this time. The suits upstairs aren't going to tolerate any more delays, you understand? We need proof that this stuff is real. No more failures, Jerry. Am I understood?"

Jerry nodded. "Understood."

Six Weeks Later

Peabo showed his new ISF badge to the corporal at the entrance to Marine Base Quantico, and the marine waved him through. It took him another fifteen minutes to drive through the giant base, following the printed instructions he'd been given at his recruiting station in DC. He passed two other checkpoints and countless turns before parking in front of an unmarked concrete building. The lot had room for maybe a hundred cars, but his was one of only four present, and there wasn't another soul in sight.

He swiped his badge at the building's unmanned entrance, and the metal door lowered into the ground. Peabo stepped across the threshold, and the door immediately sprang up and shut with a loud metallic clang.

A set of blinding lights beamed directly onto him.

"Mr. Smith, welcome to STAG."

STAG was shorthand for the Special Technologies Analysis Group. It was one of the few facts Peabo had been told prior to accepting the position, and it didn't really explain anything. He was also told that STAG was a division of the ISF that worked with cutting-edge technology, but they couldn't share much about it until he handed in his SF86 forms, which were the papers he needed to fill out to get his security clearance straightened out. It was pretty clear that whatever it was they did here, it was covert stuff that no civilians were ever supposed to know about.

"Please step forward and place your feet onto the red tiles located in front of the inner door. Look straight ahead with your arms at your sides."

Peabo did as the disembodied voice instructed. A green light flashed into his eyes, and several clicks sounded from somewhere nearby. He felt a sudden change in air pressure, and his ears popped.

"Identity confirmed. Do you have your paperwork filled out as instructed?"

Peabo held up the folder that contained his completed SF86 forms. "Yes."

The metal door lowered before him, revealing a middle-aged woman on the other side. She was attractive, raven-haired, and wore an exotic perfume that lingered in the air as she motioned him forward and held out her hand.

"Your paperwork, please."

Peabo stepped through the doorway into a lobby, and just as before, the door behind him whooshed upward. As he handed over his forms, he glanced back at the door nervously. It had to weigh hundreds of pounds.

"Anyone ever get squished by the overzealous hydraulics attached to that thing?"

The woman chuckled as she beckoned him forward. "Don't worry, those doors all have sensors. It's startling at first, but trust me, you get used to it. And they definitely help enforce the no-tailgating rule, which I'm sure they went over with you during your security briefing. One person through a badged-in entrance at a time."

She spoke with a slight New York accent, but not the kind Peabo remembered hearing on the streets. Hers had a posh sound to it, the kind he imagined belonged on Park Avenue. The sound of her heels clicked rapidly on the marble floor, and he fast-walked to catch up to her.

"Ma'am, do you have any idea how long it'll be before I'm told what I'll be doing?"

"It's not *ma'am*, it's Susan. And to answer your question… it varies."

She led him into a brightly-lit hallway dotted with closed

office doors. A sign up ahead read CLASSROOMS and had an arrow pointing to the right.

"I know you've been brought in for one of the test-engineer slots, but seeing as your forms have been given a high priority, I'm guessing it might be a project that I don't have clearance for. These forms sometimes take months to process, especially for Top Secret clearances, but when the intel guys get a fire lit under their butts, stuff can happen quickly. Either way, I wouldn't worry too much about it. You've got some specialized training ahead of you that you'll need to finish before you can even begin your assignment."

She stopped at the open door of a small classroom with a dozen chairs and a projector hanging from the ceiling projecting the word "STAG" on the white wall.

"Grab a seat and relax," she said. "I'll send in the instructor as soon as he arrives."

Before she could leave, Peabo asked, "Is there a supply cabinet where I can get a pencil and notebook or something? I was told to bring nothing into work, that I'd be given everything I need."

The woman tilted her head and stared at him for a few seconds before saying, "You won't need anything for this type of class."

As she walked away, Peabo couldn't help but wonder: *What the hell kind of classroom training doesn't need me to take notes?*

Peabo stared at the clock on the wall as the minutes ticked by. The woman had given no indication of how long it would be before the instructor arrived, but just before nine a.m., he began to hear the sounds of people walking along the corridor. The place was slowly waking up.

Then the classroom door swung open and a middle-aged man in glasses and a lab coat walked in. He plopped himself on top of the desk at the front of the room, shifted slightly so he was facing Peabo, and gave him a warm smile.

"Good morning, Mr. Smith. I'm sure you have a bunch of questions. But instead of asking them, let's dive into a visualization exercise. Okay?"

Peabo wasn't sure what that even meant, but he agreed. "Sure."

"Great. I want you to close your eyes and think of your childhood home. Don't worry if you lived in several places, just pick the one you remember the best. Imagine you're standing outside, in front of it. Do you have that image in your head?"

Peabo closed his eyes and nodded. "I do."

"This next part might sound strange, but eventually you'll see why I'm doing this. Imagine a bunch of naked people on oversized versions of those Big Wheels we used to ride around as kids."

With an uncomfortable smile, Peabo recalled some of the memories he had from the one time he'd ever visited a nude beach. It wasn't a pretty sight.

"Now imagine that these naked people are riding past you. Sweaty. Jiggling. Lots of grunting as they go by. They ride right up to your home, and instead of stopping, they crash into the door, and bodies are flung in every direction. Broken parts of the Big Wheels come rolling back toward you.

"You weave your way past the awkward scene and step into your home. You pause, appreciating the sunlight streaming in, and you notice that it's shining down onto Big Bird. Yes, the same one from *Sesame Street.* I'm sure you're familiar with him.

"The big bright yellow bird from *Sesame Street* waves at you from his perch on an enormous tan horse. Your nose tickles a bit as if you accidentally inhale one of his downy yellow feathers."

Peabo shook his head as he wondered what in the world kind of training this was.

"The inside of your home smells a bit like the horse as you walk into the kitchen, where you find the Swedish chef from the Muppets. He says a string of gobbledygook as he rapidly chops vegetables, which fly in every direction.

"You turn and walk into the living room, and there you find Madonna writhing around on your coffee table singing 'Like A Virgin.' And then you open your eyes.

"Go ahead, open your eyes."

Peabo opened his eyes and saw that the instructor was now pacing back and forth at the front of the classroom.

"Mr. Smith, have you ever seen those people who can stare at a deck of cards, spread out face up, or maybe several decks of cards, and after just a few minutes they can recite, in order, the layout of all of them? Or maybe they can do the same trick with hundreds of phone numbers, or people's names. Ever seen people perform those feats on TV?"

"Sure." There were plenty of times Peabo had wished he could do that kind of stuff when he was studying for tests.

The instructor pulled up a chair, turned it around, and sat facing Peabo. "Would it surprise you to hear that these people weren't savants? Most of the people who can do those things have average intellect as well as average memories. They've simply trained themselves through techniques that I'll teach you. And these aren't new techniques, either; this is stuff that the ancient Greeks used to do all the time. Thousands of years ago, we didn't have near-instant access to the world's knowledge, so it was much more common to exercise the memory in ways that might seem unnecessary now.

"I'll give you an example: do you remember the phone number for the home you grew up in?"

Peabo nodded.

"Okay, but I'd wager that you don't remember most, if any, of the numbers you dial frequently today. Am I right?"

Peabo smiled and nodded. The guy was right. There was a local Chinese restaurant that he called every week, but he'd never needed to memorize their number—it was programmed into his phone.

"Think about it," said the instructor. "Over the years, we've made it very easy for us humans to offload our memories to outside devices. Whether it's papyrus scrolls, books, photos, computers, or smartphones, we created ways of storing our memories so that they'll never be lost—as long as we don't lose the storage device. But before such advances, people had no choice but to remember things… or lose them forever.

"And there's a tradeoff. We now lean so heavily on technology, we've stopped training ourselves to remember things. To have the facts right there"—he snapped his fingers—"whenever you need them."

He drummed his fingers on the back of the chair. "Mr. Smith, what I'm going to teach you to do is something that's already part of our human toolbox. It's just a tool that we rarely use. And when we're done, the way you remember things will have changed. We're going to leverage the parts of your brain associated with spatial and visual recognition, and turn those parts into an assistant of sorts—an assistant that will help you remember things like our ancient ancestors used to.

"I could talk at length about the science behind the technique, going in-depth on the topic of elaborative encoding, but instead, let's talk about something more practical: something called the baker/Baker paradox. It goes like this.

"Imagine I walk up to a person and tell them, 'Please remember that there is someone named Baker.' And then I go to another person, to whom I say, 'Please remember that there is a person who is a baker.' Now, imagine I come back to these same people some time later and ask them each to recall what I said to them. It is much more likely that the second person—the one who was told about a man who *is* a baker—would remember that fact than it is that the first person—the one who was told about someone with the *name* of Baker—would remember. Do you have any theories as to why that might be?"

Peabo pondered the question for a moment. "Well, when

you said the guy was a baker, I suppose I had a visual of some guy with a chef's hat or something, whereas some guy named Baker gave me no such image or connection."

The instructor smiled. "Exactly right. The name 'Baker' is just a bit of data bouncing around in your head, but the *concept* of *a baker* has a bunch of potential cognitive connections it can make. You might remember the smell of freshly baked bread, funny white hats, flour everywhere. All of those things, those details, images, connections… they help you in recalling that random piece of data you were asked to remember."

Peabo nodded. It made sense.

"In general," continued the instructor, "humans are not good at remembering random facts and figures. But we have *exceptional* visual and spatial memories. For example, if I asked you to repeat the first ten words that I spoke to you upon entering the classroom, you'd probably have a hard time of it. But what if I asked you who was riding on the horse?"

Peabo smiled at the image that popped into his mind's eye. "Big Bird. And it was a tan horse."

The instructor grinned. "And now, the lesson begins."

CHAPTER TWO

Peabo walked into the conference room, paused as he realized someone had gotten there before him, and smiled at the familiar face at the table. "Hey, Nolan. Did you get your five hundred bucks?"

Nolan laughed as Peabo took a seat. "Are you kidding me? When you owe the government, you damn well better pay on time; if they owe you, well, they *will* pay you, but on their own schedule. At least they *acknowledged* that they owed me something. I got an email saying that Peabo Smith had started his probationary period. Speaking of which, I didn't know your name was Peabo. That's a pretty cool name."

"I suppose, but no one calls me that—just Bo. And yes, my dad was a huge fan of the singer." Peabo immediately regretted mentioning his father. He'd died only a year ago in a car accident, and it still tore him up inside. "So, are you here for the same briefing I am?"

Nolan shrugged. "No idea. This meeting just landed on my calendar, and here I am."

At that moment a gray-haired man entered the room. He wore a lab coat, but underneath was an expensive suit, and Peabo got the impression this was no ordinary lab tech. The man closed the door behind him, then pressed a button on a handheld remote. The lock clicked, and there was a sudden change in air pressure. He then took a seat at the table and nodded to both Nolan and Peabo.

"Mr. Tomlinson, Mr. Smith, I'm Jerry Callaway, Director of STAG. I'm the guy who's going to brief you on the basics of your assignment."

Peabo leaned forward. "Does this mean I received my clearances?"

"Yes. You were cleared as of last night, which allows me to brief you both at the same time. In fact, you two are going to be working as a team. One backing up the other. But before I continue…"

He pulled an index card from his suit jacket and began reading from it. "I am formally informing you that both audio and visual recordings are being made of whatever transpires in this room. The data I'm about to divulge is classified in nature and you are obligated to keep all that is said in this room in confidence. Violating such confidence will result in immediate termination and federal prosecution."

He looked up from the card. "Do you both understand what I've said and realize that violating this confidence may subject you to many years in federal prison?"

"I understand," Peabo and Nolan said at the same time.

Callaway nodded. “I need you two to realize that I’m reading you into a highly classified government project. You aren’t allowed to discuss any details or even the *existence* of this project with anyone outside of a controlled list of other read-in members. You will be provided with a secure USB key that, coupled with a biometric verification, will give you access to secure facilities on this site. Only in these SCIFs will you—”

“Um, sir?” Nolan lifted his hand. “Just to be sure we’re all on the same page, can you go over what a skiff is?”

Without missing a beat, the director said, “Sensitive Compartmented Information Facility. S-C-I-F. Just think of it as a secured facility for classified material. In the SCIF you’ll have access to the identification of the other read-in members and other material that you’ll be given clear instructions on how to handle. No information from a SCIF leaves that room—ever.

“Now, I’m sure you guys are wondering what you’ll be doing. To begin with, I need to give you a bit of background. STAG works on cutting-edge research in a variety of fields; some of what our researchers work on would seem like total science fiction to the public. The project you two have been recruited to help us on is one of the most cutting-edge projects we have, and its goals are the loftiest ones we’ve ever set. We believe it will revolutionize how humanity looks at the universe.”

“The universe?” Nolan said skeptically.

“Yes, Mr. Tomlinson, the universe. I’m sure you’ve both heard of the concept of the multiverse? Universes other than our own. And unless your hobby is researching highly speculative scientific topics, you've probably never heard of brane cosmology." The director held up his hand as Peabo was about to ask a question. "And no, I'm not talking about the human brain, but brane as derived from the word membrane. Give me a second and I'll explain. This topic of brane cosmology just so happens to be an area STAG is heavily focused on. To be honest, a couple of years ago, I wouldn't have thought it possible, but…"

He must have seen the confused looks on the men's faces, as he paused.

"Think of it this way." The director held up both hands with the palms facing each other. There was only a hair's breadth separating them. "Imagine my left hand is our universe and my right hand is some other universe whose reality we're not even sure of. Each universe is like a bubble, with just a tiny membrane separating the two realities. They're infinitely close, and yet they might as well be infinitely far apart. Until now. We've come up with something that will allow us to pierce the veil between these two universes. Just image having our consciousness travel to another dimension, another world, and then come back."

He slid a folder across the table. "Here. Take a look."

Peabo opened the manila folder and set it between him and Nolan. Inside were several grainy photographs, low-resolution images of some arid wasteland.

"What you're looking at," said Callaway, "is a place that none of us could see even with our most powerful telescopes. That"—he gestured to the photograph Peabo had just flipped to —"is a planet from a completely different universe. It doesn't exist in our view of reality. And yet there it is. It's a planet that seems to have breathable air. It's just a bit cooler than this room is right now, and we detected the scent of burning wood."

Peabo knew he should probably be in read-only mode, especially in front of the guy who could probably get him insta-fired, but he had to ask.

"I don't get it, sir. Are you saying this is from a different universe? And yet… you're describing smells. Temperature readings. Does that mean someone's *been* there?"

"All good questions," said Callaway. "Yes, this is a different universe… and yes, someone's been there… in a way. We didn't take a rocket, if that's what you're thinking. Didn't need to. As I said, this other universe is infinitely close. It's like going from one side of a coin to the flip side; it's a short route, you just have to find a way to drill through. And that's what we did. However, we haven't yet found a way to send anything physical through that hole. Thus far we've only been able to send a digitized stream of data—a consciousness, if you will—from here to there.

"Which explains how we got the sorts of data we did—smells and the like. We transmitted the equivalent of a lab rat consciousness across, maintained a connection to it, and got some data back from the other side."

Peabo looked again at the grainy photos. "And this is what the rat saw?"

Callaway nodded. "Yes. But remember, we didn't physically transport anything across. This photo, in essence, represents what the mind perceived across the tunnel between our universes."

Peabo's own mind was reeling. He tried to make sense of it all. "It's like… it's like pointing a laser into a black hole. You know that the light will get warped and twisted, but it *will* survive the transition past the event horizon. It'll just never get back out again." He looked up at the director. "But you've figured out how to get the data back out."

Callaway gave him a thoughtful look. "Peabo, you don't know how close you are to the truth of it. Yes, we've managed to crack the problem of getting a signal back. No black holes involved, of course."

Nolan looked up from the pictures. "So is that what we're supposed to do? You want to send our *minds* to this other universe?"

The director smiled. "In a word: yes."

Peabo was about to speak, but Callaway held up a hand.

"It's not as crazy as it sounds," he said. "You guys won't actually go anywhere—you'll remain safe and sound in the launch room. Only your conscious mind will connect to the remote location. If you've ever seen the movie *Avatar*, it's a lot like that. You'll see and hear and smell all sorts of things as your consciousness is transported to another place. It won't be like Neil Armstrong setting foot on the moon—your feet will never leave Earth—but it'll be much more historic. You two can be the first people, in mind if not in body, to enter another *universe*."

It was a lot to take in, and Peabo had a lot of questions. But one was first and foremost.

"Why us?" he said. "In particular, what's with wanting a couple of guys with martial arts experience?"

The director nodded. "Brilliant question. When we did our first experiment, all we expected was to get a remote viewing of a foreign place—like a TV camera peeking into Narnia or Oz. But when the consciousness arrived at its destination, it became clear that the mind sent across had taken on some form of… well, a body. We can't explain it—for all we know, our laws of physics may not work the same way in that place—but the energy we sent through the connection instantly triggered some physical manifestation. Almost like an ROV."

An ROV was a remotely operated vehicle. Peabo had used them when surveilling abandoned buildings back in his Army days. Quite different from remote-controlling a body in a different universe.

The director continued. "Currently, we can only maintain the connection for a short time, but eventually, we hope to make these trips last longer, so we can do a bit of exploration. And since we have no idea what's out there… well, just as a precaution, it stands to reason that we might want you to be able to defend yourself. Just in case.

"That's also one of the reasons why we're sending you both at the same time. So you'll have each other's backs. But also so we'll have two different points of view, so you can see each other. Even if all you're able to do is look at each other and figure out what's going on with these so-called bodies… that alone could be incredibly valuable."

"And if our bodies are just floating blobs of energy?" Nolan asked.

"Then we'll have learned *that*," said Callaway. "We're exploring an unknown frontier here, gentlemen. We just don't know what to expect. Which is why it's best to be prepared for any eventuality."

"When are we supposed to go?" Peabo asked. He'd been hoping that this project would be a way back into some type of action, but this wasn't the kind of action he'd anticipated. He wasn't sure if what he was feeling was excitement or nausea.

"Soon. We're just waiting for the arrival of the transmission serum. The serum externalizes your brain's signals into a data stream that we can then monitor during your exploration phase. But it's probably better if I have the scientists explain. In fact, I'm sure you two have tons of questions, and you'll come up with lots more once this all sinks in, so I've arranged for you to have plenty of time to talk to the project leads."

He leaned back and smiled proudly. "Gentlemen, I can't emphasize enough how key your roles are in this project. I'm not joking when I say this is bigger than Neil Armstrong and Buzz Aldrin's little trip to the moon's surface. And if I'm being quite honest… I'm a bit envious of you both." The director paused, staring at nothing in particular, and then chuckled. "I really wish I could go with you… but maybe in one of our future missions."

Without waiting for more questions, the director stood and pressed the button on his handheld remote. There was a whoosh of air as the pressure adjusted, then he gathered up the photos, shook both of their hands, and was out the door.

Peabo turned to Nolan. "Well? What do you think?"

Nolan laughed nervously. "Oh, it's no big deal, right? I mean, going to another universe can't be worse than going to some parts of DC after dark. Plus, bonus: there's a chance we'll have to fight aliens with eight arms and three heads with nothing but our bare fists."

His new partner held up his fists, showing his scarred knuckles that had seen many a fight. Being in the same dojo, he'd sparred with the guy dozens of times and knew just how tough he was. Even though Nolan had lost half of his pinkie on his right hand in a wood shop accident, it didn't affect his ability to brawl. He stared at Nolan with the typical cauliflower ears of someone who'd been wrestling for years and knew that he'd be a great guy to have on his six in this world, but in that world… did any of this really matter?

Nolan drummed his fingers on the conference room table and shook his head. "I didn't think the movie *Men in Black* was real, but now I'm starting to wonder. I think we might be working for the same government organization those guys did."

Peabo smiled. "Well, I always fancied myself a Will Smith type."

"You wish. Apart from both of you being black, there's no resemblance whatsoever, my friend. For one thing, the man's good-looking, and you… well, you're no Will Smith. Sorry, Bo. Looks like I'll have to take on that role."

Peabo laughed. "Gee, thanks. So, you've seen *Men in Black*. Have you seen *Avatar*?"

Nolan shook his head. "Nope."

"Then we should rent it. It's actually pretty cool."

"No need to rent it," said a voice from the doorway. Peabo turned to see a short man in a lab coat standing there. "We have it on site. It's a staff favorite." He held out a hand. "Nice to meet you both. I'm Ed Baker, one of the project leads. Let's get you guys to the SCIF. We've got a lot to talk about."

From the day Peabo had been made aware of the details of his assignment, he'd begun having dreams about the place he was about to visit. The tension he felt was just like what he felt before a mission when he was in the Special Forces, and in many ways, the preparation was similar as well. Except that instead of being given satellite reconnaissance photos of the target to study, he'd been given grainy images of an arid land.

Now, a mere two days later, he was in an isolated room fifty feet under Marine Base Quantico.

Launch Room Beta.

He lay back in what looked like a dentist's chair, with an IV hooked up to his arm and wires trailing off of him. The light in here was intense, so much so that he had to squint to even see all the monitoring equipment packed in around him. A nurse gave him a warm smile as she hooked a bag of yellow fluid to his IV. Another nurse stood nearby, fiddling with the equipment.

A speaker in the ceiling crackled, and a man's voice spoke. *"Tomlinson is now at ready-stage. Launch Room Beta, report in."*

One of the nurses picked up a red phone on the wall and said, "We're go for launch."

She then lowered a periscope-like device from the ceiling and pressed a viewfinder against Peabo's eyes. "Pay attention to the flashing lights," she said. "It'll help the scanners synchronize with your brain signals, and once the serum is in you, it'll help turn whatever you see over there into a coherent stream of data for the computers to interpret."

As Peabo looked into the viewfinder, he felt warmth creeping up his arm and up into his neck. The serum. As the world around him faded, he heard the man's voice come over the speaker again.

"Tomlinson launched."

Then everything faded to black. Peabo felt as though he were immersed in a sensory deprivation tank, a disembodied mind.

"Smith launched."

And then he was rocked by the sound of rolling thunder. It was so loud, he felt the vibrations in his chest.

He fell to his knees, and then to all fours, feeling sand crunch between his fingers. An overwhelming nausea washed over him, and it was all he could do to fight it back down.

Slowly, the roaring in his ears subsided. It was only then that he realized that his eyes were squeezed tightly shut.

He opened them.

And gasped at what he saw.

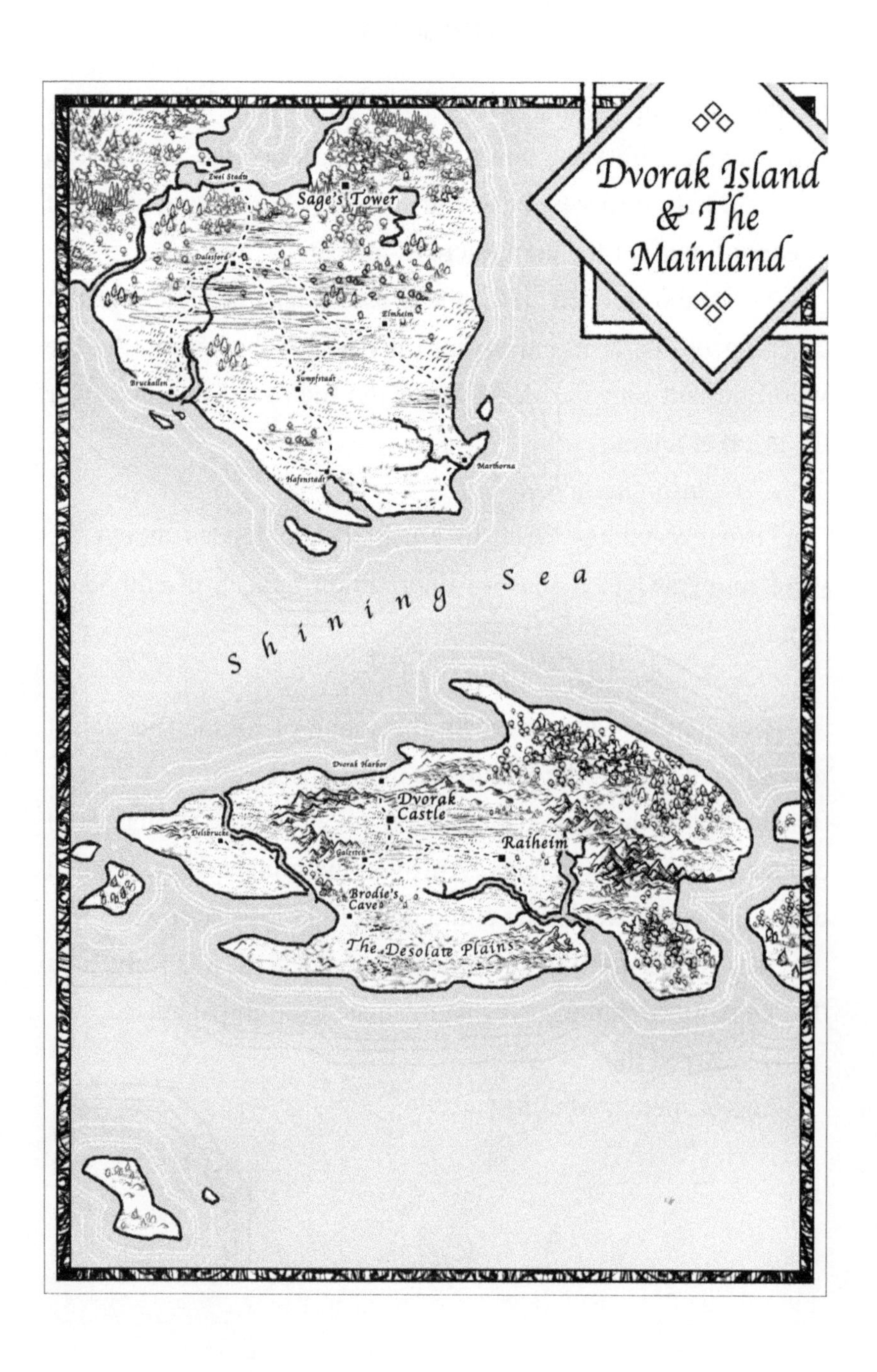
Dvorak Island
& The
Mainland
Zwei Stadte
Sage's Tower
Dalesford
Elmheim
Bruckallen
Sumpfstadt
Marthorna
Hafenstadt
Shining Sea
Dvorak Harbor
Dvorak
Castle
Delsbrucke
Raiheim
Brodie's
Cave
The Desolate Plains

CHAPTER THREE

"Here you go, sir." A grizzled old bartender placed a large mug of dark ale on the counter in front of Brodie. "That'll be two silver royals."

The short man plopped down his payment, sipped at the sudsy drink and grimaced at the sour, watered-down taste of the aboveworlder drink.

"Good stuff, isn't it?"

Brodie tossed the barkeep a thumbs-up and silently cursed the brewmaster who'd concocted the ale and his entire ancestry that preceded him.

As the bartender wandered away, one of the nearby patrons at the bar leaned over and spoke under his breath, "You're being really kind to that old man by not calling his stuff the mule vomit that it is. I've been drinking his brew all my life, and I know you Myrkheimers are used to much better."

Brodie turned his gaze to the middle-aged farmer who'd

just drained his mug and slammed it back onto the counter. “You’ve been to Myrkheim?”

The farmer let out a wet burp and shook his head. “No, not all the way there. I was never the adventuring type, I just did some trading on occasion in Metamorphic.” The man's gaze seemed to lose focus as he smiled about another time and place. “Aye, that was some glorious brew I remember having there. I’ve never had the like since.” He focused again on Brodie. “You up here for the festival or to trade?”

Brodie was about to respond when the entrance to the bar slammed open and a tall, barrel-chested man yelled, “Whose damned forest pony is that outside?”

“He’s mine, friend.” Brodie yelled back and hopped off his stool. “What’s the matter?”

The man sported a guild medallion on his chest, a member of the fighter’s guild, and someone who was used to getting the respect due to someone of his rank. But as he glared down at the approaching dwarf, an expression of uncertainty bloomed on his face. “As I walked past your damned pony it licked half of the grease paint off my face. I was going to—”

“You were going to what?" Brodie growled ominously. "Dress up and pretend to be something you’re not?” Despite the difference in height, Brodie stood toe-to-toe with the behemoth and grinned up at the man who’d drawn a series of black lines across his face and chest.

“Hah!” One of the patrons yelled from across the bar. “He looks like a plainswalker that’s melting.”

The fighter grimaced and yelled back, “Shut up, farmer boy.” He turned his gaze back to Brodie, who’d pulled his own guild medallion out from under his tunic. The man did a double-take as he looked at the dwarf's medallion, and took a step back.

Brodie stepped closer and gave the large man a broad smile. "Friend, you were saying something about my pony?"

The man took a deep breath and shook his head. "I'm sorry. It was my mistake." The behemoth turned and raced out of the building.

The farmer who'd been talking to him at the bar walked up to Brodie and laughed. "You sure took the wind out of his sails." He looked down at Brodie, noticed the medallion and his eyes widened. "Oh my. No wonder he looked like the Nameless One had just chased him out of here."

Brodie tucked the medallion back under his tunic when the world flashed with a white brilliance that temporarily blinded him.

He felt a tremor building in his chest. A wave of nausea hit him just like last time. But last time was nearly thirty years ago, and he'd convinced himself it wouldn't happened again. The queasy feeling grew within the pit of his stomach as the world seemed to rock back and forth.

And then suddenly, everything flashed back into existence.

The farmer looked at Brodie with an odd expression. "Sir, are you okay? You were looking a bit unsteady on your feet for a second."

Brodie's heart raced and he knew that nobody else had seen or heard what he'd just felt. "It's happened again."

With a furrowed brow, the farmer said, "What happened again?"

"Nothing." Brodie raced out of the building as if the Nameless One were in fact chasing him.

Peabo was looking upon a world that had been wiped clean of all life. All around him was a desolate gray plain. It looked like it had been blasted with a blowtorch. Everything had an otherworldly look, almost as if he'd landed on the moon.

He pulled in a deep breath, filling his lungs with cool air, and pushed himself to his knees. He looked at his hands, his arms, the clothes he wore, if that's what they were…

"How is this possible?" he wondered aloud. His voice sounded unusually deep and gravelly to his own ears.

His mind raced. This was supposed to be some sort of visit via a remote link—but there was nothing about this that felt remote. He was most definitely *here*. And in a body that most definitely wasn't his. He had two arms and two legs—he was basically humanlike, much to his relief—but his skin color was unlike anything he'd ever seen. Like stained oak, it had a base of brown with dark striations. The markings were random, almost like a lightning pattern of tattoos, but all over his body. And as he examined himself, he realized he was built like a tank. He now had a powerlifter's build, with much of his bulk gathered in massive thighs and an overly broad chest.

He rose to his feet, feeling very off-balance, and scanned the area for Nolan. He'd heard the announcement over the speaker back in Launch Room Beta—he knew his friend had "launched" before him. And then he saw someone approaching in the distance.

With a sigh of relief, he began walking and then jogging toward the figure. And as he drew closer, the first thing he noticed was that the figure wasn't on foot—he was on a horse.

The second thing he noticed was that the figure *wasn't* Nolan.

Peabo stopped right where he was. If he really was in another world… was he now the first human to spot alien life? Confirm once and for all that there was more than just us in this universe—well, any universe?

Whoever this unknown rider was, they dismounted and jogged toward him. It was a man, bearded and short—maybe four feet tall. His clothes looked to be made of some sort of leather and cloth, sewn together with skill. They fit him well, and as Peabo glanced down at his own body, he found that the clothes he was wearing were similar.

The strange man uttered a stream of harsh guttural noises that sounded more like clicks and growls than any language Peabo had ever heard before—and yet Peabo understood them. His ears heard the odd vocalizations, but in his mind he heard, "He said you'd come. And you have come."

Peabo looked past the man to the horse, which, like the man, was too small. As he watched, the horse flicked a long tongue at some invisible annoyance with a whip-like crack.

Peabo took a step back. *A miniature horse with a frog-like tongue.* Either this was a hallucination induced by whatever drug they'd pumped him full of… or he really was in another universe.

And he wasn't alone.

He focused on the man in front of him. *He said you'd come*. That was what the man had said. Did the "he" in that sentence refer to Nolan?

"Did Nolan send you?" Peabo asked in English.

The man tilted his head and frowned. Then he spoke in English as well, though it was very halting and hard to understand. "I and I go. Must go I with I." He pointed back toward his horse, or whatever that thing was, then looked back at Peabo and spoke in the harsher, inhuman language. "Follow me. I'll hide you from the Seekers. You understand me, right?"

Again, though the language was alien, Peabo's mind told him its meaning. He nodded.

The tiny man hopped nimbly onto his steed and began riding back in the direction from which he'd come. He didn't even look back to see if Peabo was following. And Peabo wondered if he even should. Could this stranger be trusted? How could it be possible for Nolan to have met this guy already? They'd left only seconds apart.

Peabo panned his gaze across the horizon and saw nothing. Where was Nolan? They were supposed to have each other's backs.

"The mission won't last longer than five minutes. We don't have the energy capacity to sustain the connection for any longer."

The scientists had made it very clear. It was a quick in-and-out, and he'd already eaten up at least two minutes just getting his feet under him and talking with the tiny man.

The man who was likely Peabo's only chance of finding Nolan. His only lifeline.

Making up his mind, Peabo followed at a jog. He tried keeping track of the elapsed time in his head.

Three minutes.

Despite traveling on foot while the man rode a horse, Peabo had no trouble keeping up. This new body of his seemed to have speed and stamina to spare. He caught up and ran alongside his escort, knowing that this was about all he was going to see of this world.

Four minutes.

The horse put on a burst of speed, and Peabo pushed to keep up. And somehow, he did. It was amazing—even though this body was built like a defensive lineman, he was running like a gazelle. It was exhilarating.

Five minutes.

That was it. Any second now he'd wake up in the underground lab.

And yet he didn't. Another thirty seconds elapsed. Still nothing. Maybe he was off on his calculations? But when his mental clock ticked over to seven minutes, he knew that wasn't it. And that's when he began to worry. *Why am I not going back?*

At around the ten-minute mark, the arid landscape gave way to something green—a forest of giant pines. The shift was abrupt, as if a line had been drawn between forest and plain. At least the trees looked familiar. Peabo was no botanist, but they sure looked like pine trees, just like the ones he knew from back home. He smiled as the familiar scent greeted him.

As the little man approached the trees, the one directly in front of him—it had to be a good eighty feet tall—shuddered, and its mass of thick roots ripped themselves out of the soil. The *entire tree* shifted two paces to the right, uncovering a dark cave entrance—and then the roots grasped at the dirt and buried themselves back into the soil once more.

Peabo stopped dead in his tracks. "How…?"

The man dismounted and gave his horse a slap. It grunted and raced into the forest. "Hide first," said the stranger. "*Then* questions."

The man's demand pushed aside Peabo's worry about the time that had elapsed—and replaced it with a new one. A wave of suspicion washed over him.

"Before I go any further, tell me where Nolan is," he said.

The little man paused, as if uncertain. Then he beckoned. "I will take you to him." He clearly understood English.

Instead of leading Peabo into the cave, the little man set off along a path that wound through the woods. Peabo followed. And as he walked, he felt as though everything, literally everything, was watching him. The very forest bristled with motion.

The stranger stopped in front of a mound of fist-sized rocks and pointed at it. "My friend, he is now gone."

Peabo felt the blood drain from his face. "Are you saying Nolan's dead? How's that even… how long ago?"

The tiny man shrugged. "Almost thirty turns of the seasons he is gone. But he said you would come, and you have come."

An ear-splitting squawk erupted from somewhere above, and the man's eyes widened. "Seekers are coming. Come. Hide."

Peabo stared for a few long seconds at the mound, his mind racing. Thirty turns of the season? Thirty *years*? Impossible. *All* of this was impossible.

The squawk erupted again, louder than before.

"Hurry!" said the little man, and began racing back the way they'd come.

Peabo hustled after him, and together they ducked into the cave. Behind him he heard the giant tree uprooting itself, and then the light coming through the cave's entrance dimmed.

One thing was clear: wherever Peabo was, he wasn't going back out in that direction.

The tunnel sloped down, and the little man scrambled ahead of Peabo at a rapid pace. Peabo found that it took only seconds for his new body's eyes to adjust to the darkness—which was far less dark than he had anticipated. It seemed that every surface had a faint glow, and to his surprise, the stranger glowed as well—even brighter than everything else. The cave was thick with the pungent odor of dirt and… mushroom. The soil was probably full of fungal spores.

After a couple of minutes of following the twists and turns of this underground passage—Peabo trying not to strike his head on the many roots that poked their way through the ceiling—they entered a chamber that was tall enough for him to finally stop crouching. It was wide and spacious and looked to be some sort of semi-permanent camp. It featured two low beds, complete with wooden frames and mattresses, one about twice the size of the other, as if the little man had expected a larger guest. A table was laden with what might be food, and along one wall was an array of chests, one of which was open to reveal an assortment of tools. All of this was illuminated by a central campfire that gave off no smoke or flame.

"This place is safe," said the man. "You can rest. Or maybe you're hungry?" He motioned to the table, which had two chairs—also in two different sizes.

I shouldn't be here, thought Peabo. *This guy is confused. Nolan's probably up there wondering where the hell I am.*

He shook his head. "I appreciate your help, but the person I'm looking for couldn't possibly have come here a long time ago. We were supposed to arrive together, and he's—"

"Nolan Tomlinson," said the little man.

This was only the second time the man had spoken English, but his pronunciation was perfect.

Peabo was dumbstruck. "You… you met Nolan?"

The stranger fell right back into the unknown language that Peabo's mind was somehow translating for him. "He was a plainswalker, like you. Not many will brave the Seekers to cross the Desolate Plains. When he first came, he also spoke your strange language. Aingish it's called, right?"

"English."

"Ingish. Yes. He left something for you, too. For the one who comes after him."

As the man walked over to one of the chests and began rummaging through its contents, Peabo tried to make sense of all this. Nolan *had* been here, and he *had* met this little man. That was proven by the fact the man knew Nolan's last name, which Peabo was certain he hadn't shared. But… if the little man was telling the truth, then Nolan was dead. And had been dead for thirty years.

How? They'd left only seconds apart, and should have arrived only seconds apart. Could these worlds be running on such a different timescale that a few seconds translated to thirty years?

Peabo did some quick math. The researchers had explained that they hoped to be able to hold the connection open for about five minutes. If a few seconds translated to thirty years in this world, then five minutes would mean…

About two thousand years.

He would be stuck here for the rest of his life—and then some.

I'm screwed.

"Aha!" The man straightened up, holding a small wooden box, which he offered to Peabo. "Nolan entrusted me to give this to you when you arrived."

The box was heavy considering its size. Peabo opened it to find it contained a yellowed scrap of paper and a pile of metal ingots of various colors.

"Sit, relax," said the man. "This is your place to be for now."

Peabo took a seat at the table, set the box down, and picked up the paper. It was thicker than regular paper, probably some kind of parchment. And there was writing on it. In English.

Bo,

I don't know what happened. I don't know why I'm here and you're not. There's so much I don't know. But if by some miracle you're reading this, let me share with you the one thing I know with absolute certainty.

We got screwed.

That five-minute trip we were promised has become a lifetime.

Yeah. Sorry I signed you up for this.

And I still never got my five hundred bucks.

I don't know what I can do for you but offer a few pieces of advice. Maybe you can at least avoid making the same mistakes I made.

First piece of advice: don't admit to anyone but Brodie that you're from another planet or universe or whatever. I spent the first two years of my life here killing the bounty hunters who were looking for me because there were reports of a new foreigner on the island. Try to lay low.

Brodie, however, is cool. You can trust him. In fact, I'm pretty sure I'd have died within the first hour of being here if he hadn't convinced me to leave the Desolate Plains and get away from the Seekers, which are some kind of giant bird, like a pterodactyl with feathers. I've seen a couple from afar, but thankfully they don't seem to care about anything unless you're on that cursed plain of theirs.

I'm assuming you've met Brodie—he's the dwarf guy who gave you this letter, if all went well. Brodie isn't his real name—it's something like Brodislav, with a few clicks and tweets mixed in—but he's okay with the nickname. And by the way, I never taught him how to read or write English, so even he can't read this note, though I wouldn't mind if he did. Nobody on this planet, or in this universe, can read it. We've got our own secret code language, you and me.

Second piece of advice: forget about anything you think you know about how science works. The stuff I've seen here will make your hair—if you still have any, I didn't—turn white. Also, evidently I can read minds in this universe. It's a plainswalker thing, but be careful. There are others who can read minds as well, so learn to cloak your thoughts. Brodie can help with that.

Third piece of advice: learn the common language, and I mean learn it like you never learned anything before. Because everyone, even a plainswalker, speaks Common in this place. If you don't... you're going to have a bounty hunter on your ass pretty damn quick.

Fourth piece of advice: work on your katas. I don't know if you ended up anything like me, but I ended up being almost seven feet tall and strong as an ox. But my balance was awful and my flexibility was worse. It took some work to get back into fighting shape. And believe me, you'll need fighting skills in this world.

For what it's worth, I'm also leaving you some cash, or at least what passes for cash in these parts. Brodie has agreed to pass that on to you when you arrive... assuming I'm not here to do it myself. And increasingly, I fear that will be the case.

Fifth, and most important, piece of advice: Adapt to this world as quickly as you can... because I'm sorry to tell you, you're stuck here.

My friend, I wish I had better news for you. Again, I'm really sorry I got you sucked into this.

All the best,
Nolan

The parchment fell from Peabo's hand. Nolan really had been here. Had been here for years.

And now he was dead.

Peabo didn't need to remove those rocks from the mound to verify it. He knew it was true.

He swallowed hard, took a deep breath, and let it out slowly. Then he looked over to the little man—Brodie—who'd been watching silently all this time, a look of concern on his face.

"Brodie, is it okay if I get some sleep? I need to clear my head before I do anything else."

The man nodded and gave him a reassuring smile. "You have a lot to learn before it's time for you to visit the above-world. I'll teach you what you need to know, and like Nolan, we will work out an arrangement that benefits us both. Are you also a fighter, like Nolan was?"

Peabo nodded. "I suppose so."

"Nolan preferred daggers and a sword he called a katana. Is that…?"

"Yes, we both had similar training."

"Excellent. That *will* come in handy." Brodie walked over

to a different chest, retrieved some blankets, and laid them on the larger bed. "Go ahead and rest. I need to go get some supplies, but I'll be back in a quarter of a day."

Brodie then turned and walked directly into what Peabo had thought was a decoration on the wall—a simple straw mat with odd symbols drawn on it. But the mat parted, letting Brodie pass, and the yellow tendrils weaved themselves back together after he was through, leaving no visible seam.

Peabo stepped up to the mat and put his hand on it. It felt solid, yet clearly it was some kind of door. A door that didn't seem interested in letting *him* pass. He pressed hard against it, and it didn't move an inch.

He shrugged and moved his arms in circles to loosen them. He'd built up a lot of tension and he was feeling it. Or… this body was. But he could no longer think of this as some remote body he was controlling. He was stuck here, which meant this was as much his body as the one he'd been born with.

He lay down on the bed, which was surprisingly comfortable, and pulled the top blanket over him. It wasn't made of any cloth he recognized, but felt instead like a long, thin, pounded-out layer of sponge. He sniffed it, and again caught a whiff of mushrooms. But just a mild smell, like when he'd worked at a salad bar and had to slice up ten pounds of button mushrooms. It was earthy and fresh, and he found it pleasant.

Peabo let out a yawn and rolled over on his side, bunching up some of the blanket to form a pillow. His mind wandered, and the light in the room grew dimmer. Before he knew it, he was asleep.

CHAPTER FOUR

By the time Peabo had woken up, Brodie had come and gone, leaving behind a basket full of odd-looking root vegetables on the table. Even though the bed was comfortable, he hadn't slept well. He'd been startled awake several times and each time he'd felt a sense of panic at his new surroundings. Now that he was fully awake and pacing the floor of the underground hide-away, his mind filled with doubt about Brodie, this situation, and most of all, what had really happened to Nolan.

Peabo walked to the wall of bark that blocked the entrance to the cave and wondered aloud, "How the hell do I get out of this cave?"

Suddenly, the wall lurched forward and the tree that had been blocking the entrance uprooted itself and shifted to the side, as if on command.

Peabo stared open-mouthed at what had just happened, collected his wits and scrambled out of the cave and into the strange forest. He patted the trunk of the giant tree and shook his head. “Thanks, buddy.”

Gathering his bearings, Peabo spied the trail that he’d taken earlier and walked purposefully along the path, all the while trying to ignore the weird sense of everything staring at him. Even the grass fluttered unnaturally without a breeze, as if each blade turned to stare at the new creature walking past it. It took all of a minute for him to find the mound of rocks when a chill breeze blew across the gravesite, raising goosebumps all over his body.

He *knew* Brodie was lying to him. This was all some kind of elaborate hoax. The letter, the little hints of knowledge the dwarf seemed to have were all some kind of trick. He had no idea what the game was that the little man was playing, but it started with the mound of rocks laying before him.

Peabo crouched at the edge of the gravesite, hesitated for a second and then began digging.

Time passed without him noticing as he moved what had to have been a few thousand pounds of fist-sized rocks. Peabo figured this was all for show and by the time he got to the bottom of the pile, there’d be nothing to see.

He was wrong.

As he lifted a particularly large rock off the ever-diminishing pile, Peabo’s eyes widened as he spotted a strip of braided leather. It looked like the end of a belt.

With his heart racing, Peabo hurried with the excavation, uncovering more fragments of leather and cloth. Another chill raced up his spine as he spotted a long bone the size of a femur. “Holy crap…”

Peabo took in a deep breath and tried to calm his racing heart.

He continued removing rocks until an entire skeleton lay before him. Whoever this was had been buried for a long time. The leather he'd been wearing had mostly rotted and the few pieces of cloth that remained were more coarsely woven strings than cloth anymore.

His mind raced back to Saddam's killing fields. He'd witnessed the discovery of bodies buried a decade earlier and they looked nothing like this. Those bodies still stunk of death, a putrid smell that was hard to describe, but would linger in the tastebuds of his mind forever.

This gravesite had nothing of the sort. It actually smelled clean, sort of like the forest all around him.

"There's no way this could be Nolan—" and the words stuck in his throat as he caught sight of the skeleton's right hand. He then looked at the left hand and shivered as if his blood had turned to ice in his veins.

Peabo crouched on all fours and studied the skeleton's right hand. "I'll be damned…" Remembering that he'd been asked to vocalize things so that the signal going back would have as much data as possible, he said, "There's a missing joint on the skeleton's right hand, fifth finger. The distal joint looks to have been cut cleanly by something and the end of the bone had healed naturally. Despite what I'd been told regarding only our consciousness being transported, it seems like some parts of us must have come across or at least the description of such, because I can confirm the identity of the deceased as being

Nolan Tomlinson. Nolan had a childhood injury to the same finger.

"It seems to be the case that his death preceded my arrival by a very long period of time. Certainly years if not decades, and I'm wondering if anyone back home will ever hear what I'm saying."

His words echoed back to him in the lonely forest and the meaning struck him to his core. A sense of dread washed over Peabo as he stared at the pile of bones that belonged to his long-deceased partner. An iron band of anxiety threatened to crush the breath out of him as a million thoughts raced through his head.

None of this was supposed to have happened… yet it had. There was no doubt about it, and he needed to face the reality of it all.

He bowed his head for a moment, struggling to control the raw emotions that threatened to tear him apart. As he stared impotently at Nolan, a sense of calm fell over him, and he felt the presence of his mother. His mind drifted back in time to his father's gravesite. The words of the prayer she'd offered to his father on the day they'd buried him came pouring forth. They echoed loudly through the alien forest, with nobody as a witness other than the God he wasn't sure existed. "God, filled with mercy, dwelling in the heights of heaven, bring Nolan to rest beneath the wings of your divine presence, amid the ranks of the holy and the pure, glowing like the brilliance of the skies and the souls of our beloved and our blameless who went to their eternal place of rest. May You who are the source of mercy, shelter him beneath Your wings eternally, that he may rest in peace. Amen."

Peabo pulled in a shuddering breath and whispered, "I didn't have your six, Nolan. I'm sorry about that."

Standing on the edge of the forest, Peabo stared across the Desolate Plains and wondered aloud, "How screwed am I?"

One of the last instructions he'd received before coming across replayed in his mind. *"Mister Smith, remember when you're over there to vocalize your reports. Even though we'll see what your brain experiences, having a vocalization actually helps us decode some of the data. It's like a duplicate data stream in another part of your brain."*

"I don't see the point of vocalizing anything. If time goes by so much faster over here than back home, my entire life and death will just be a blip on STAG's radar." Peabo's face contorted with a sour expression. "What the hell happens when I die here? Am I going to just wake up in that chair? Am I going to even remember any of this at all? Or maybe my mind will be so screwed up, I'll be nuts when I finally am back home… this all sucks."

A deafening screech erupted somewhere up in the sky and for a moment the world fell under shadow as something huge flew over him.

With Peabo's ears ringing, he spotted a creature out of a nightmare several hundred feet up in the air.

"What the hell is that?" Peabo whispered into the air as he took several steps back, into the forest.

It looked like a pterodactyl. The creature resembled a huge bird-like dinosaur with wings and feathers. He heard the leathery flap from the downstroke of its wings and suddenly felt the crackling energy of static electricity building up all over him. The creature banked on wings that were easily one hundred feet long and Peabo was pummeled with a shower of broken sticks and leaves as a hot downdraft blew through the forest.

"Are you crazy?" Brodie's voice broke through the din as he grabbed Peabo's arm. "If you want to get eaten, this is a sure way to do it. Is that what you want?"

"No!" Peabo was startled by the man's voice and tore his gaze from the nightmare flying above. "I just wanted to have a look."

"Idiot move, plainswalker. Follow me." The tiny man turned in the direction of the cave and ran faster than Peabo thought was possible for someone with such short legs.

Somewhere behind Peabo, a raucous shriek echoed through the forest and he sprinted after Brodie, trying to keep up.

After a minute of ducking branches and almost sprawling headlong as he tripped over a hidden root, Peabo spied Brodie waiting at the entrance to the cave, motioning for him to go in.

As Peabo ducked into the cave the tiny man growled, "The Seekers don't care if you're just wanting to look. To them, you're a tasty snack invading their territory. Hopefully, that's a lesson learned."

As Brodie entered the cave, the tree sealed the entrance from the noise coming from the frustrated Seeker.

Peabo felt a pang of guilt.

Brodie hadn't lied to him. And as far as he could tell, everything he'd been told up until now was the truth. He most definitely wasn't in Kansas anymore.

"Do you mind if I ask you a few questions?" Peabo and his new companion were laying in their beds, trying to get some sleep.

"Sleep, plainswalker. Have you heard of it?" Brodie grumped and turned to his side. "If it'll get me to my slumber more quickly, go ahead and ask. I can't guarantee I'll have answers, but I'll try."

"The seekers… what are they?"

"They're creatures who attack those who set foot on the Desolate Plains. I thought that was fairly obvious."

"But why? What's on the Desolate Plains that they're guarding?"

"How should I know, plainswalker? Any group who's attempted to explore those wretched, lifeless plains have either never been seen again or they've returned bloody and half-dead with those wretched creatures terrorizing them the entire time. It's obvious that they're territorial creatures, and maybe they're guarding their nests. Let me put it simply, I know of no person who has attempted to cross through the Desolate Plains and not regretted the attempt."

Peabo imagined what the breeding ground for dozens of those giant dinosaur-like creatures might look like and frowned. He mentally scratched off any plans he might have had of exploring in that direction. "Okay, what about this plainswalker thing? I mean, I know I'm one, but what does that even mean? Is it some kind of race? Am I very different than others?"

Brodie lay back in his bed and stroked his beard as he stared up at the ceiling. "Lots of questions, many of them are not simply answered. Let's start with the basics. A plainswalker is what you are, that we have no doubt—"

"How do you know? Is everyone your height and I'm very tall compared to most people?"

Brodie chuckled. "Those of us who live primarily underground are shorter than the aboveworlders you'll encounter. You are of a similar size to the aboveworlders, maybe a bit bigger, but not terribly so. The markings on your skin give you away as a plainswalker."

Peabo looked at his bare arm and frowned. In this world, his skin had a general brown coloration to it, but there were markings that looked like complex forked lightning bolts all over his skin. They were dark brown and looked like tattoos."

"The myth of the plainswalker is a thing out of our ancient past. To be honest, the history of the plainswalker is only known in fragments. The story goes that there was an ancient war long long ago, and it was through the help of a plainswalker that the war was won. It's funny that there's so little known of that time, but one of the few things everyone seems to recall is the tale of the plainswalker. The enigmatic figure who appeared on the Desolate Plains and saved the day. That's the history of it all."

"So, are there other plainswalkers around? Was Nolan a plainswalker as well?"

"Yes, Nolan was a plainswalker, and I can't even begin to express how shocked I was when he appeared. I had almost lost faith that such a being had ever existed. There are many who believe that there are a race of plainswalkers that live somewhere on the Desolate Plains, but the truth is that there are no others. There have been stories of people seeing ghost-like images of a plainswalker walking around the island, seemingly looking for something along the shore, but I've never seen such a thing. To the best of *my* knowledge, you are the third known plainswalker to have ever existed. Like I said, we know very little for certain. However, there's a story that claims that one day the plainswalker will return to right things that are wrong in the world."

Peabo frowned. "What does that even mean? What's wrong in this world? And how can some stranger fix it?"

Brodie snorted. "It's just a tale parents tell their kids. It's hard to put much meaning behind such things, and as to what's wrong in this world... you ask ten people that question, you'll get eleven answers."

Sitting in silence, Peabo absorbed what his newfound mentor had said and he sensed that Brodie wasn't exactly sharing everything he knew. "I don't mean to be rude, but I'm curious. Why are you helping me?"

"I have reasons that are my own." Brodie's voice held a

serious tone. "You can trust on my oath that I mean for you to fulfill whatever it is that you're destined to do."

"And what is that?"

"I have no idea. But I will help you as much as I can."

Peabo's mind flashed back to Nolan's grave. "Can you tell me how Nolan died?"

"It was a bounty hunter who killed him."

"Wait a minute, but if there's some legend about how a plainswalker is supposed to come back to fix whatever's wrong in the world, and Nolan arrived and got killed, what does that say about the legend?"

"He was not the one." Brodie responded matter-of-factly.

"Clearly, but…" Feeling his heart begin to race, Peabo pressed his head deeper into the pillow, breathing as deeply and slowly as he could. "How am I going to avoid the attention of a bounty hunter if it's so obvious that I'm a plainswalker."

"That was thirty years ago, my new friend. I'm certain any bounty hunter that had been actively seeking a plainswalker has since died or grown disinterested after Nolan's death. And besides, there are yearly festivals where villagers sometimes dress up as famous people from the past—a plainswalker being one such person. Such a festival has just occurred, so I think for now, things should be relatively safe for you. As long as we keep you as inconspicuous as possible, things should be fine. Now, let's get some sleep. Tomorrow will be a long day."

Peabo closed his eyes and within minutes, he heard Brodie's soft snore.

The idea that he was in a new world, in a new body, and with an unknown mission was more than unnerving.

His stomach gurgled as he thought about home, his mother, and in his mind's eye he pictured himself lying on a reclining chair with all sorts of wires and tubes hanging from him.

Was he really stuck in this world until he died? And if he died in this world, what then?

As he felt his anxiety increasing, he willed himself to focus on the here and now. None of these things were things he could do anything about.

He was in this world to stay, and he needed to focus on whatever this mission turned out to be. As a former Special Forces soldier, he'd been trained to have contingencies for his contingencies, and this was no different. Plan A had gone to hell, so this was going to be plan B.

As he thought about what his new plans could be, his mind began to wander and exhaustion finally claimed him.

Thirty seconds elapsed when suddenly a dim light appeared just above Brodie's head. The small man turned to his side and studied Peabo's sleeping form. With a grim expression he made a sweeping hand gesture toward the large man and the plainswalker's body glowed for an instant, and then the room was cloaked in complete darkness.

CHAPTER FIVE

Peabo's mouth watered as he breathed in the spices from the thick brown stew that Brodie was preparing. Mushroom stew was one of Brodie's favorite things to make, which was a good thing, as it was among the tastiest of his dishes. Pretty much everything he made involved mushrooms of one kind of another, but this stew also included some cubed vegetables that looked like waxy potatoes but tasted more like carrots.

Peabo had now been living in this underground room with Brodie for over six weeks, learning the language known as Common, which evidently was spoken by nearly everyone on this world. It felt like he was back in elementary school, which didn't bring back good memories. He'd always been good at math and science, but languages were never his thing, and the weird grammar rules of Common proved to be a real challenge. The memorization tricks he'd learned proved to be a godsend, but even they were of little use when it came to pronunciation. It took dogged amounts of practice to master the weird clicks and vocalizations.

He was proud of himself though, because he was becoming far more adept with the language than he ever thought he would be. And now those strange vocalizations sounded more to him like a Scottish brogue. In fact, now whenever Brodie spoke, he reminded Peabo of one of the dwarves from *Lord of the Rings*. Even the little man's mannerisms fit the image.

Brodie set out the pot of stew and ladled up two wooden bowls, and the two of them sat down across from each other at the table. As they dug in, another lesson began.

"Okay," said Brodie. "I'm shutting my mind from your plainswalker prying ability. You've got the basics of Common, so you don't need to depend on listening to the meaning of my words anymore."

"Wait a minute—"

"Trust me, you're better off. I should have done this a while ago, because now I'm afraid it's become a crutch. Let me warn you," Brodie said, wagging a thick finger at him, "you'll be able to read the thoughts of many people you encounter in the future, but there are many like me who can prevent such things, and normally do. Starting today, I'm treating you like any other citizen of this world. So, citizen, tell me what you know about Myrkheim. And say it in Common."

The mental silence that followed was disturbing. Peabo had gotten used to always having a sense of his companion's thoughts—the little man was a regular mental chatterbox—but now… nothing. Brodie wasn't kidding when he said he'd cut him off.

Peabo let his breath out slowly as he thought about Myrkheim and what he'd been taught.

"Myrkheim is what most people call the passages beneath the surface. It's a multi-level underground world with many different nations. But Myrkheim also refers to a specific city deep below ground—a city very few aboveworlders actually know of, and fewer still have seen. Everyone living below ground is relatively short—"

"No," Brodie snapped, jabbing his empty spoon in Peabo's direction. "You aboveworlders are taller than what's normal."

Peabo chuckled at the short man's gruff reaction. He shoveled more stew into his mouth and continued. "In Myrkheim there are two major races that tend to keep to themselves. One is the trpaslík," he pointed at Brodie, "which you are one of. The aboveworlders call you guys dwarves. Your people are mostly farmers, traders, and miners, and you often journey up to the surface to exchange goods with the aboveworlders. You have your own language and religion.

"The second major race is the šotek, who live in the lower depths of Myrkheim. The Common word for šotek is goblin, and they rarely venture aboveground, especially during the day, because of their aversion to bright light."

Brodie nodded. "Good enough. My people are also frontiersmen. I've known some who have explored below the great ocean to the main continent. We are an adventuresome lot, when given inspiration."

"What inspires you to explore?"

"Treasures. Knowledge. Adventure. Why? Does that seem odd to you?"

"No, just curious. Are there a lot of unexplored areas in this world?"

"Of course," Brodie responded, looking surprised. "Is where you come from… do they no longer have any places that are unknown?"

Peabo shrugged. "I guess long ago we did. And I guess in some ways, we still do." He thought about where he was now—about the possibility of infinite universes. That certainly qualified as "unknown areas." Whether across continents, space, or even universes… humanity was always exploring, pushing the frontiers of something.

"How's my Common coming along?" he asked.

Brodie snorted. "You sound like a drunk aboveworlder, slurring all your words. You'll pass, but you'll probably need a few years of smoothing out. Now tell me about the world above us."

"In the aboveworld," Peabo began, "the main race I'll encounter is taller than you, but on average a bit smaller than me. Like the dwarves, they include a number of farmers and traders, and live in settlements. And you mentioned that they may want to hire me for my fighting skills. Can I ask why that's something that's in demand?"

Brodie bunched up his thick eyebrows in puzzlement. "I would have thought that your encounter with the Seekers would have answered that question. The world above, like the one below, isn't tame. There are many things in this world that will attempt to kill you. Steal from you. Eat you. Enslave you. A person with fighting skills will always have work to do."

Peabo finished the rest of his stew, the spices tingling on his tongue. "When do you think I'll be ready to go out there and meet some of these aboveworlders? I assume there's a town nearby, since you're always getting supplies."

Brodie grunted. "You have a lot to learn still. But..." He rose from his seat, went to his storage chests, and withdrew a bundle wrapped in cloth. He tossed it to Peabo. "Open it."

Peabo unwrapped it and smiled. Inside was an outfit that looked a lot like a karate gi, colored in a mottled brown and green, like natural camouflage. In addition to the shirt and pants, both made from a thick cloth that was tightly woven and smooth to the touch, was a vest of some kind of tanned leather, very similar to something he'd find at home.

"Those will serve you well for our first journey to Raiheim," Brodie said.

"*Our* journey?"

Brodie scoffed. "You aren't ready to venture out alone. Raiheim is an aboveworlder town. Mostly decent farming folk and refugees from Castle Dvorak who cannot stand the city life any longer. Now hold on, I have something more for you."

Brodie pulled out a pair of long wooden boxes from his storage, and he set these on the table. "These were Nolan's. I'm sure he'd want you to have them."

Peabo lifted the lid of the first box to reveal two gleaming metal daggers. Their handles were wrapped in what looked like paracord, but knowing this place, the paracord was probably another form of plant he hadn't encountered yet. He picked one up, and it felt comfortable in his hand, its edge razor-sharp. Also in the box was a leather shoulder harness that would make it easy to carry the knives and have quick access to them.

The second box was much longer, and when Peabo opened it, his cheeks ached with the force of his smile. Inside was a large, sheathed katana.

He removed its sheath, and the wavy pattern along the blade's edge told him everything he needed to know. This was no mean sparring weapon like the one he'd practiced with for countless hours in the dojo. This was a working sword.

And then he saw the base of the blade, and he let out a quiet "Whoa." There, Nolan had carved a Japanese symbol for four bodies. He must have done combat with this, and the symbol indicated this was a four-body sword—meaning it had sliced through the equivalent of four bodies with one slice. Peabo had heard of such swords before, but they were museum pieces. Nobody actually did cadaver tests anymore… at least not on Earth.

He lifted the sword carefully, and the first thing he noticed was its balance. It took almost no effort for him to move with the blade as he stood and made a few test cuts in the air.

Brodie took a few steps back. "That was made to Nolan's specifications, by my people. You'll find the aboveworlders lack the skill to make such a thing. You are pleased?"

"Pleased?" Peabo laughed. "I could never have dreamed of owning something of this quality back home."

"And where is home, plainswalker?"

Peabo pointed the sword at Brodie, its tip not wavering

even a millimeter. "On the far side of the Desolate Plain, near a village with no name on a beach along the great ocean."

Brodie nodded with approval. "Good. I think you're ready."

Brodie's horse slowed when the first signs of Raiheim appeared ahead. He dismounted and turned to Peabo, who had made the roughly ten-mile journey on foot, running alongside.

"How are you feeling?"

"Fantastic," Peabo said truthfully. "Honestly, it feels like I just finished a warmup. I'm ready for action."

"Pffft..." Brodie shook his head. "You plainswalkers are a mystery. You'd put forest ponies out of business if only we could figure out how to put a saddle on you and get you to take a bit."

Peabo laughed and rolled his shoulders. His joints felt nice and loose. Maybe a ten-mile run really was just a warmup for this body. Back on Earth, he'd have been dying after a run like that.

Brodie smacked the pony's hindquarters and sent it racing back the way they'd come.

Peabo frowned. "Brodie, you didn't remove the saddle."

"Why would I do that?" Brodie asked. "You expect me to carry it on my head? Besides, the saddle isn't even mine."

"It's not?"

"No. Those ponies are... rented. There are merchants within the forest who raise the forest ponies for us

Myrkheimers to use. But don't worry—he knows how to get back home."

Brodie led Peabo along a worn path between cultivated fields with rows and rows of crops. The scent of freshly-tilled soil wrapped Peabo in its loamy embrace, reminding him of his grandparents' farm in Alabama. Back then he was a kid from the suburbs, but his visits to their farm were etched deeply in his memory. Now, as he breathed deeply of his childhood, he couldn't help but smile.

"Before we figure out where you'll stay long-term," said Brodie, "the first thing we'll need to do is get you officially on the books so you can get hired off and support yourself."

"Makes sense," said Peabo. "What does that entail?"

"It'll cost one gold royal for the testing and certification—and Nolan left you about one hundred royals. Now, normally..." Brodie glanced around and lowered his voice. "Normally a father would bring his child to the testing, pay the fee, and register as the child's responsible party. That entitles the father to a ten percent cut of the child's earnings in the future."

"Ten percent?"

Brodie shrugged. "Aye, it may seem like a lot, but it's usually how the parents can afford to live once they're too old to work. In this case, since you don't have a parent here... I'll be playing that role. Now don't go thinking I'm trying to steal a cut of your earnings; if you don't register a responsible party when you get certified, the fighting guild will just keep that ten percent anyway. Either way, someone's taking the ten percent, so you're not losing anything."

"What does the guild do with the ten percent when they keep it?"

The small man shrugged. "They claim it goes to paying for overhead, but between you and me, I don't trust anyone with my money but myself." He looked up at Peabo. "Does the proposed arrangement bother you?"

"Not at all." Peabo grinned as he looked down at the little man who was barely half his height and probably a third his weight. "Should I call you Dad?"

"Shut up," Brodie harrumphed.

As they approached the outskirts of town, Peabo finally got his first good look at the people of this world. They looked a lot like humans—like anyone he'd have seen in any town back home—except their builds were a bit on the lanky side, everyone seemed to have dark hair, and their skin coloration varied from pale beige to almost mahogany. There didn't seem to be much difference in height between the men and women, although the women did seem to be thinner. And their clothes were similar to Peabo's own: a loose-fitting overcoat, another layer underneath, and some basic trousers.

As the two newcomers walked into town, Peabo and Brodie got more than their share of furtive glances, but no one reacted as if an alien was walking in their midst.

The roads were packed dirt, and the buildings, none of which were more than two stories, reminded Peabo of the old west. Simple wooden construction, glass windows, and the occasional wagon hitched. One was hitched to an animal that looked like a cross between a Clydesdale and an ox. The thing probably weighed thousands of pounds and could tear the town apart, but it stood calmly on the side of the street, held only by a thin leash tied to a post.

The breeze shifted, and Peabo detected the scent of cooking meat. His mouth watered; he hadn't had meat since he'd arrived in this universe, and the smell made him homesick… and hungry.

Brodie led him to a wide building with a sign that read, "Fighters' Guild." A grizzled old man stood at the entrance, and when he took in Peabo, his eyes widened.

"Oh my, you're a big one."

"I'm here to register my son for testing," said Brodie.

The man looked back and forth between Brodie, his head moving up and down to take them both in. "Like father like son, eh?" He chuckled. "Well, if you have a gold royal on you, I can start the testing right away. We had a cancellation this morning."

Brodie pulled out a small gold bar and handed it over. "Let's get him done then."

The old man pointed at the scabbarded katana hanging from Peabo's waist. "Your father will have to hold your weapon during the testing."

Peabo handed Brodie the sword, and the old man led them both inside.

"Karina!" he called. "I've got a test to run. Can you help this gentleman with the paperwork?"

A middle-aged woman with a sour expression peeked up from a desk and waved Brodie over.

The old man then turned to Peabo. "What's your name, son?"

"Peabo."

"An unusual name. I like it." He led him to an apparatus that looked surprisingly like a bench press. "Are you familiar with the testing process?"

Peabo tried to maintain a stone-like expression despite his anxiety. He wanted to avoid any obvious mistakes that would label him as someone who didn't belong here. But that was difficult, as he wasn't sure exactly how much he was supposed to know. "My father told me some, but not all of it."

"Well, there's not much to it. We just want to measure the various attributes that will contribute to your initial rating. The better you do, the easier it will be to find you jobs that you're qualified for. We'll begin with the strength test." The man patted the long bench. "Lie down on here, and we'll get started."

Peabo laid himself on the bench, feeling relieved that he'd at least start by doing something familiar. This thing really was much like the bench presses he'd used back home.

The man pressed a pin into a stack of weights and grabbed a clipboard. "Okay, Peabo. Just press up on the bar until the weight is lifted from the stack, then hold it there."

Peabo did as he was asked. The small stack of weight felt like nothing.

"Very good. Now slowly lower the weight, and lift it back up ten times."

Peabo did as he was instructed. It took almost no effort at all.

"Okay, good. I'll add a bit more weight, and we'll do it again. We'll keep at it until it's too much for you to lift."

They went through several more rounds of this, the man putting more weight on each time. At first it was easy, but by the end, Peabo was struggling.

"Okay, only one more round for this test, young man. Give it your all. Same as before, lift, and then ten slow repetitions."

Peabo grunted as he lifted what turned out to be the entire stack of weights. As he raised and lowered the weights, drenched in sweat, he found that it felt good to push hard against something that was resisting so strongly.

Before he knew it, the old man was saying, "Okay, you're done."

Peabo lowered the stack, sat up on the bench, and moved his arms back and forth. The delicious feeling of blood circulating in his muscles made him feel more alive than he had since coming here.

"How'd I do?" he asked.

"How did you do?" The old man chuckled and shook his head. "Let's just move on to the next tests. I'll share all the results with you when you're done."

They moved to a table, and the old man instructed Peabo to take a seat and roll up his sleeve.

Peabo did as he was asked. "What are we testing now?"

The old man pulled out a leather strap. "We're going to see how well your body reacts to being injured and how quickly it recovers." He winked. "Don't worry, it'll just sting a bit. Hold out your forearm and don't move."

Peabo extended his right arm across the table, and the old man smacked his forearm with the leather strap—hard. Peabo had to grit his teeth against the pain.

The man quickly grabbed a wooden frame that contained hourglasses of various sizes, and turned it over. Peabo supposed this was what passed for a stopwatch on this world.

A strap-shaped welt quickly appeared across his forearm. He tried to keep an internal count of the elapsed time, and was surprised when the welt faded away and disappeared altogether in less than two minutes.

The man scribbled something in the chart. "Three more tests to go."

Peabo wasn't sure how well he'd done on his tests, except for the strength one. He'd lifted all the weights they had, so surely he'd gotten top marks there. After the strap test, they'd tested his reflexes, which made sense for a fighting guild, but the last two tests didn't make any sense to him at all. In the first, he had to make up a story and tell it to an audience, almost like reciting a play. And in the second he was given a series of questions about what he'd do when faced with two bad choices —which would he pick, and why?

He was given a short break afterward, and he and Brodie got a snack at a nearby market stand before returning to the guild, where the woman with the sour expression announced, "I have your results."

They stood in front of her desk, and she pulled out a medallion that looked to Peabo like a military-style dog tag, except the metal had a shimmering opalescence. She put it into a device with a long lever attached, laid several metal dies on top of it, and pulled hard on the lever. Then she took out the medallion and strung it onto a leather rope.

"Peabo," she said, "you're now officially a level one member of the guild." She looked up at him and gasped, "Oh my." The woman's eyes grew wide and she smiled. "That's an excellent job on the skin markings. You should really do it again for the next season's festival, you might win a top prize. I swear, you look so much like a plainswalker you'd fool the Nameless One himself."

Peabo returned the smile as she handed him the medallion. He looked at the symbols now cut into the medallion, but they meant nothing to him. The metal was warm to the touch, and when he tilted it, its color shifted, almost like the images on those cheap hologram cards that came in Cracker Jack boxes.

"You should be proud," the woman said to Brodie. "Your son should easily be able to find work with these test scores. His strength is at the top of our ability to measure. He also got top marks on constitution, so he should be a tough nut to crack. He did very well on dexterity scores, and fairly well on intelligence. All in all, very promising."

She turned back to Peabo. "Be sure to wear your guild credentials at all times. There will be fines if you're caught in public without it. Understood?"

Peabo looped the braided leather over his head. "Understood."

* * *

Upon leaving the guild, Brodie announced he would take Peabo to the booking agent, where, he explained, he'd be able to find upcoming guild jobs that he might be qualified for. But on the way there, they were slowed by a gathering in the middle of the town square. A group in brightly colored outfits made of what looked like shiny silk—a stark contrast to the undyed clothes with muted earth tones that everyone else wore—stood before a rudely constructed wooden platform. On top of the platform were two little girls, about ten years old, and a woman who had obviously been crying. All three of them had blonde hair, which Peabo hadn't seen on anyone else in the town.

"Looks like people from the city," Brodie said. He jerked his head toward a man off to the right. "See the soldier with the broadsword strapped on his back? That's a guard from Castle Dvorak, the island's capital city. I'm guessing we have some government folk here for inspections or something."

A man stepped onto the platform and put the narrow end of a wooden cone in front of his mouth.

"Everyone, everyone, lend me your ears. The people of Dvorak Island are in for a rare treat from the mainland."

The man's voice was surprisingly loud and easily penetrated the din of the square. Hushing sounds spread through the crowd, and the speaker waited patiently until everyone's eyes were on him before continuing.

"You have no doubt heard of the Sage's Tower on the king's promenade. You are also no doubt aware that very few things that come from the tower are ever made available to the common man to purchase. Until today."

The announcer panned his arm toward the three people on the platform.

"Dívka smrti... the king's famous blood maidens. Only one

in a thousand are chosen for such training in the Sage's Tower, and the training lasts a full ten years before they are qualified to pair with someone out of a noble house. But occasionally, there are issues before the training is completed. That was the case for two of these lovelies, who were found to be lacking after three and five years, respectively." He pointed to one of the little girls. "*The first is Josefa. She can be made a matched pair with one of you, if the price is right. Let's start the bidding at fifteen gold royals..."*

Several men immediately raised their hands, and a bidding frenzy began. The girl looked excited as the bids increased, and the final bid was nearly one hundred gold royals. The winning bidder, an older man, approached the platform with a bag of money, and the girl hopped down the stairs happily to meet him.

"You people break my heart," said the announcer. *"Ninety-five gold royals was an absolute steal."* He shook his head and pointed to the other young girl. *"Baruska has two more years of training than Josefa. I will start the bidding at thirty-five gold royals."*

Bile rose in Peabo's throat as he watched a bunch of old men slobbering over themselves for a girl who didn't look like she'd even hit puberty. A "matched pair" could only mean one thing, and it made him want to throw up. But he noted that Brodie was watching in fascination, apparently unbothered by any of it. What kind of society supported such a thing?

When the bidding ended, the second girl went off with the winner—again, an older man—and only the woman was left. Unlike the girls, who'd somehow been thrilled at the prospect of being purchased by some old lech, the woman looked miserable. Her face was red and splotchy from crying.

"Ladies and gentlemen, our last item is a once-in-a-lifetime opportunity. This is Nicole, a fully trained *blood maiden. She completed her training three years ago, but through no fault of her own, her partner was killed..."*

A murmur rippled through the crowd, and Peabo heard hateful whispers.

"Disgusting."

"Unreliable wench."

"Probably killed him."

The crowd's *unvoiced* thoughts were even worse as they echoed loudly in his head. For him, they might as well have been yelling the epithets.

Stone her!

Bury her alive!

She should be left as a sacrifice to the old gods!

The announcer, apparently sensing the mood of the audience, said, *"I'm going to be very generous and start the bidding at a mere twenty royals!"*

But in contrast to the frenzy of bids that had met the two girls, the woman found herself standing before a thinning crowd. People were actually walking away now, many shaking their heads with looks of disgust.

Peabo suddenly got an idea. He raised his hand. "Five gold royals!"

Brodie grabbed his arm. "What do you think you're doing?"

Peabo shrugged out of Brodie's grip. "You'll see."

The announcer shifted his gaze to Peabo, and his eyes widened. *"A plainswalker? Aha, the man painted like a plainswalker has a bid. We have a bid of five, does anyone want to bid ten?"*

More people left. No one raised their voice to bid.

"Seven?" said the announcer, hopefully.

Still no bids.

The announcer frowned. *"Six, then?"*

A few seconds passed, and not only were there no other bids, there was practically no one left in the square.

The announcer looked Peabo in the eye. *"Plainswalker, do you have the five gold royals?"*

Peabo counted out five gold bars from his pocket and held them up.

The announcer was obviously disappointed. He stared at the gold for a few long seconds, then grimaced and said, *"Five gold it is!"* He looked at Nicole, snapped his fingers, and pointed at Peabo.

Nicole looked no more or less miserable than before as she climbed down the stairs and met Peabo in front of the platform. She was even taller than most people he had seen in the town, only an inch or two shorter than Peabo himself.

Peabo tilted his head toward her and whispered, "I'll make this right for you."

If the words had any effect on her, she didn't show it.

A man at a table beside the platform, apparently the announcer's partner, beckoned them forward. "Five gold royals," he said gruffly.

Peabo set down the gold bars, and the merchant weighed

each of them before nodding his approval. Then he pulled out a thin metal tube.

"Are you two ready for the pairing?"

Nicole, who looked resigned to her fate, held out her index finger. But Peabo had no idea what was going on. He looked back at Brodie, who was standing back about ten feet and merely shrugged. Clearly the little man wanted no part of this —whatever *this* was.

"Now you, plainswalker," said the merchant.

Peabo turned back to see that Nicole had stuck her finger in one end of the tube. Apparently he was supposed to stick his finger in the other end. The thing looked a bit like a Chinese finger trap, but it was made of metal. And… was it glowing? Or was that just a trick of the light?

There didn't seem to be any other direction to go but forward, so Peabo took a deep breath and stuck his index finger in the other end of the tube.

It immediately clamped down with a click, pricking the tip of his finger. The tube brightened, its glow now unmistakable. Peabo felt a warmth spread up his finger, into his hand, and up his arm.

Nicole gasped, pulled her finger out of the tube, and licked the dot of blood off its tip. And to Peabo's surprise, she smiled. Following her lead, he removed his finger as well.

The merchant turned away and began packing up. Apparently his job was done here.

Nicole looked up at Peabo. "Thank you," she said. Her voice was soft and timid. "What may I call you?"

Peabo took a close look at her for the first time. Her eyes

were shockingly blue—like the eyes of a Siberian Husky. Her long blond hair was gathered into a single braid that fell below her shoulders. And despite the swollen eyes and splotchy face from all the crying, she was attractive, especially now that she was smiling.

He returned the smile. "You can call me Peabo." He put a hand on her elbow and led her away from the merchant and the platform, not wanting to be overheard. "But I want you to understand, you owe me nothing. I saw how upset you were, and I didn't want you to be obligated to anyone because they bought you like a slave. So you're free now. Go wherever you like. Maybe back to your family?"

Nicole looked confused for a moment, and then her face turned ghostly white. Her chin quivered as she asked in a quavering voice, "Are you dismissing me?"

Dismissing? What did that mean? He tried to read her thoughts, to better figure out what she was talking about, but he sensed nothing from her mind. Still, he didn't require mind-reading to see the agitation on her face.

When he looked over at Brodie for help, the little man shook his head vehemently.

"Did I somehow fail you already?" Nicole asked.

Peabo turned back to her. "No, that's not it. I just didn't want you to be sold like an item at a market—nobody deserves that. So all I'm saying is that I… well, I paid so that you wouldn't be stuck with the merchant trying to sell you elsewhere. And trust me, you don't want to be stuck with someone like me either. You don't even know me, and—"

"Since when does that matter?" Nicole's voice was stronger

now, tinged with anger. "We're partners now. You own me, as much as I own you."

Own me?

"Now wait a minute. There's been a misunderstanding. I just want to give you your freedom."

The woman's back stiffened. "I don't want it!"

Brodie appeared at Peabo's side. "Blood maiden, please accept my apology on the young man's behalf. The boy is a bit… well, let's just say he doesn't understand. He needs to be taught a few things about how this all works."

He looked up at Peabo and sighed. "I'm sorry, my boy, but you two are now a matched pair. This young lady is now yours, and you are hers, and she will *never* betray you." He looked at Nicole. "Right?"

"I couldn't possibly," she retorted.

Brodie patted Peabo on the back and gave him a wistful smile. "Well. I've done what I can for you, my friend, but it seems our paths together, at least for now, are done."

"Wait, what?" said Peabo. "I thought we were… I thought we had an arrangement."

"We do. But then you did this… which I hadn't anticipated at all." Brodie glanced at the woman, who was glaring at them both. "How could I have even guessed such a thing would happen in this lonely part of the world? I didn't plan for a blood maiden to be involved. They are dedicated to protecting the mainland nobility. For all I know, she's the first blood maiden to have set foot on this island—ever."

As Peabo stood there in utter confusion, Brodie turned to Nicole. "He's already certified with the guild, level one, but with top scores where it matters. You'll help him adapt to a fighter's life?"

Nicole looked back and forth between Peabo and Brodie, a frown still on her face. Then she stepped closer to Peabo. "I'll advise him as best I can."

Brodie gestured for Peabo to lean down, then spoke in a low voice. "You can tell her the truth about you and your special situation—but only after you've settled down somewhere. And be sure to speak in private. It was good knowing you, my boy. I'm sure our paths will cross again."

Peabo straightened. "Brodie, I don't understand any of this. What's going on?"

Brodie ignored the question and handed Nicole a small gold ring. "If I'm needed, this will reach me." And then he turned and walked away.

Peabo watched him go with a feeling of both resentment and confusion. His only friend in this place had simply abandoned him. Just like that.

Why?

He looked at Nicole. Was he... *married* to this woman? Was that what he'd just gotten himself into?

Nicole raised an eyebrow. "For someone as big and strong as you, I swear you look like you're about to cry."

"Maybe I am," Peabo responded truthfully. The loss of Brodie had hit him harder than he would have expected.

"Now, now." She looped her arm through his. "Whatever's wrong, we'll figure it out together. Where do we live?"

Peabo stared blankly at her, then held up his pouch, filled

with the remainder of his money. “I don’t live anywhere. Brodie was going to help me find a place.”

She looked into the pouch and nodded. “In that case, I guess we know what needs taking care of first.” She pulled at his arm. “Let’s go.”

CHAPTER SIX

Peabo watched with awe and a little bit of fear as Nicole gave instructions to the workmen who were emptying the two-room wood-framed building that was going to be their new home. The farmer who owned the place had been using it for storage.

"Make sure all of the junk is removed and it's swept out or I'll hunt each and every one of you down," Nicole snapped.

One of the men staggered past, carrying a heavy crate. His mind yelled, *"Nameless One, please make her stop staring at me with those demon eyes of hers!"*

Yes, Nicole definitely had these men cowed. The workmen made haste to do as she instructed, and Peabo found himself looking at his new "partner" with a smile. Long gone was the crying woman on the stage whom he'd mistaken for a victim. In her place was a smart, confident woman, sure of herself. And frugal too, which Peabo appreciated; he'd always been one to pinch pennies.

Nicole turned away from the workmen and gave Peabo a wink. "It'll be a few hours before they're done, so why don't we go eat our lunch?" She held up the basket they'd picked up at the market and nodded to the nearest hill. "How about we go up there and get to know each other? And you can explain what your friend meant when he said you have a 'special situation.'"

They remained silent as they walked up the slope. Peabo spent the entire time wondering what he was going to say. When at last they had settled down to eat, it was Nicole who broke the silence.

She patted her chest. "Peabo, I can feel your heart racing. You're nervous. But you needn't be. Believe me, I'll never betray your confidence. Tell me what's on your mind."

Peabo frowned. Brodie *had* told him he could trust this woman.

He took a deep breath. *Here goes nothing.*

"The thing is," he began, "I'm not really from this world…"

There was a lot about Nicole that puzzled Peabo, but the one thing weighing on him most was how weird it was to not hear her thoughts. He'd gotten used to being able to hear the low murmur of noise associated with people's thoughts, an ability that evidently was an attribute of being a plainswalker, yet from Nicole, he sensed nothing. She was just like Brodie, after he'd shut himself off.

He reached into the basket, grabbed what looked like a red apple, and took a big bite. He immediately regretted it.

Nicole laughed. “You’re not supposed to eat a fire radish like that.”

His eyes watered, and he chewed quickly and grimaced as he swallowed. “Well, I guess I have a lot to learn.”

“If you’re willing to learn, I’m willing to teach. Now—you’ve told me your story, fantastic as it is, and I’m sure you’d like to know mine. What questions do you have?”

Peabo started with the question that was top of mind. “Why can’t I hear your thoughts?”

“You can hear people’s thoughts?” Nicole’s eyes widened.

Feeling self-conscious, Peabo lowered his voice. “I guess it’s a plainswalker thing—”

"Wait a minute, a plainswalker?” She grabbed his hand and rubbed her thumb across some of the markings on his skin. She looked up with furrowed brows. “Those markings aren’t of grease-paint? Are you… are you seriously telling me you’re a plainswalker? A real one?”

Peabo felt the heat of her gaze as it focused on him. “I’m afraid so. Anyway, I could hear Brodie’s thoughts at first, and then he did something that made me not able to hear him. But when I walked through town, I was able to sense most people’s thoughts. What’s the difference between you and Brodie and most of the other people?”

Nicole tilted her head as her ice-blue eyes bore into him, blinked a few times and let out a snorting type of laugh. “Well, I know you’re ‘new’ to this world…” she said in a tone that implied she wasn’t yet prepared to completely believe his story, "but your friend Brodie is not just a simple Myrkheimer. I sensed who he was the moment I was near him. But as for me —it's part of my training. I always have my thoughts shielded, even when I sleep. After all these years, it's almost impossible for me to turn that off. I'm sorry."

"I wasn't complaining, I just don't know what's normal and what isn't for certain things. I've been here for almost two months now, but most of that was underground with Brodie, learning how to speak Common. And sure, we talked about a lot of things, but there's so much I just don't know about this place. For all I know, blood maidens can sprout wings and fly away, and that might be normal."

"You can't fly?" Nicole asked, surprised.

Peabo stared at her with incredulity for several seconds before she winked and laughed.

"I'm just teasing you. Go ahead, ask me another question."

"Okay… What is a blood maiden? And… what does it mean that we're a matched pair?"

Her bright-blue eyes focused intensely on him. "The proper term for what I am in the old language is *dívka smrti*—but in Common, I'm called a blood maiden, and the term fits. Not because of our common reputation for being assassins—"

"You're an *assassin*?"

"No, but our training gives us many of the same skills that would be needed."

"You keep referring to your training. What kind of training do you go through?"

"It's rather complicated…" For a moment, Nicole held a pained expression. "As I mentioned earlier, among some of the general population, we're thought of as assassins, but that's the least of who and what we are. The teaching in the Sage's Tower is very rigorous and strict. We learn everything there is to know about our history, combat, science, and philosophy, and yes, we even learn a bit about how to take a life.

"But the term 'blood maiden' comes from the matching ceremony—where our fingertips were pierced and your blood commingled with mine. I'm now a part of you as much as you're a part of me; nothing can undo that but death. And through my training, I can now detect you wherever you are. I can feel your heartbeat literally next to my own. Even if you were on the other side of the island, if I closed my eyes, I'd be able to sense what direction I'd need to go to find you."

"How is that possible?" Peabo asked.

Nicole shrugged. "Do you ask how it is that you breathe? Some things just are."

"Does that mean we're married?"

She looked amused. "You mean as in life partners? Have babies together?"

"Well…" His face burned from embarrassment.

"No, that's not what we are. I love you more than any woman will ever love you. You're a part of me now. But that isn't the same thing as a wife. Think of me as a sister. And blood maidens cannot bear children. That's not my role in this life."

Peabo wasn't sure how to react to that. "I'm sorry."

"Why would you be sorry? I'm doing exactly what I've always wanted. Next question."

Peabo wanted to ask about the way the crowd had reacted

to her, all the offensive things they whispered about her. Why had they behaved that way? But it felt rude—too personal and embarrassing. So he opted for something more practical.

"What now?" he said. "We have a home. What's next?"

She nodded at the sword attached to his belt. "Do you know how to use that thing?"

"Yes."

"Good." She stood and brushed off her hands. "Then I think it's time you show me what I'm working with."

Peabo's legs flew out from under him and he landed hard on his back, his breath whooshing from his lungs. When he hopped back up onto his feet, he saw phantom pinpricks of light and struggled to catch his breath.

Nicole didn't press her attack, but her look of confidence made it clear that he had very much underestimated her.

He shifted his fighting stance, trying to take advantage of his longer reach, and snapped out a jab. She flicked it away effortlessly.

Rolling his shoulders, he pushed forward with a rain of jabs, followed by a series of front kicks. She blocked or avoided them all, without giving up any ground.

He saw her punch coming, but before he could even move his hand into position to block it, she connected and pulled back, showing perfect control.

With a shout of frustration, he surged forward. He attacked, she blocked, and then she tagged him with a shot that would have been to the groin, but thankfully she altered its trajectory at the last second and tapped him on the thigh instead.

Out of breath, Peabo motion for them to stop. "Okay, that was utterly pathetic on my part. I feel like I'm a kid fighting against my teacher."

Nicole smiled. "Don't be so hard on yourself. I can see you're well trained."

"A load of good that does me when I can't even move fast enough to block anything you're hitting me with. You move faster than I've ever seen *anyone* move."

Nicole sat cross-legged on the grass and motioned for him to follow suit. "I'm a level seven dívka smrti, which makes me a pretty good fighter, whether hand-to-hand or with weapons. Don't compare yourself to me; that'll just frustrate you. Let's focus on you." She held out her hand. "Show me your medallion."

Peabo handed it to her, and she wiped the sweat from it and pointed at the symbols.

"See? You have excellent strength and dexterity ratings, and a very strong constitution. Your attributes make you a natural fighter. You just need to advance in levels."

"You say that as if I'm supposed to understand what that means."

"It's not complicated. Everyone starts at level one, like you," Nicole explained. "And most people, unless they're of certain professions, will remain at level one; they'll simply never have an opportunity or reason to advance. But as a fighter, you'll want to advance as fast as you can."

"Why? Because I'll get paid more?"

"Well, there is that benefit, but there's far more to it. When you advance a level, it means that you become in essence more of what you already are. If you're naturally strong, advancing to the next level means you'll be a bit stronger. Fast reflexes will become faster, and so on."

Nicole dug out a similar medallion from under her tunic and put it next to his. "See the symbol on the left? Yours is a one while mine is a seven. When you advance, your medallion will automatically reflect the change in your body. In your case, I'd expect you to see rapid benefits to speed and strength. You're naturally very gifted in both."

Peabo chuckled. "A fat lot of good that did me when sparring against you. What are your strengths?"

Nicole's cheeks turned a slight shade of pink. "Mine are a bit unusual. To even qualify for training as a dívka smrti, I had to have top marks."

"In what?"

"In everything. It's a real privilege to be selected."

"So what you're saying is… you're a good person to have watching my back."

She smiled. "I'd hope so."

"All right, and if I want to advance to the next level? What do I need to do?"

Nicole stood and began packing up their things. "First, let's go back and see if our place is ready to move into. We'll cover the rest of your training tomorrow." She winked. "I have a few ideas."

While Nicole arranged things the way she liked them in the cramped kitchen, Peabo was in effect sent to his room to get him out of the way. He didn't mind; in fact, after an exceptionally eventful day, he was relieved to get a chance to lie down and rest for a bit. It took him all of about five minutes to fall into a restless sleep.

It was the sort of light sleep that felt somewhat surreal, because he was thinking about things, flitting from one worry to another, yet he caught himself snoring on occasion. In this semi-asleep state he smelled something cooking; it smelled like fried onions, which he loved. That made him think of Nicole in the kitchen, which in turn made him wonder about the sleeping arrangements. There was only one bed, and hardly enough room to squeeze in another bed. This was going to be awkward.

Suddenly, flashes of someone else's thoughts intruded on his own. When he heard the bedroom window opening, he opened his eyes and turned his head to look.

Only… his head didn't move. Other than his eyelids, his muscles weren't responding. It was as if he was a quadriplegic. He couldn't move at all.

From the corner of his eye, he saw a shadowy figure starting to climb through the window. He heard the intruder's breathing, a harsh wheezing, like someone having an asthma attack.

He wanted to scream, to move, to do something, but all he could do was blink.

"Peabo?" said Nicole through the closed bedroom door. "What's wrong? I feel your heart racing."

The figure was halfway through the window, but at the sound of Nicole's voice, it backed away and receded from Peabo's awareness.

The bedroom door opened, pouring light into the room.

"Are you okay?" Nicole said.

Peabo couldn't respond. What was wrong with him? Was it some otherworldly sickness? An allergy to the unfamiliar foods he'd eaten today?

Nicole rushed into the room, slammed the window shut, and leaned over him. "Close only one eye if you can't move."

He closed his right eye.

"Damn!" She grabbed one of the daggers he'd left on the table by the bed and sliced open her thumb. It began bleeding, and she shoved it into his mouth. "You've been spelled. My blood will help with the symptoms."

He tasted her blood on his tongue and felt it pooling in the back of his throat, but he couldn't swallow it. Nicole forcefully lifted him into a sitting position and tilted his head back. The blood slid down his throat, and within seconds he was able to croak out one gurgling word.

"Someone..."

She held him up and put her thumb back into his mouth. "Suck hard on the cut. It'll help you."

He found he was able to do as she instructed, and in about a minute he was free of whatever "spell" had been put upon him. Once again his muscles were his own.

"At first I thought I was dreaming," he said. "I sensed someone's thoughts and saw someone at the window, and I couldn't move."

"One second." Nicole raced from the room and returned with a large wooden bar that she placed across the window, preventing entry. Then she disappeared once more. Peabo caught the smell of something burning.

He grabbed his brace of daggers and hobbled after her, his legs wobbly. "Don't you think we should go after whoever that was?"

She turned from the stove to face him. "Do you sense their thoughts anymore?"

He paused and cleared his mind. "No. I don't think so."

Nicole scraped what she could salvage from their dinner onto a serving dish. "Then they've already left, and there's no sense in going after them now. Whatever they wanted, they needed the element of surprise, which they've lost."

"What happened to me? Why couldn't I move?" Peabo shuddered at the helplessness he'd felt. He could have had his throat sliced open and there wouldn't have been a thing he could have done about it.

She motioned to the dining table. "Sit and I'll explain."

Peabo pointed at Nicole's hand. "Your thumb is still bleeding. Let me wrap it in something."

She shook her head. "It's fine. I heal very quickly. Sit."

Peabo sat down, and she doled out portions of what looked like stir-fried vegetables, rice, and something that might have been meat… but was probably just another kind of mushroom. Then she sat down and began eating.

"In this world," she began, "everything the mind does sends signals to those nearby. This isn't commonly understood by most, but I learned many things during my training in the

Sage's Tower. Those signals of thought, they take many forms, and you're able to sense one of those forms.

"At all times, people are unwittingly transmitting these signals. But there are some who transmit these signals *intentionally*—and what they send is not just their thoughts. They send transmissions that affect other people, causing help or harm. Or, as in your case, causing paralysis."

"Okay… I kind of understand… I guess. And why did your blood help with that?"

"As a part of my training, my body was infused with certain… treatments." She looked uncomfortable. "These treatments make *dívka smrti* immune to the effects of most spells and poison. They're also why we cannot have children. When I shared my blood with you, it acted like a healing potion, speeding up your body's natural process of removing the spell's effects."

Peabo's mind raced. This all felt too close to magic. But this wasn't Earth. It wasn't even the same universe that Earth was in. And the laws of physics were probably somehow different. He recalled what Nolan had said in his note.

Forget about anything you think you know about how science works.

Nicole reached across the table and touched his hand. "I feel your heart racing again. Are you okay?"

Her ability to sense his heartbeat—that was yet another thing he couldn't explain.

He nodded. "I guess I'm realizing more and more that I'm really not in my old world anymore." He returned her gaze. "I want to be sure I understand. If that person had tried the same trick on you, it wouldn't have worked?"

"No. I wouldn't have been affected at all."

"And how common is it to be able to do whatever that person did?"

"It's not common. But rogue mages do exist. Mostly those with some basic talent that they never developed very far, but is strong enough for them to eke out a dangerous living."

"So you think this was just some thief?" Peabo asked. "Breaking in on the very first night we're here, and while we're in the house?"

Nicole waved dismissively. "Think about it. All day workmen were here preparing this place for us. Something was obviously going on. Maybe this rogue was notified and was overconfident with his skills."

"Or maybe *not* so overconfident," Peabo said. "If you hadn't sensed me…"

"But I did, and yes, he was unprepared for that. He had counted on facing a helpless opponent." She smiled. "But trust me, I am not helpless."

Peabo frowned. It was frightening to think just how close to death he had been.

Nicole squeezed his hand again. "Don't worry. I will protect you, Peabo. And soon, this'll be less of a concern. The higher your level, the less likely it is you'll be affected by such spells."

"You said you have plans for me tomorrow. You're going to show me how to advance in these levels?"

She chuckled. "Don't get too excited. It's a lot of work, and it takes a long time. But yes, I'll show you what you need to know. Our life's adventure together starts tomorrow."

Nicole stood guard in the doorway as Peabo slept. She'd lied to him when she told him the intruder was probably some common thief. Whoever had paralyzed Peabo had to be at least a level three healer or a level five conductor—and there was no way a tiny farmhouse like this would draw the interest of such a spellcaster.

Unless they'd been sent.

But sent for what reason? Was Peabo the target, or was she? There were those on the mainland who would rather have seen her dead than humiliated. But if Peabo really was what he claimed to be, a plainswalker, that was something entirely different. If the legends of the plainswalker were true, Peabo was supposed to be some form of foil against the reawakening of the twin Gods. It was hard for her to imagine such a latent power in the form of someone as weak and defenseless as the man laying in her bed. If someone knew that a real plainswalker was walking the lands, any number of high-powered people from the mainland might want to control such a man. And she, of all people, was paired to him.

Peabo yelled and shot up into a sitting position, a haunted expression on his face.

"Shh, it was just a dream," she said, walking toward the bed. But then she realized he was still dreaming. Behind closed eyelids, his eyes darted back and forth.

She sat on the edge of the bed and spoke in a soothing whisper. "It's okay. Nicole's here, and I'm watching over you. Lie back down. Go to sleep."

He did as she asked—and then released a shuddering sob. He was weeping in his sleep. She could feel his emotions lying just beneath the surface.

Had the intruder done more damage than she knew about?

Nicole scooted closer and closed her eyes. She hated to invade his privacy, but she needed to know…

She placed her hands on his broad shoulders, holding him physically while she nestled her mind into his. This was the most intimate connection that two people could make, and she almost pulled away. The memories of her previous partner's death were still so raw; when he died, it had felt as though she were the one being stabbed in the heart. But she willed herself to hold the connection with Peabo. She was here for him. And in her mind's eye, she saw what he saw. Felt what he felt.

She saw an older woman and man, dark-skinned and smiling. They were his parents. He was feeling an almost overwhelming sorrow at the knowledge that he'd never see them again. Never be able to talk to his mother again.

She saw glimpses of a world very foreign to her. A world with devices that let you see others in faraway places, wagons that moved without anything to pull them, ships that transported people in the air. It was fantastic magic, but it meant nothing to Peabo. He didn't miss those things. He cared only about the loss of his parents.

Nicole slowly pulled her mind away and found herself spooning with this stranger who meant everything to her. She breathed in deeply of his scent and felt his heartbeat slow to a more normal pace. The dreams had faded for him, but they remained foremost in her thoughts.

He really was from another world. And now he was scared and lonely—much like she had been ever since her prior partner's death. They were so different… and so similar.

She rolled away from him and returned to her vigil in the doorway. Somewhere out there in the darkness was a formidable opponent. Nicole prayed that it was mere chance that had brought the intruder to their window, but she didn't believe it.

Not for a moment.

CHAPTER SEVEN

Peabo stood by as Nicole tried to get them some work from the farmer they were renting their home from. The farmer was a stout man, heavily muscled, but Nicole towered over him. And yet in contrast to the overbearing attitude she'd maintained with the workers the day before, now she was quite friendly and cordial. She'd been prodding to find out what work he might need done, and had uncovered that he had a rat infestation in one of his fields.

"But I can't offer you anything for looking into it," the man said. "I've already offered it to the guild for them to take care of."

Nicole tilted her head. "And have they?"

"Well, no… and I gave them the job at the beginning of the growing season, which is almost over. Still, a contract is a contract."

Nicole put her hand on the man's shoulder. "How about we

look into your problem for free then? You don't need a contract with us, just point us in the direction of the problem and we'll see what we can do."

The farmer frowned. "I don't suppose it would be against my honor to just point you in the direction of the nest." He nodded to the northeast field. "One of my boys saw a mound of them rats off near the far end of the fire radish field. They only saw the one mound, but you know where there's one, there are probably dozens more we just haven't seen."

"Excellent," said Nicole. "Do you care what we do with the carcasses?"

"You're serious?" the farmer said, looking doubtful. "Just the two of you are doing this?"

"Of course we're serious," Nicole replied.

The man shrugged. "In that case, I'll give you the choice. Either bury the carcasses, or I can lend you a wagon so you can bring them back. If you do that, I'll have the missus smoke and dry the meat, and we can split it."

Peabo's stomach turned at the idea, but Nicole clasped hands with the farmer. "That sounds like a great deal. We'll be back this evening. You just have the smoker ready."

A few minutes later they were taking a small four-wheeled wagon out into the field, Peabo pushing and Nicole pulling.

"What does pest control have to do with advancing my level?" Peabo asked.

Nicole chuckled. "It's easier for me to show you than to explain."

"These aren't rats," Peabo said.

Nicole had just kicked an anthill, sending thousands of black ants scurrying forth.

"We'll get to the rats in a second. This is just a demonstration. I want you to pick up one of those ants and squish it between your fingers."

"Why not just stomp on them?"

She glared at him.

Peabo sighed. "Fine. You're the boss." He picked up an ant, squeezed, and felt a pop. "Okay, I killed an ant. What's that supposed to prove?"

"Do it again, but this time look at the ant as you're squeezing. Tell me if you see anything."

Peabo repeated the procedure, and this time he looked closely. When he killed the ant, he saw a pinprick spark.

"You mean that tiny spark?" he said. "Is that what you're trying to get me to see?"

"Yes. That little spark is what the sages in the tower call a life essence. All creatures have one. The sages say that a portion of a life's essence is made visible to the person who exposed that essence. In other words, there's a link created between the defeated creature's essence and yours. In killing the ant, you absorb their essence—and by doing so, you've made yourself stronger."

"And the more of those essences I collect, the closer I get to another level?"

Nicole gave him a friendly smack on the back. "See? You're not as dumb as you look."

"Gee, thanks."

"Now, on to something larger. We'll never get anywhere killing ants. The bigger the animal, the larger the essence."

They continued on through the field until they came upon a mound of dirt that rose about six feet above the soil. A scratching sound came from the grasses to one side, and Peabo looked to see a furry face peeking out from the tall grasses. It was a rat—but it was the size of a beagle. Probably a thirty-pounder.

The animal surged toward him, its orange incisors flashing in the sunlight, and Peabo instinctively pulled his katana, leaped to the side, and with a practiced slice decapitated the thing.

"Nicely done," said Nicole. "Now, what do you see?"

Just above the twitching body of the dead rat was a shimmering ball of light. It crackled like a ball of raw electricity.

"Is that the essence?" he asked.

Nicole shrugged. "I can't see it. As I said, only the one who exposed the essence can see it. If we'd both contributed to the creature's death, we'd each see a different portion—mine might be bigger or smaller, depending on how much I'd contributed. But hurry now—you don't want the essence to dissipate."

Peabo was confused. "What am I supposed to do?"

"Just touch it."

Peabo reached forward cautiously. When his fingertips came within a few inches of the blob of light, it moved toward him. He yanked back his hand.

Nicole rolled her eyes. "It won't hurt you. Just touch it."

Peabo again reached toward the light. It moved toward his

outstretched fingers, and this time he didn't pull away. It enveloped his hand, then vanished. He hadn't felt a thing.

He looked at Nicole. "The ball of light wrapped itself around my hand, and now it's gone. Is that what's supposed to happen?"

She nodded. "Your body absorbed the essence. You've taken your first step. Now that you understand what we're doing, we can get to work." She nodded at the mound of dirt. "I'll help you with this first nest, just so you can get the rhythm of it, but the ones afterwards, I'll want you to do it."

"Okay. Let's do it." Peabo tried to sound confident, but the size of the mound had him feeling a bit nervous.

Nicole gathered up a bundle of dried grasses, then pulled out some kind of firestarting device and clicked it a few times, setting the grasses aflame. She tossed the burning bundle into a hole at the top of the nest. It took ten or fifteen seconds before the first puffs of smoke began rising out of the mound, but after a full minute, the mound looked like a miniature volcano, with smoke coming out of the top.

She stepped back, a knife in each hand. "Remember," she said, "if you see an essence, grab it before it disappears."

Two rats emerged from other holes at the base of the mound. Nicole dispatched one with a swipe and Peabo skewered the other. But they were only the first two of many; suddenly it seemed as though they were everywhere at once.

"They're disoriented from the smoke, so attack them as soon as they surface," Nicole instructed, taking out two more.

Peabo slashed one rat, then another, and another.

"Remember the essences!" Nicole called out. Peabo noticed

she was swiping her hand above a twitching corpse, likely collecting her own essence bounty.

It wasn't easy to grab the orbs while at the same time defending against the onslaught of rats, but he managed not to let a single orb slip away. By the time they were done, he figured he had killed about fifty rats, and Nicole had probably killed another twenty more. Peabo was sweating and splattered with bits of gore. But Nicole was calm as ever. She had backed out of the fight midway.

As they started collecting the corpses and tossing them onto the wagon, he asked her about that.

"I told you I was only here to help you get started," she said. "You need to be the one to kill the rats, if we're going to get you to level two."

"What about you? Don't you need the essences as well?"

Nicole gave him a look that implied he'd said something stupid, but her tone was mild. "With several hundred of these, maybe a thousand, you'll probably get to a new level. But for me to level up from rats, I'd probably have to make the entire species go extinct. No, these essences are worthless at my level, but for you, they're perfect."

Peabo tossed another rat on the wagon. "Did you just say I have to kill a *thousand* of these things?

Nicole laughed. "The path to advancement lies on the corpses of your enemies."

Peabo shook his head. "When I got up this morning, I didn't imagine I'd be killing a thousand rats today. But if that's what it takes… let's do this."

"How will I know if I've gotten a level?" Peabo asked.

"Trust me, you'll know."

Peabo was nearing exhaustion. He'd been clearing out rats' nests all day, and it wasn't easy. The smoke left them dazed and confused, but it also seemed to piss them off. Those suckers were fast, and when they got past his defenses, those teeth of theirs could really take a chunk out of him. Nicole refused to help, but she did give him some pointers along the way—things like he needed to loosen his grip on the sword so his hand didn't cramp, and that he needed to think of the killing as almost like a dance.

It was the "dance" comment that made things click for him. When he approached the fight that way, his balance was better distributed, his movements smoother. There was a rhythm to it—attack, collect the essence, and turn to face another foe. His karate master had been trying to improve his sword work for years, but in one day Nicole had done more for him with only a few words of advice.

He cut down another rat and absorbed its essence. "I think that's the last of them from this nest," he said.

But he'd spoken too soon. The now-familiar scrabbling of claws presaged the emergence of the largest rat he'd seen yet. This one had to weigh at least a hundred pounds, and it immediately charged right at him.

He jumped to the side and swiped down with his bloodied katana. That should have resulted in a decapitation—it had done so with the other rats—but instead he merely wedged his blade into the top of the rat's head. This rat wasn't only bigger, it was faster, nimbler, and had dodged what would otherwise have been a killing blow.

Still, it had a sword stuck into its skull, and it wasn't going anywhere.

Peabo pulled his dagger and flung it at the rat. It landed with a meaty thwack at the juncture of the rodent's neck and shoulders. Blood gushed from the wound, and the creature fell over, shuddered, and then lay still.

"That must have been the queen of the nest," Nicole said, and let out a big yawn. "She's a big one."

Peabo looked up at her. "Are you bored, or just tired?"

"I'm fine." She motioned toward the rat. "Finish her off."

Peabo pulled his katana from the rat's skull, then retrieved the dagger. Back on Earth, he would have felt bad for killing an animal, but this one… well, he had no illusions about what she would have done to him. This was a harsher world than his own. Or maybe it was simply that this world had exposed him to the harshness he'd been privileged enough to never have to see back on Earth.

When the ball of essence bubbled up from the rat's carcass, he reached out to it. Previously, he'd felt nothing when coming into contact with an essence, but this time, a tingling sensation traveled up his arm and spread throughout his body. It was almost like he'd stuck his finger in an electric socket. Except it wasn't painful. It was… invigorating.

The exhaustion he'd felt vanished as goose bumps rose on every inch of his skin.

He looked over at Nicole. She looked different. Clearer

somehow, as if his vision had improved. Then he breathed in deeply, feeling a shiver of exhilaration run up and down his spine. The smell of combat was everywhere. Hanging in the air was the coppery scent of blood. He sensed the chlorophyll from the grass, the scent of the freshly turned soil, the musky smell of the rats, and even his own sweat—and every odor was so much more intense than ever before.

"Congratulations," said Nicole. "That was well-earned."

"I leveled up, didn't I? Do I look different?"

"No, but I saw your reaction. It's almost an erotic feeling, don't you think?"

That wasn't exactly how Peabo would have described it, but he nodded. He was tingling with energy. And he felt stronger. He felt more… everything. Like an improved version of himself. He wanted to dispatch just one more rat so he could test out these new abilities.

In fact, he wanted to do today all over again.

"That was almost indescribable," he said. "Can we do this again tomorrow?"

Nicole laughed. "You're adorably naïve. Let's see how you feel tomorrow morning. In the meantime, let's get the wagon back to the farmer. We've got plenty for his wife to process."

The next morning, lying in bed, Peabo moaned. Every inch of his body ached.

Nicole rolled over to face him and smiled sympathetically. "I suppose you're not ready to do it all over again today?"

Peabo tried sitting up, but Nicole pushed him back down and shook her head.

"I was kidding, you big bag of radishes. You need a few days to take it easy. Your shoulders and arms are probably the worst off—do you want me to massage them?"

"No, that's uh… that's okay," he stammered.

She tilted her head. "Why not? You'll feel better afterwards."

Peabo felt his face getting warm. He prayed that with his mahogany skin tone it didn't show. Nicole had worn only a long thin shirt to bed, and he was suddenly all too aware of that fact.

"I'll be fine," he said.

She shrugged. "Okay then, I'll prepare breakfast."

She rolled out of bed, took off her shirt, got dressed, and left the bedroom. If Peabo's face was warm before that nude display, it was burning hot now.

He wondered what he'd gotten himself into with this lady. Not only was she some kind of Amazon superhero woman, she was… attractive. And yet their relationship was very strange. They were more than married, but not married at all.

Treat her like a sister, she'd said. Peabo had been an only child, but he was pretty sure that most brothers didn't see their adult sisters naked.

It took three days before Peabo was back in fighting shape. For the first two days, his body was unbelievably sore, so much so that he even broke down and let Nicole massage his stiff arms and shoulders. At first this had seemed like a huge mistake, since she seemingly had only two modes for her massages: off and painful. But though it hurt like hell when she did it, afterward he felt a lot better.

Now, as they walked into town, Peabo was feeling no aftereffects whatsoever. And it wasn't only his body that felt better; *he* felt better too. The last time he'd walked into this town, with Brodie—that was only days ago but it felt like ages—he'd been nervous, an outsider. But now, with Nicole by his side, he felt comfortable. He was still an outsider, and there was a lot he didn't know, but he was sure she wouldn't let him get into a bad situation.

"Do you know where the booking agent is in this place?" Nicole asked.

"Not exactly, but I know the general direction." He pointed. "Brodie was leading me that way, through the market, when you caught my eye."

"I 'caught your eye'?" Nicole said, raising an eyebrow. "Is *that* what happened?"

"Well… I mean… you had a sort of presence about you, even though you'd been crying."

"I don't think you really mean it, but you can be sweet sometimes… for a plainswalker."

They walked across the square, and soon enough they found what they were looking for. In front of a squat building was a large chalkboard filled with scrawled messages that Peabo couldn't make sense of. He could read Common now, but this chicken scratch was a mystery all the same.

Sitting at a table in front of the chalkboard was a teen boy. He saw them approaching and called out to them. "Hey there, are you guilded? Interested in some easy coin?"

Nicole frowned at the chalkboard. "What do you have that's a bit challenging?"

The teen leaned forward and examined their medallions. "Let's see. You're a level two, and…" His eyes widened as he looked at Nicole's medallion. "Level seven! Wow, you're not kidding… you do want something challenging. There's not a lot on the board, but let me have a talk with my uncle. He's got some things that might be worth your time, Miss…?"

"Nicole."

"Miss Nicole. I'll be right back." The teen disappeared inside.

"Well, you sure impressed the kid," Peabo said to Nicole.

"I doubt he's ever seen a seven before out here in the hinterlands. Which also means he probably won't have many interesting jobs, but it's worth a shot. Maybe they've spotted some stray hobgoblin scouts or something."

Three men exited the building. Front and center was an older gentleman in leathers, and flanking him to either side were two men in chain mail.

The older man addressed Nicole directly. "I'm sorry, ma'am, but we can't have you in a group, especially one with a higher-level challenge."

Nicole stiffened. "Why is that?"

The man frowned, glanced at Peabo, and shook his head. "I'm sorry, but given your background, there's nothing for you here."

Nicole looked like she was about to assault the man, so Peabo stepped in quickly. "What about one of the lower-level challenges then? What's available?"

The agent let out a sigh. "Listen, sir, I don't want any trouble. But the folks around here know about your partner's history. Nobody's going to trust a failed maiden on their team."

Peabo barely controlled a sudden surge of rage. He growled, "She's the finest person you'll ever hope to—"

Nicole put a hand on his arm. "Let's go."

"No," said Peabo. "This is crap." Peabo hadn't felt so angry on behalf of anyone else… ever. As a former soldier, he'd participated in missions where lives had been lost, but he'd never been in a real fistfight in his life. At the moment, he so wanted to beat the living daylights out of these three men.

"Trust me. Let's go," said Nicole, her voice somehow projecting directly into his head. And the look she gave him brooked no argument.

Peabo let out a deep breath, stepped away from the booking agent's table, and walked away, with Nicole holding his arm.

"I don't understand," he said. "Why do the people here hate you?"

"Peabo…" Her voice was soft, almost whispering. "People like me… we're feared as demonic fighters and defenders. But almost none of us have lived past a failure."

"But you *didn't* fail," Peabo said. "You told me that you were sent to take care of something and your partner was killed while you were gone. You couldn't have been in two places at once."

"Agreed, but it doesn't matter." Nicole looked at him and

smiled. "Thanks for defending me, but it wasn't necessary. And you can go back there if you want. They would likely still give *you* an assignment."

Peabo draped his arm over her shoulders. "No chance. We're a team. If I've learned nothing else in this strange place, it's that you and I are working together from here on in."

She grabbed his hand. "Thank you. But we are eventually going to run out of money, so… are you up for fighting something other than rats?"

"Sure. What do you have in mind?"

She gave him a wicked grin. "We're going to cut out the middle man."

Before Peabo could ask what she meant by that, she'd fast-walked into the path of a balding man hurrying down the street toward the booking agent. He was dressed in what looked like monk's robes.

"Brother, can I help you?" she said.

He stopped, startled, and shook his head. "No, no… this is something for the guild."

Nicole showed her medallion, then motioned for Peabo to do the same. "We're guilded, and can probably work a quick deal with you if you like. What's the problem?"

The man looked uncertain, but then nodded. "Father Karl… he's been dead all these five years, but I came into the monastery this morning, and…" He began crying. "Well, he's leading the morning service. Everyone ran, but he's still in there. I'm afraid of what he might do."

Peabo's jaw dropped. This guy had just described a zombie.

He must have misunderstood what the monk had said, or he'd misspoken.

But Nicole was as calm as ever. "Okay, how about this. No money, but if you can supply us with healing elixirs, at least two dozen, then we have a deal."

The monk nodded vigorously, his jowls jiggling. "That's fair. Very fair. But please don't… I mean, Father Jakub was a good man. I don't want him hurt."

"He's already dead," said Nicole, giving the monk a withering stare. "Trust me, he won't feel a thing."

Peabo's eyes widened. He hadn't misunderstood. How was this possible?

The monk wrung his hands. "Well… okay. When can you do it? We have congregants expected for the midday service, and we can't have Father Jakub just… It's just wrong, and the smell is horrific."

"We'll take care of it right now. Which way to the church?"

The monk pointed with a trembling hand. "It's just on the north end of town. Right next to the graveyard."

"Rest easy, brother. Consider your problem resolved." Nicole motioned to Peabo, and they began jogging to the north.

Behind them the monk yelled, "May the Nameless One put his blessings upon you!"

CHAPTER EIGHT

As Peabo stepped into the church, the smell hit him immediately. It reminded him of urine. No, it was stronger than that. Ammonia.

"Don't breathe deeply," Nicole cautioned. "The scent of the undead can make you dizzy."

Peabo was more than happy to breathe shallowly. He pulled out his dagger and katana, and Nicole had her daggers at the ready as they moved forward down the church's central aisle. But despite the strength of the odor, he saw nothing.

It suddenly dawned on Peabo that he had no idea what he was looking for, nor what the rules of engagement were. It was one thing being in a war, where you knew that anyone not wearing your uniform was likely the enemy. But this wasn't a war, at least not that he knew of. There had to be some laws in this place, yet he didn't have the first clue what they might be.

The word she'd used for the thing they were looking for wasn't one he was familiar with. In Common it translated into "not dead," but in the way she'd used it, he'd automatically translated it to "undead." Did that mean what he thought it meant?

"Are these things dangerous? Are we supposed to kill it?"

"Yes on both counts." Nicole put her hand to her ear. "Can you hear any thoughts coming from it?"

Peabo stood still, and he heard something. A buzzing sound. No, not a sound—he was hearing someone's thoughts… but they were confused, jumbled. Was that the mind of the undead priest?

He pointed toward the side of the church. "It's coming from over there. Outside, I think."

Nicole raised her eyebrows. "The graveyard is over that way. Come."

As they slipped back out of the church, a desperate voice shouted from the direction of the graveyard.

"Ah! Oh please, Nameless One, keep it away!"

Peabo and Nicole raced around to the side of the church and stopped short. At the edge of the graveyard stood a dirt-encrusted figure, wearing torn, filthy clothing. He was more skeleton than flesh. At his feet was another man, a living man, bloody and terrified.

Peabo hesitated for only a moment before lunging at the shambling corpse. He struck with the katana, lopping off one arm at the shoulder.

But the undead man didn't even seem to mind. He spun

toward Peabo and attacked. Peabo dodged just as Nicole appeared with a tree limb in hand and slammed the skeletal creature in the chest. Several ribs fell to the ground, and the skeleton had to wheel its remaining arm to catch its balance.

Seizing the opening, Peabo brought his sword down on the base of the creature's neck. He sliced right through it, and the moment he did, the entire collection of bones and rags collapsed into a motionless pile on the ground.

A large shimmering ball of energy rose from the remains. Peabo and Nicole both scooped up their share.

The living man on the ground cried out. "He's raised another!"

Peabo turned to find another skeleton standing in the graveyard. And this one was truly only a skeleton, with no rags to speak of; it must have been buried for much longer than the previous creature.

Nicole raced ahead and slammed the thick tree branch against the skeleton's knee. The crack of shattered bone echoed across the graveyard. Again Peabo took advantage of the opportunity, decapitating the creature with a single vicious stroke from behind, and again the headless body collapsed.

They collected the essence, then Nicole nodded toward the far end of the graveyard. "There he is."

Peabo couldn't see what she was looking at—the far end of the graveyard was all deep shadows—but he had no doubt there was something there. The smell from that direction was overpowering.

Nicole dropped the tree limb and pulled out her daggers.

"The blades work better against the juicy undead," she explained.

They moved closer, into the shadows. And that was when Peabo saw the yellow glow of the creature's eyes.

"Holy crap, what *is* that?"

"It's a zombie," said Nicole.

The creature was rocking back and forth in the shadows. It closed its eyes, practically vanishing in the gloom, and made a rhythmic gurgling sound as though it was trying to pray or sing through ruined vocal cords. The static from the creature's mind was getting louder, too.

"I thought zombies were mindless killers," Peabo said.

"What would give you that idea? Just be careful. If this Father Jakub was able to raise two of his dead parishioners, he was probably a decently leveled cleric when he was alive. Let's move in. Same strategy as before. I'll distract, you go for the head."

Peabo adjusted the grip on his katana. "Fine. But I'm going to have lots of questions for you later."

Nicole raced forward. The zombie reacted with surprising swiftness, raising a thick wooden staff and swinging it at her head, missing by only inches. Peabo came in right behind her and sliced at the arm holding the staff, thinking he would lop it off as he'd done with the first skeleton. But instead the sword bit heavily into the flesh before striking something solid, sending powerful vibrations back up the blade.

What the hell are this thing's bones made of?

Nicole ducked another attack, and with preternatural speed

she slashed at the front of the undead's neck. A hissing exited from the new hole in its throat, and the smell grew even stronger.

Peabo came around behind the zombie priest and brought his katana down hard on the back of the thing's neck. He felt the blade dig between the vertebrae. It didn't go all the way in, but it left the head tilting at an unnatural angle.

With a loud keening, the priest turned and swung its staff viciously. Peabo just barely managed to block the heavy attack with his sword.

That's when Nicole delivered the final blow. With one of her daggers she severed the head, and the priest collapsed.

"Holy crap," said Peabo. "That thing was tough for a dead guy." His sword arm was tingling from having blocked that last attack. Evidently undead were stronger than they looked.

Nicole smiled and shook her head as if to say, *You don't know what tough is.* And he probably didn't. Peabo knew so little about this world.

They absorbed the priest's essence, then returned to the injured man, who had levered himself up against a tombstone. It looked like one of his legs was injured.

"What happened here?" she asked.

The man still looked terrified. "I don't know. I was visiting my mother's grave, and I smelled something awful. Next thing I knew, a skeleton came up out of the ground and attacked me. I owe you my life. If you hadn't arrived..."

Peabo was about to say that the guy didn't owe them anything, but Nicole tossed him a glare that silenced him.

"We are guilded and would expect no less than two hundred gold royals for such a service," she said.

"Two *hundred*?" said the man, looking shocked. "I cannot afford such a price. I am sorry. But…" He opened the pouch attached to his belt and poured its contents onto the ground. "I have … twenty-eight gold royals and seven silver."

Nicole sighed with exasperation.

"I'm sorry," the man pleaded, "but the crops are not doing well this season and I have a sick—"

"Fine," said Nicole, cutting him off. "Give me twenty-five gold and we're even."

"Oh, thank you, thank you." The man's eyes teared as he counted out the gold bars into Nicole's outstretched hand. "May the Nameless One bless you for your kindness."

Nicole turned and strode away, motioning for Peabo to follow.

As they walked, Peabo glanced back over his shoulder at the injured man, who was now hobbling north. "Did you really need to take most of that guy's money? I feel bad for him."

Nicole shook her head. "You are naïve. Did you see his boots, made of finely tooled hide? His fine linen vest, his silver-studded belt, those two gold rings? That man was wearing at least fifty gold worth of clothing and jewelry alone. I was half-tempted to strip him naked and send him on his way. Twenty-five gold? Bah!" She made a disgusted sound.

Nicole led them back toward the center of town. But as Peabo followed along, he had to ask about what had just happened.

"Is that a normal thing—dead things suddenly becoming reanimated?"

"It's not *normal*, but it can happen." Nicole shook her head grimly. "Now isn't the time to go over the science of the undead. I spent nearly a year studying it at the Sage's Tower, and it's a morbid topic. Trust me, you'll be happier not knowing."

But then she smiled. "Let's go find that monk. I believe he owes us some potions."

"Remember, don't unbar the door at night."

Nicole had given him that warning over and over again. But warning or no warning, sometimes nature called. And since for once Nicole was sleeping—instead of hovering over him like a mother hen—he took the opportunity to rise and go relieve himself.

He did miss having a toilet. A ceramic piss pot was not the same thing at all. No running water, no toilets, no hot showers, or even cold ones. And yet this place, this world… it was beginning to feel like home.

As he returned to the bedroom, the light from the lantern sent a warm glow over the sleeping Nicole—which in turn sent a warm glow through him. She was beautiful. She had undone her braid and the gossamer blonde threads splayed across her face and fell over the swell of her chest. And despite how strong she was, she had a narrow waist and full hips.

During waking hours, he didn't think about her in any way

other than a business partner. He didn't dare to, because he suspected she could read his mind. Hopefully she couldn't do it while she slept, because right now, he was feeling very conflicted about her. They had never hugged or kissed or done anything a couple might do, and yet he cared more about her than most of the girls he'd dated.

And yet he knew she didn't feel the same. She was still largely silent about her past, but it was clear that she was still mourning the loss of someone else. Of her prior partner.

He blew out the lamp, shrouding the room in darkness, and climbed back into bed.

"Are you okay?" said Nicole, her sleepy voice rising out of the gloom.

"I'm fine. Just needed to use the pot."

Nicole rolled over, and he sensed her body relaxing as she fell back asleep.

But Peabo only stared into the darkness, wondering how many sheep he needed to count before he'd get some rest.

In the underground city of Metamorphic, Brodie sat in the darkness of his private room. He had come here to avoid distractions, because when he talked with the head of the church, he couldn't risk losing his focus. Though he didn't wear the trappings of his office, Brodie was one of the highest-level priests in the church of the Nameless One, and that meant it was his duty to let the prelate know what had happened with the plainswalker.

He pulled his high priest's ring from a hidden pocket—in the darkness it gave off a light blue glow—and tapped out a message on its surface, using the holy code he'd been taught when he'd achieved level seven. The prelate wore the sister copy of this same ring, and Brodie pictured the series of taps wending its way through the miles that separated the two rings. At this very moment, the prelate would be feeling Brodie's communication come through in the form of vibrations on his finger.

With his message sent, and his heart beating loudly in his chest, Brodie waited. The prelate's answer came quickly, and Brodie's own ring vibrated in a pattern of short and long pulses that he easily translated.

"What do you mean he isn't with you any longer? Watcher, the plainswalker's welfare is in your hands. I would have thought you'd learned a lesson from your first mistake."

The words were relatively mild, but Brodie felt the rebuke like a slap in the face. When the head of the church referred to him by the title of Watcher, it was always a slap in the face. Brodie had failed as a Watcher almost thirty years ago—when Nolan had been poisoned.

Few people knew what a Watcher's true duties were. Most thought they were responsible for keeping the people of Myrkheim aware of the goings-on of the aboveworld. But although Brodie did this, it wasn't a Watcher's true purpose at all. The Watcher—an ancient title, originating with the first breaths of the church—was entrusted with two sacred responsibilities.

Watch for the arrival of the plainswalker.

And keep him safe.

Only two duties. And Brodie had failed at the most important one.

Nolan had told him that one day, another plainswalker would arrive. Brodie wasn't convinced—or at least, he wasn't convinced it would happen during his own lifetime—but after Nolan's death, the thought gave him a glimmer of hope that he might redeem his failure. And he'd spent the intervening years planning what he'd do differently with the next plainswalker, if he ever had the chance.

All of that planning had been torn to pieces with the arrival of the blood maiden. How in all the hells could he have anticipated *that*? And had he made a mistake, leaving Peabo with the woman?

He replied to the prelate on his ring. *"Prelate, I apologize for the unexpected news. But our plainswalker is headstrong, and before I could intervene, he managed to get paired with a blood maiden. Would you have me do something different?"*

The ring soon vibrated with the prelate's response. *"A blood maiden on the island? That is unexpected, but perhaps it is also fortunate. She will be heavily invested in keeping him safe. The ancient tablets say that the plainswalker will find his way, and we must trust in that. But Watcher, you must go to her and give her a ring to communicate to you with if she needs assistance. She will have been trained on its usage."*

Brodie replied. *"Thank you, and understood. I will contact you again when I have more to say."*

Then he let out a sigh of relief. He had already given her a ring. Now all he had to do was wait.

"I know you can inject your thoughts into my head," said Peabo as he ate breakfast with Nicole the next morning—an omelet heavy with spiced rat sausage. "Can you read my mind as well?"

Nicole shook her head. "Not in the way you're thinking. What I can do is sense your emotions when I'm near you—though that often gives me a pretty good clue to what's going on in that head of yours."

Peabo struggled to suppress his thoughts from last night. Of course, this only made them race to the fore of his mind. Trying to distract himself, he asked, "How exactly does that work?"

If Nicole sensed what he'd been thinking about, she didn't show it. She wiped her mouth and leaned back in her chair. "The technical details are hard to explain without a lot of background that you don't have. But the short version is, you and I are tuned to each other—we have a link. That's how I can hear and feel the things your body is doing, like how fast your heart is beating; it's like an invisible signal that I can feel. And when I send my thoughts to you, I'm using that link to send energy from one place to another. The truth is, everyone is transmitting invisible signals like these at all times—about who they are, what they're doing, what they're thinking. It's just that as a paired couple, we can sense each other's transmissions."

"I can't sense yours," Peabo said.

Nicole waved dismissively. "You're just too low level. In time you'll be able to sense me and send me your thoughts without speaking. Remember how I said leveling improves who you already are? These abilities are part of that."

Peabo frowned. "Okay, so everyone's sending out these signals, but normally no one can receive them. It's only because you and I are linked that we can read each other's signals. Right? So how is it that I can sometimes read *everyone's* thoughts? Or at least, most people's thoughts."

Nicole shrugged as though this were obvious. "Because you're a plainswalker. Listen, even as someone who's studied plainswalkers in the tower, I know little. There's not much in the chronicles about the origins of your abilities and exactly how they work. Hell, most people in the mainland have never even heard of a plainswalker. The earliest stories about the plainswalker are incomplete and it seems like the island-dwellers are the ones who are most familiar with the legends. After all, the plainswalker was supposed to have been born on the island."

Peabo frowned. He wasn't exactly born on the island, but if the previous plainswalkers all appeared like he had, that statement was as true as anything else. "And the story most people are told is that the plainswalker came from the Desolate Plains? What do you know of that?"

Nicole shrugged. "That's the same story everyone on the island is told. The truth is, nobody has explored that part of the island to verify where the plainswalker came from."

"Because of the Seekers?"

"Yes, among other things." Nicole narrowed her eyes at Peabo. "I forget how little you know about this world, plainswalker. Do you have other questions I can answer for you?"

Peabo had tons of questions, but he started with the one that had been on his mind ever since the encounter with the zombie priest.

"Well, I'd like to talk about this whole undead thing for a second," Peabo said, chewing on a gristly piece of rat sausage. "Where I come from, the dead stay dead. How are corpses able to suddenly come alive here?"

"You really want to get into this?" Nicole asked.

"If I'm stuck in a new world, I might as well understand what's going on in it."

Nicole sighed, then pointed from her head to his. "These transmissions we talked about—sending messages between us—they require energy, just like every other action we take. But a dead person, as you might imagine, doesn't exactly have much in the way of energy. Unless someone with very specific training transmits massive quantities of energy into them."

"You mean… into the dead body," Peabo said. What she described was gruesome, but also fascinating. To him it sounded like magic, but in this world it seemed to be a legitimate science.

"Yes, exactly."

"So corpses don't just come back to life on their own," Peabo said. "Someone has to reanimate them."

"Yes, of course." Nicole paused. "Have you ever beheaded anything other than a rat?"

Surprised by the question, Peabo thought back to a childhood memory. Back on his grandfather's farm, he'd watched his grandfather prepare a fresh chicken for supper. Step one: beheading it.

"I've seen it done," he said.

"Then you've seen the convulsions of the body. The body can still move, at least while its heart still beats, but the mind is no longer attached to give direction to it, so those movements are purposeless and uncoordinated. Undead are like that to an extent. Mindless vessels that can be infused with energy, by someone with the right training. But still, even their bodies must be coordinated by a brain. And once you removed that brain… the body collapses."

"Easier said than done," Peabo grunted. "So, what about Father Karl. Now that he's dead *again*, I was wondering who would have raised him in the first place? I assume someone had to have done that, right? I presume the dead don't normally come back to life."

"No, they don't." Nicole's brow furrowed. She remained silent for a few seconds before saying, "I don't know who would have done it, but that's actually something I was planning on looking into. And while I do that, I want you to see if there's anyone at the market selling a decent mace. As you observed, the crunchy undead are difficult to fight with edged weapons."

Peabo nodded. "I agree. A blunt weapon would be good to have."

Nicole smiled warmly. "I'm glad we agree. Just don't spend too much."

"Wait, you're not going with me to the market?"

"Do you need me to?"

"No, I guess. But what will you be doing?"

"Just a little research," Nicole said, shoveling a spoonful of eggs into her mouth.

"Care to elaborate?"

"There are a couple of things I'm wondering about. The first is our home intruder. It has to have been either a mage or cleric that paralyzed you. And second is that priest, who could only have been reanimated by someone especially powerful. I don't know if the two incidents are connected, but if it turns out there's a high-level necromancer in the area... well, that doesn't usually bode well for the people in the vicinity."

"Necromancer? That's really a thing?"

"Of course. A necromancer is nothing but a skilled cleric who's gone in a bad direction. But no decent community would tolerate one in their midst—unless you *want* an army of undead destroying everything you ever cared about."

"Has that happened before?" Peabo asked uneasily. The existence of undead was bad enough, but the idea that someone would raise an army of those things...

Nicole reached across the table and squeezed his hand. "Not in a long time. More often than not, there are enough good people around to stop maniacs like that."

Peabo was glad to hear there were good people to do that kind of thing. He just hoped he didn't have to be one of them.

Standing before a table featuring assorted weaponry, Peabo examined the mace in his hand. It looked well made, the handle wrapped in leather, but when he swung it, it didn't feel right. The balance was off. He put it back on the table.

"Do you have anything heavier and more solidly constructed?" he asked. "Like a footman's mace?" That was the type of mace Nicole had recommended he get.

The merchant held up a finger. "One moment." He snapped his fingers at another worker, who looked like his son. "Olaf, watch the store. I'll be right back."

The merchant disappeared into his smithy and returned a minute later with three different maces. He was also rolling a small section of a log with the shove of his boot. He set the maces on the table, and one of them immediately caught Peabo's eye. It had a large head with six flanges, raised surfaces designed to dig in and break things… like bones.

Peabo picked it up and swung it a bit. The handle was comfortable, and the balance was smooth. There was no rattling, nothing loose about it.

"That one took me almost two months to get right," said the merchant. He stood the log upright. "Go ahead. Test it."

Peabo took a light swing at the log, sending bark flying. He then gave the log a heavier hit, and then another and another. On the last strike, the log cracked.

The merchant smiled. "Satisfied?"

Peabo was impressed, but he tried not to look it. "How much?"

"Twenty-five gold royals."

Peabo made a choking sound. Nicole had told him that he'd

be getting ripped off if he paid more than eight. "Two gold," he countered.

"Pfft!" The merchant waved dismissively. "Don't insult my merchandise. Thirty gold."

Peabo frowned. This wasn't the way negotiations were supposed to work. "Five gold."

The merchant shook his head. "The materials alone are worth ten. Do you realize how long it took me to find the vibration-dampening barrier mushroom for the handle material? Those greedy bastard dwarves control the market on that stuff. Twenty gold, not a copper less."

Peabo squeezed the handle and found it had a slight give. No wonder it felt so good hitting with it.

He reminded himself of Nicole's instruction: *Don't pay more than eight gold.* But he *really* liked this mace.

"I only have fifteen gold," he said.

The merchant frowned. "Show me."

Peabo wondered what Nicole would do to him if he spent it all; somehow, she had automatically become the keeper of their finances. But he pulled out the pouch and dumped the fifteen small bars of gold onto the table.

The merchant looked back and forth between the small pile of gold and Peabo, a look of disappointment on his face. Peabo heard the man's inner voice grumbling to himself. *If only I hadn't been muscled out by the others in Dvorak, I wouldn't be haggling like this with a cheap fool who paints himself like a plainswalker. In the city I'd have customers who could afford quality pieces.*

"You're lucky I'm in a generous mood," said the merchant. He spit on the ground and extended his hand. "Deal."

Peabo shook the man's hand, and just like that he was the owner of a mace that made him very happy. He actually grinned as he gave it one final swish through the air. The end of the handle featured a thick leather braid, and he used that to hang the mace on his waistband. It was on the opposite hip from his katana, and somehow the combination felt right.

Peabo walked proudly through the merchants' square. He had no money to spend, but he perused the stalls of breads and fruit. And rat meat. Evidently the farmer must have sold the smoked rat meat, because every other merchant seemed to have some form of it for sale.

He paused before a woman selling sweets, but it wasn't the sweets that caught his eye, but the vendor herself. She didn't look out of the ordinary—just a dark-haired woman dressed like everyone else in Raiheim—but something about her made the hairs on the back of his neck stand on end.

The vendor looked at him, and her eyes grew surprisingly large. She pulled something from a small bag hanging from her waist and leaned forward with her arm extended. "Plainswalker, I have something you might relish. The first one is always free…"

Her voice was surprisingly warm and breathy as she offered him a brown jelly-like candy.

Peabo smiled politely and waved the treat away. The vendor leaned forward, pushing the treat closer, but Peabo was saved from having to decline again when two teens, tussling with each other, practically knocked him over, and a woman, presumably their mother, yelled, "Itzik! Stop fighting with your brother!"

Taking advantage of the commotion, Peabo continued on his way, patting the handle of the mace. He really wanted to test it out on something *crunchy*, like Nicole said. But at the thought of Nicole, he winced. She was going to give him so much grief for spending above his budget.

He shook his head. This relationship was just like being married—but without the benefits.

"Fifteen gold?" said Nicole. "I told you no more than eight!"

Peabo looked like a puppy who'd just been kicked. "The other stuff the merchant had was crap, and this was by far the best thing I'd seen all morning."

She sighed. "Fine. What's done is done. Show me this grand weapon of yours."

Peabo handed over the mace, and Nicole hefted it in one hand. It was well balanced, and the grip was particularly comfortable. The weaponsmith who made it had taken pride in its construction. Was it worth fifteen gold? Probably not. But it was a solid choice for a blunt weapon.

"Well?" said Peabo expectantly. "What do you think?"

Nicole scowled as she handed the weapon back. "It's an adequate weapon—but you still overpaid."

"I'm sorry—"

"No, it's my fault. I should have gone with you." Then she allowed a smile to creep onto her face. "Besides, we can afford the extra seven gold." She pulled out a pouch and tossed it onto the table. "Almost fifty gold in there. I don't know about you, but I didn't exactly want to eat hundreds of pounds of smoked rat, so I worked out a deal with the farmer's wife. She sold most of it, and that's our cut."

"Brilliant!" said Peabo. "I did see a lot of rat meat for sale in the market square."

"I don't doubt it. Did you see anything else of interest?"

Peabo shrugged. "Nothing in particular. Although there was one vendor who triggered my uncanny valley reaction."

"What is *that*?"

"Oh… um, it's kind of hard to explain." Peabo scratched at his chin. "Do people draw portraits around here?"

"Of course."

"Okay, so imagine a portrait. The nicer and more detailed and accurate it is, the better it is, right? But now imagine a master painter, who paints a portrait so accurate that you can't quite tell whether it's a painting or it's real. When your mind has trouble telling if it's real or not, that makes people uncomfortable. Almost like the painting is staring back at them. Or at least, back where I'm from we sometimes have that kind of reaction. We call that 'the uncanny valley.' Do you know what I mean?"

Nicole felt a shiver run down her spine. She knew exactly what he meant.

"You saw a person that made you feel that way?" she asked.

Peabo nodded. "Yeah. Like I said, it was just a vendor who—"

Nicole hopped up from her chair. “Show me.”

Peabo’s eyes widened. “Why? What’s wrong?”

“What you just described is something I’ve only encountered once before. And if it’s what I think it is, there’s a very dangerous creature occupying the guise of that merchant.”

“What? You mean like a doppelganger?”

She shrugged. “I’m unfamiliar with that term. We call it a skinwalker. And if you really have spotted one… then people have already died because of it.”

CHAPTER NINE

Peabo and Nicole watched the waning market activity as early evening fell and customers drifted away. Eventually, one merchant packed up for the evening, and as if that were a signal, that led to the rest of them packing up their wares. But Peabo and Nicole held their position as the woman they'd been surveilling departed, moving a small pushcart filled with bags of unsold candies from her stall. Leaving the square, she moved west, out of the town and into the countryside.

"You're right," Nicole whispered. "I sense the same wrongness about her."

Just watching her walk didn't raise any alarms for Peabo. He'd learned that there wasn't any stereotypical walk for a woman. Nicole was quite capable of walking with a swish of her hips or with a soldier's crispness depending on the situation. But there was *something* about this woman. Something about the face, the shape of her neck. It was that damned uncanny valley.

Nicole leaned closer, her breath warm on his cheek. "Let's follow at a distance. But walk normally… there's nowhere out here to hide."

When the merchant was about a quarter mile down the road, Peabo and Nicole left the shadows of the market. Nicole grabbed Peabo's hand and held it.

"Trust me," she said, "it's much less suspicious if it sees a couple walking rather than two individuals."

He gave her hand a squeeze. She was right. If he looked behind him on a dark street and saw two shadows following him, he'd immediately think muggers. But two people holding hands would look perfectly benign.

The insects began chirping as the sun dipped below the horizon. The sky was filled with an ever-darkening reddish glow. They followed the merchant for about fifteen minutes before she veered off the main road toward a small, isolated home. Nicole pulled Peabo to the side of the road, out of sight of the front door, and crouched in the tall grasses.

Peabo began to feel nervous about the plan. "Are you sure we're not imagining things?" he whispered. "How can we know?"

"We can't take a chance," Nicole said. "These are dangerous things, these skinwalkers. I learned about them in the Sage's Tower. Most people don't even know they exist anymore. It is said that there were once many more of them, sowing chaos wherever they went. But when one of those things took the place of a king, it started a war against the skinwalkers, an attempt to wipe them out. It did not succeed completely. And this thing we are following, it is one of them. That valley you talked about, I sensed it too, the moment I saw the thing."

Peabo still felt uneasy with the idea of attacking a woman. Even a fake woman.

Nicole nodded toward the house. "I'd prefer to just burn the place down around it, but there might be someone else in there. Can you sense anything?"

Peabo focused on the building, but didn't sense any whispers of stray thoughts. "Nothing, not even the skinwalker."

"I was afraid of that. Give me your hands."

He held out his hands. Nicole grabbed them, closed her eyes, and began soundlessly moving her lips. Peabo watched in surprise as both of their hands began to *glow*. And then he heard a faint hum, almost like the sound a fluorescent bulb makes when it's first switched on. The sound was coming from their joined hands.

What the hell was going on?

The glow faded, and Nicole opened her eyes. "One more," she said. She started the same noiseless murmuring, and the glow returned, but this time with a slightly different coloration.

Peabo felt a warmth creeping up his arms. Whatever she was doing, it gave him a feeling of power. No, not power. *Awareness*. And even when the glow faded again, he sensed something lingering there, on his skin.

"What did you just do?" he whispered.

"Just a few blessings." Nicole stood. "Come, let's go. No matter what it looks like, don't underestimate it. This thing will be very fast and very strong. You knock on the door, draw it out. I'll try to attack from behind. We clear?"

Peabo drew his katana and forced himself to dismiss the image of the woman in the market. On every conceivable level, this felt wrong… but he trusted Nicole's instinct, even if he didn't trust his own.

Nicole moved past the entrance and positioned herself so she'd be behind the door when it swung open. Then Peabo walked right up to the front door and knocked.

"Merchant," he bellowed, "I have the money I owe you."

He sensed nothing behind the door, no thoughts whatsoever.

But he heard the creak of a wooden plank.

Tightening his grip on his sword, Peabo took a step back.

The door swung open. But the person on the other side wasn't the merchant from the market. In fact, the person Peabo saw standing before him…

It's not possible.

"Mom?" he said.

His mother stepped forward with a look of concern—a look he'd seen on her face many times. "Peabo? What's wrong?"

At that moment, Nicole attacked.

Peabo's mother hissed and spun around with preternatural speed, blocking Nicole's attack and swiping at her with elongated claws. Only then did Peabo realize he'd been fooled. He slashed his katana hard at the creature's back and connected with a meaty thwack.

But the skinwalker's reaction was quick. It yanked back, pulling the sword from his grip, the weapon still lodged between two of its ribs, and struck a blow against his left arm that sent him wheeling backward.

Nicole renewed her attack, sending a heavy kick into the creature's chest.

His left arm burning from the attack, Peabo drew his mace with his right and smashed it with all of his strength into the back of the creature's head, caving it in with a sickening crunch. The creature staggered, then looked back and forth between him and Nicole, changing forms as it did so, shifting from a grotesque image of Peabo's mother, and then looking just like Nicole, and the vendor, and several other people he didn't recognize.

Its eyes glowed white for a moment, and then it shuddered one last time and collapsed onto the ground.

Peabo reached across his waist to awkwardly hook the mace onto his waistband. His left arm was dripping blood, and he felt a burn where she'd cut him.

He turned to Nicole. "I'm sorry, I shouldn't have hesitated. But she…"

Nicole put a hand on his shoulder. "It's okay. I should have warned you that those things are very intelligent and can pluck thoughts from an unshielded mind. Show me your arm."

He lifted his arm, and she began probing at the wounds. A light hovered just above her, like a lightning bug on steroids, but this was no flying insect.

"Ow!" he cried as she dug into his arm.

"It's a clean wound. Just hold still." Nicole closed her eyes and gripped his slashed bicep and forearm tightly. Her fingertips began glowing and he felt warmth blooming from her touch.

He was reminded of a famous quotation by Arthur C. Clarke, one he'd read ages ago in a literature class. *Any sufficiently advanced technology is indistinguishable from magic.* Most of that class had been a waste of time, but that quote had stuck with him. It was true, even in a place as odd as this one. There was always an explanation; there was no such thing as magic.

Yet it sure seemed like magic when Nicole pressed the edges of his gashes together and they stayed closed, the pain rapidly fading.

After about thirty seconds, she opened her eyes, the glow faded from her fingertips and she looked more tired than he'd ever seen her. "How's your arm now?"

Peabo slowly bent his arm, and to his surprise, he felt no burning or pain at all—just some deep bruising. If it weren't for the holes in his shirt sleeve and the bloodstains, he wouldn't believe he'd been sliced open at all.

"How did you do that?" he asked.

"I'm dual specialized," Nicole said, "including some limited healing skills."

Peabo pumped his arm cautiously. "Well, I appreciate whatever it is you did. Losing an arm to infection doesn't seem like a good way to go."

He retrieved his sword from the body of the skinwalker, which was rapidly dissolving into a dark-gray goo—and smelled like boiled chicken. The largest globe of essence he'd yet seen drifted toward him, and he silently absorbed it.

"Is there a way to tell how close I am to a new level?" he asked.

Nicole shook her head. "There are some on the mainland that can measure such things, and of course at the Sage's Tower, but here, no. There's no way of knowing."

She crept cautiously through the open doorway, and Peabo followed. He was instantly hit by the smell of a rotting corpse, a scent he was unfortunately familiar with, having seen the open graves in Iraq left by Saddam's forces. Sure enough, the broken body of a woman lay at the far side of the one-room home.

"Looks like the creature killed the homeowner," he said. "What else is there to see?"

"I don't know. Anything that might give us a hint as to what brought such a thing to this remote area of the kingdom. Skinwalkers are very rare. They normally reside in various levels of Myrkheim, mostly because being in the aboveworld is dangerous to them—and because there's more of us up here who have instinctive memories of what they've done and can detect them."

Peabo scanned the room. It looked more like a storage facility than a home, and just walking through the room was like navigating an obstacle course. Nicole didn't try to navigate; she was like a bulldozer, turning over furniture and yanking open drawers.

Peabo was more delicate. He peeked in various boxes and shelves, finding mostly clothing and kitchenware. In one basket he found a sack filled with something that looked like yellow sand but smelled sweet like molasses. Probably unrefined sugar.

He made his way over to the homeowner's corpse. He had to cover his mouth and nose as he approached, as the smell was nauseating. Not nearly as bad as the monstrosity from the graveyard, but still awful. The woman might once have been pretty, but there was no way of knowing now, and her clothes were stained from the fluids that had leaked from her shrunken corpse. "If things decompose in the same way here as back home, this woman looks like she's been dead at least two weeks."

Nicole turned from the desk she was tearing apart, glanced at the body, and nodded.

Clutched in one of the dead woman's hands was what looked like a butter knife, and in the other…

"What do we have here?" he said aloud.

He pulled from her hand a piece of parchment, and read the handwritten note aloud. *"You were my eyes. I told you there'd be consequences if you didn't report in.* It's signed, *D.*"

He turned to Nicole. "What does that mean?"

She shrugged. "Sounds like she made some kind of deal and didn't fulfill her end. Though I wouldn't have expected someone to send a skinwalker as punishment. I didn't realize they would even work on a contract basis."

Peabo moved past the body to the straw mattress in the corner. Lifting it up, he spotted a glint of shining metal. "Well, look at that," he exclaimed. "A sword!"

Just as he grasped the hilt, Nicole yelled, "Don't!"

Too late.

The moment Peabo closed his fingers around the hilt, he felt a surge of energy wash through him. The world shimmered, and for the briefest of moments, he felt invincible, like the strongest person that had ever lived.

Then the feeling ebbed, leaving him short of breath but smiling nonetheless.

"Whoa," he said. "I just leveled."

He turned to Nicole, who sighed with relief.

"How's that possible?" he asked.

"You appear to have stumbled upon an item that's been imbued with special properties."

Peabo pulled the sword from its scabbard and looked at the blade. "You're saying there was an essence in a sword? And just because I picked it up, I absorbed it?"

"Yes. It's as simple as that."

"No, it's not." Peabo shook his head. "Surely I'm not the first person to ever pick up this sword."

Nicole smiled. "I'm impressed. You really are smarter than you look." She nodded at the sword. "At some point in the past, probably long ago, someone imbued that sword with that essence you just absorbed. Its next owner then gained that essence. But once he possessed it, the sword no longer had it. He could give that sword away, and nobody would gain anything from it, because that prior owner still held the essence within him."

Peabo's eyes widened. "But if that owner dies…"

"Exactly," said Nicole. "If that owner dies, the essence returns to the sword. And the first person to pick it up *after* that takes on the essence. You're getting the hang of how things work. Still—you shouldn't have touched it without me checking it first. It could have been cursed, and I would have been displeased if it had turned you into a pile of sand."

Peabo wasn't sure if she was joking or not. He expected not.

"Now stop fooling around and come over here," she said. "I've found something."

He walked over and found her holding a wooden box. Inside were two rings. She held one glowing hand over it for a moment, then picked up one of the rings and threw it aside. "That one had a curse on it."

"How do you know?" Peabo asked.

She shrugged. "It's a thing I can do." She picked up the other ring. "But this one looks like it's worth keeping."

Peabo shook his head. "It looks identical to the first one."

She slipped it on and smiled. "Yes. I like this one."

"So, are we just robbing the place now?" Peabo said.

Nicole rolled her eyes. "Whoever owned these things no longer has any use for it. Now, let's get out of here. Why the skinwalker was here is still a mystery, but you leveled up, and that was more than worth our while. At level three, and with a decent weapon," she nodded toward Peabo's new sword, "one of these days you might *actually* be helpful in a fight."

Peabo held his katana in one hand and the new sword in the other, while Nicole rolled a log out in front of him. Then she held out her hands, and he handed both weapons to her, hilt-first.

She looked down the length of both of them. "Good. The cutting edges are of the same angle, so all we need to do is compensate for weight."

She wrapped a strip of leather around the base of the katana's blade. Midway through the wrapping, she added several silver royals, and when she was done, she tied off the leather with a simple knot.

"Okay, let me explain what I'm doing."

"I'd appreciate that," Peabo said drily.

Nicole placed the hilts of both swords on the ground and gripped them by the flats of their blades. "The two swords have approximately the same cutting geometry, and now their weight is about even. So they should bite into the soft wood equally well. However, I don't believe everything is equal in this case; I believe this sword is likely imbued with some special characteristics, and I want to prove it.

"This imbuing… it's like leveling up. I'd expect that your strength, stamina, and reflexes all improved when you reached level three. These are key characteristics of who you are. Swords have their own special characteristics that can be improved beyond what you see."

"You mean that the sword can level up as well?"

"Yes. Though it's not easy to do. It takes a lot of skill and know-how to be able to force essences into inanimate materials."

It hadn't dawned on Peabo that a sword could get stronger or sharper due to something other than its physical materials and form, but it made sense… in this world. He was now stronger and quicker than he'd been this morning, and yet he was no more muscular than before.

"Now we begin the experiment," said Nicole. With the hilts on the ground, she held the blades at an even height above the log, and let go. They both dropped and thumped into the wood.

The difference was immediately apparent. The blade of the katana had dug into the log about half an inch deep. The new sword, by contrast, looked to have dug in about one and a half inches.

"Wow," Peabo said.

Nicole repeated the test a second time to be sure, and got the same result. She then returned the new sword to him, hilt first.

"It somehow seems appropriate that you've reached level three and have a level three enhanced sword. I assume you don't mind if I begin using your old weapon, do you?"

"Of course not."

Peabo felt a moment of regret at the thought that the katana had been Nolan's, but he was dying to try out the new, enhanced sword. It felt particularly good in his hand, and he had a feeling he and this sword would soon become well acquainted.

"Nicole, you *do* realize that I'm willing to cook, right? It feels weird having you always cook for me."

Nicole set a bowl of stewed vegetables on the table, beside

another large bowl of what served as this world's version of wild rice. "First of all, I *like* to cook. Second of all, you don't know what half of the ingredients are and will end up poisoning us if you try to make anything."

"Ouch," said Peabo. "You don't mince words, do you?"

"You'll live."

He ate a spoonful of the spiced stew, and it reminded him of an Indian curry. Even back home, he knew better than to try to make his own curry. He was lucky that she liked to cook.

He began wolfing it down. He knew he was hungry, but for the next several minutes he must have looked like he was engaging in an eating contest. He served himself seconds, and then thirds. He was relieved to see that Nicole was eating a lot, too; at least he wasn't being piggish alone.

"This is fantastic," he said. "I can't believe I'm eating so much."

"You just leveled," she said matter-of-factly. "That gives you an appetite."

"Why are you eating so much?" he asked. "Did you level too?"

"No, but I did expend a lot of energy, so I need to replenish."

"I noticed you looked really tired after you treated my arm. Did that take a lot out of you?"

"Being a weaver is a lot harder than it may look."

"A weaver?" Peabo asked.

Nicole sat back. "The ability to weave forces is very rare. But it's also a selection criterion for being allowed to train as a blood maiden—though few know this. The art of weaving…

it's difficult to explain to someone who's never experienced it themselves. Even for those who were born with the skill, it's very complicated. People spend their entire lives studying it and still master only small facets of the weaving arts."

Peabo chuckled. "I graduated number two in my class at a top-notch university, and was starting on my PhD. I'm not used to people telling me how complicated something might be."

She raised an eyebrow. "I don't know what any of that means."

"Sorry—I guess it just means that I'm not as stupid as I look, as you love to point out. If you can, I'd love for you to teach me how this works. All the complicated details."

"Are you serious?" Nicole asked. She looked genuinely surprised.

"Why wouldn't I be?"

For a long moment she stared at him, saying nothing. And then her eyes glistened, and tears ran down her cheeks.

Surprised by the sudden show of emotion, Peabo went around the table, kneeled beside her chair, and put his arms around her. "I'm sorry. Did I say something wrong?"

She leaned into him and began crying on his shoulder.

Peabo couldn't believe it. The woman had been an emotional rock since the moment they'd paired. What had he done to upset her so?

After a short while, she took a few deep shuddering breaths, straightened up, and wiped the tears from her face.

"I'm sorry about that," she said. "I just never expected to meet another person like Jakub. He was…" Her cheeks reddened. "He was as curious as you are."

"Jakub was your previous…."

"Yes. I'm sorry, I shouldn't—"

"Why wouldn't you want to talk about him? You clearly had a connection. And I'm guessing you didn't have much chance to mourn him."

One last tear rolled down her cheek. She leaned forward and gripped his hands. "What do you want to know about weaving?"

She clearly didn't want to talk about the past, and he wasn't going to push it.

He returned to his seat. "Well," he said, "let's start with how you healed my arm."

Nicole took in a deep breath. "There are two types of weavers: those who can weave the forces from outside themselves and apply them in what might be considered crude and dangerous manners, and those who can only conduct the forces from within, but who tend to have a much deeper control of their weaving. I'm one of the latter. I'm able to apply forces to speed up certain natural processes, like mending your skin, or fixing a broken bone."

"How, though? You looked like you were really focused when healing me. What are you concentrating on?"

"Interesting question." Nicole leaned back and looked up at the ceiling. "When I'm weaving, it's like I'm using a straw to mentally push the force within me to the location I'm focused on. But the force is thick, like honey, so it takes a lot of effort to push it through."

Peabo nodded. "And this force—you said it accelerates what would naturally happen? You were forcing the tissue to grow, the vessels to reattach, the nerves to merge and heal." He frowned. "Is that what the glow indicated? That things are all moving at very high speeds?"

Nicole's eyes widened. "That's exactly right. Many people think it's the Nameless One's blessings or some other mystical thing—and they actually teach that in some of the weaver guilds. But in reality, it's very small things moving very quickly in an organized manner. How did you know that? Do they teach weaving where you're from?"

Peabo laughed and shook his head. "No, but some of what you're talking about is familiar." He'd been thinking about that glow, and the only time he'd seen such a thing before was in a class, when certain gases had electricity applied to them, causing them to ionize like when the gas inside a fluorescent bulb glowed. "It's not the same as we do it back home, but it's not completely different either. What about that light you had above your head? Was that you aiming the mental straw at a spot in the air?"

"Yes and no. I *could* make a spark appear in the air, but it wouldn't last long, and it certainly wouldn't follow me once I moved from that spot. What I did is more like lighting a candle. Here, let me show you."

She retrieved a spool of an extremely thin, translucent thread, and bit off a length of about a foot. She held it up by one end and focused on it for a few seconds… and the lower end began burning, glowing brightly like an incandescent bulb's filament. As it did so, the bottom end of the thread floated up into the air, until it looked like she was holding the bottom end of a wax-less candle.

"Because the burning end is warmer, it rises up in the air," she explained. She nodded at the spool. "This stuff comes in handy in Myrkheim."

"That's amazing. So it's a portable candle." Peabo said.

"Yes, and it doesn't blow out unless I smother the flame." Nicole snuffed out the floating light between her fingers. "We can talk more about weaving tomorrow. Let's get to bed. We both need our rest."

Peabo grabbed his dish and spoon before Nicole could sweep them away, and he forced his way into the kitchen to at least help clean up. And as they stood next to each other in silence, washing their dishes, he sensed that things had changed for them. Up until now, they'd had an arrangement, but it had felt artificial. Formal. Now… now she was a real person to him, with emotions, a history, and things to share. She could teach him things that perhaps nobody else could, and she seemed to enjoy the sharing.

In this strange world, he'd somehow managed to find something he never would have expected.

A real friend.

CHAPTER TEN

Nicole's eyes snapped open. She was staring into the darkness, her heart beating loudly in her chest, and she was practically paralyzed by an overwhelming grief.

What had brought that on? Had she had a nightmare?

No. She turned on her side and stared at Peabo's broad back. *He* was the source of the emotions she felt.

She laid a hand on his side, closed her eyes, and sensed flashes of his dream.

He was dreaming about his mother.

Of course he was. The skinwalker had taken on her form, and then Peabo had been forced to attack her. It only made sense that the experience had affected him deeply.

She scooted closer and whispered in his ear. "It's okay."

Peabo stirred and whimpered in his sleep.

Nicole pressed her body against his and rested her head on his pillow. She would take care of this man. Her life hadn't gone the way she'd hoped, but now... maybe things were looking up.

And she was determined that this time, she wouldn't fail.

Peabo woke to the light of early morning pouring through the window and the smell of breakfast wafting through the open bedroom door.

"Get up, lazy bones. Food's almost ready, and we have a lot to do today."

Somehow, Nicole always knew the moment he awoke. That blood maiden link was another thing he didn't understand.

A minute later he was seated at the table, enjoying a bowl of scrambled eggs and rat sausage. Nicole was seated across the table from him, but instead of eating, she was just staring at him.

"What?" he asked.

"We need to talk." She sounded serious.

Peabo wiped his mouth and gave her his undivided attention. "Okay."

"I've noticed that you've been having trouble sleeping. And it's been worrying me. So... I peeked into your thoughts a bit."

"I thought you couldn't read my mind."

"I can't. Not really. But I can see snatches of what you're visualizing, especially when you're dreaming. Restless dreams. Last night you were crying in your sleep as you dreamed of your mother. I know what happened with the skinwalker was hard on you. But you were sleeping poorly before that, too. I figured it's time we talked about that."

Peabo felt a chill rush through him. She was right—it *had* been hard on him. He'd felt like he was killing his own mother. And as he thought of her, he saw an image of her crying. He didn't remember ever seeing her cry, but there it was. Maybe that was what he'd been dreaming about?

"I'm sorry," he said.

"Don't be sorry." Nicole reached across the table and gripped his hand. "I'm just worried about your mental health. If you don't get proper rest, it'll hurt the rest of you."

"Is that something you learned in the Sage's Tower?"

"Among other things. But talk to me. What has your sleeping mind been feeling so upset about?"

"Wouldn't you be upset if your… I'm sorry, I don't know if your parents are alive."

"They are."

"Then wouldn't you be upset for them if you'd gone missing one day and you knew they'd have no explanation for your disappearance?"

Nicole furrowed her brow. "Didn't you tell me that five seconds in your world ended up being almost thirty turns of the season here?"

Peabo nodded.

"Then you're not thinking straight. Even if you lived for a thousand turns of the season, it would only be a moment where you are from. Back in your world, you haven't gone missing. You've only been gone an instant."

Peabo's mouth dropped open. She was right. Totally right. He was an idiot.

Nicole's voice took on a softer tone. "It's really best if you think of your old life as something separate from this one. The Nameless One has granted you two lives, but you can't live them both at the same time. I'm glad you're in mine, and while you're here… there's no value in feeling guilt for having temporarily left your old one."

Peabo smiled. He'd never been a religious person, even though his parents were, but if there really was a greater power out there, it didn't want for him to worry about things he couldn't control. At the thought, he immediately felt lighter, as if he'd shed some weight that had been holding him down.

He rose from his chair and gave Nicole a hug, which she returned. "Thank you for being honest with me. And you're right, I can't live two lives at once. I'm going to live this one, and only this one."

At that moment a knock sounded on the front door, and a voice called out, "It's Brother Chesky of the Nameless One."

Peabo raised an eyebrow at Nicole, who explained.

"The monk from the church. He'd better have those healing potions for us."

"Miss Nicole, just like I promised, two dozen healing elixirs." The monk wrung his hands, looking nervous. "It was a week-long effort filled with headaches, but the Nameless One gave me the strength."

With a slight frown, Nicole unstoppered one of the bottles and sniffed at its contents. "Water-based?"

The monk nodded vigorously. "Aye, the water's from a local spring. It's what I drink… what my entire congregation drinks. It's as pure as it gets." His eyes widened. "Did you need it in some other way? I'm exhausted, but if you really—"

"No." Nicole turned to Peabo. "Is your arm still sore at all?"

Peabo flexed his left arm. "It's fine, but I can feel a bit of soreness."

"Good." She handed him the open bottle. "Drink it."

Peabo looked at the bottle with skepticism.

"It should do you well, plainswalker," said the monk with an approving nod.

Peabo shrugged. "Fine. Bottoms up." He drained the bottle with two gulps. "Bleah… tastes like algae."

"Aye, I said it's a natural spring."

It took about thirty seconds before he felt a flush of heat wash over him. The heat seemed particularly intense in his arm, and it vanished just as quickly as it had come.

"Well?" Nicole said.

Peabo flexed his arm… and smiled. "Wow. My arm feels totally better."

Nicole spit in her hand and clasped hands with the monk. "Payment accepted."

The monk let out a deep breath. "Good. I pride myself on not carrying any debts." He hesitated, then added, "There is… something else. I don't think the Nameless One would fault me for sharing something that I think you should know about…

even though it's a stain on my flock. I don't want to have this on my conscience."

"What is it, Brother Chesky?" Nicole asked.

"George, he's one of my flock… he was turned into a wight. Luckily, George's wife had a candlestick with a loose candle holder. She removed the candle holder and stabbed poor George to death with the sharpened end. We burned his corpse."

"Good," said Nicole.

Peabo saw nothing good about a wife having to kill her husband. But he had no idea what a wight was, either.

"How did he get turned?" Nicole asked.

"That's the thing that's so odd." The monk lowered his voice to a whisper. "George came home from an errand, and all Emilia noticed was a confused look to him. He didn't mindlessly attack or anything. But he did say he had met a *breathless man*."

"A breathless man?" Peabo asked.

Brother Chesky shrugged. "I don't know either. That's all he said. Anyway, the reason I'm telling you is that poor George was given instructions."

"Ah," said Nicole. "He was a puppet."

Chesky nodded. "Yes. And the instructions…" He turned to Peabo. "They spoke of you, plainswalker. George asked Emilia where their family sword was. He said he needed it to 'dispatch the plainswalker.' When Emilia refused to tell him where she'd placed the sword, George snapped… and she ended up doing what was necessary."

"Where did George live?" Nicole asked. "And before he came home like this, where had he been?"

The monk gave them the location of the man's home, then added, "He had gone to the woods bordering their farm to collect mushrooms. I don't know specifically where. I'm truly sorry about all this. But I felt I had to warn you."

As soon as the monk had left, Peabo turned to Nicole. He had a ton of questions.

But she held up a hand, forestalling him. "Grab your sword. I'll explain on the way."

Peabo found himself practically running to keep up with Nicole's long strides. "So basically," he said, summarizing what she'd explained thus far, "this wight thing is a bigger and badder version of what we fought in the graveyard."

"Close enough. And if touches you, it'll drain one of your levels."

"That's possible?"

"I just said it was, didn't I? If it touches you a second time, you'll lose another level. And if it drains you to level zero, you'll fall unconscious and wake up as a weaker version of the wight that drained you."

"And that's what happened to George?" Peabo asked.

Nicole nodded. "Presumably he was already a low level. He had no chance."

Peabo shook his head. "I could use a monster manual for this world. This stuff is out of control."

Soon they approached the forest near George's home. Nicole pointed to a spot on the ground and spoke in Peabo's head. *"You see the crushed plants?"*

He nodded. The trail was obvious, leading right through the crops toward the house. Whoever had walked this way had done so with no regard for the damage they were causing.

"Stay quiet, use the hand signals I taught you, and listen for anything unusual. Wights tend not to expose themselves in the daylight."

Peabo pulled his new sword from the scabbard as they approached the trees. He listened carefully, as instructed, only to find that he could hear nothing at all. No birds, no scurrying of mice or other animals, not even a breeze blowing through the leaves.

As they walked deeper into the woods, Nicole tracking a trail of disturbed leaves and broken twigs, the space beneath the trees grew darker, the air more oppressive. Peabo kept his head on a swivel, looking for threats.

And then he saw something of interest. He tapped Nicole on the shoulder and pointed. At the base of a tree lay a sack of mushrooms, open and spilling its contents on the forest floor.

Nicole nodded. *"This is where George found his end."* She closed her eyes and moved her lips as if soundlessly saying a prayer, and the katana in her hand glowed ever so slightly. *"I just lent the sword some of my energy,"* she explained. *"The glow comes from the excitation of the metal along its cutting edge."* She gave Peabo a wink. *"I sensed your confusion."*

They continued deeper into the woods. For the most part, even Peabo was able to see the trail. Whatever this wight was, it wasn't concerned about hiding its tracks. Not only had it left its marks on the ground, but it appeared to have plowed right through branches, some of them broken as high as Peabo's shoulder.

He couldn't help but wonder just how large this thing was.

Just when he caught the smell of death somewhere up ahead, Nicole held up a fist, signaling for them to stop. They both froze, scanning the area, and Peabo felt the cold prickle of danger on the back of his neck.

And then a nearby tree trunk practically exploded as a huge creature bounded up from beneath it, or perhaps from within it. The thing was easily a foot taller than Peabo, even though it was hunched over. Its heavily muscled build carried only the tattered remains of an orange robe, and there was madness behind its glowing yellow eyes.

But what Peabo noticed most was its wheezing breath. He'd heard that sound before. It was the same asthmatic breathing he'd heard when the figure opened the window to his bedroom.

This creature, this wight… it was the same creature that had paralyzed him without ever even having touched him.

The creature seemed to recognize Peabo too. Ignoring Nicole, it turned its gaze full upon him, its eyes shifted from yellow to almost blood-red. With a keening wail, it charged right at him.

Peabo braced himself for the impact, but Nicole leapt, swinging her brightly glowing katana with all her might at the back of the creature's exposed neck. The wight fell where it stood. Or at least its body did. Its head rolled several feet away.

Peabo still didn't move. He was half afraid the headless body would get back up. But it didn't.

"Is it dead?" he said.

"Yes, I managed to connect with a critical hit."

"Thank you."

Nicole wiped her blade clean and sheathed it. "I'm sorry I didn't leave you any essence to collect. There was no time."

"I'm just glad it's dead. Nicole, that's the intruder that paralyzed me on the first night we were together. I recognized the sound of its wheezing breath."

She raised her eyebrows. "Interesting. After we burn the body, let's check out its lair." She pointed at the exploded stump, beneath which appeared to be some kind of underground passage. "Maybe we can find out why it wanted to kill you. Go get the head, and let's set this thing on fire. Though I should warn you… you're really not going to like the smell."

The awful smell of burnt flesh still filled Peabo's nostrils as they descended into the wight's lair, which proved to be nothing more than a single underground chamber filled with the bones and half-eaten flesh of various forest creatures.

"I thought you said wights are already dead," he said. "So why was this one eating animals?"

Nicole frowned, her tiny ball of light hovering above her. "I never said wights were dead. They're not dead until you kill them. What gave you that idea?"

Peabo was confused. "You said it's like the skeletons and zombie from the graveyard. And *they're* dead, right?"

Nicole looked at him like he was an idiot. Speaking very slowly, in a condescending manner, she said, "Were they moving?"

"Yeah."

"Then they aren't dead. Dead things tend not to move."

"Right, but—"

"There's no but about it, Peabo. Maybe where you come from things are different, but around here, dead things don't move."

Peabo stood his ground. "Listen, treat me like a kid if you have to, but I don't get this. Let's start at the beginning. The skeleton that we killed back at the graveyard, it used to be a person. One that was alive, right?"

"Yes."

"And at some point the person died, right?"

"Yes."

"Okay, so when that person's skeleton decided to attack us, it was alive again?"

Nicole nodded. "Yes. Someone infused the remains of a dead person with energy. Just like when the monk infused the bottled water with some healing energy, you drank it, and it healed you. It was the monk's energy that healed you—he just gave it to you through an intermediary. The water. In this case, as I explained before, someone put their energy into the remains of a dead person."

Peabo nodded. "I understand that much. I just… I don't

understand the *how*. How energy would make a dead person reassemble, come to life, and attack us."

Nicole shrugged. "I only know the basics; the studies of the animation process were not my strong suit at the tower. But let's start with the reassembly. You know how a bar magnet has one side that likes to stick to only one particular side of another bar magnet? Does your world have magnets?"

Peabo nodded.

"Good. The bones of any living creature have a similar affinity. So once they're infused with energy, they can sort of self-assemble. That's the easy part. Their ability to think… that's where the whole thing gets rather philosophical. But I know that skeletons are incapable of rational thinking. They either attack whatever they see, or they follow very basic instructions. When creatures have more of their brain remaining, they're capable of more advanced thoughts. Zombies, for instance, although the level of intelligence varies.

"But wights… they think quite clearly. They even retain their abilities from their former life. If they were a weaver, they're still a weaver. I've heard of wights that can cast the most horrific spears of killing energy. And believe me, there's worse than that in this world.

"But to maintain their lives, they must sustain themselves. They have to eat, like any living thing. Skeletons are the exception, as they *can't* eat. If they're not reinfused with more energy, they'll eventually just fall apart once the energy runs its course. But zombies, wights, other animated creatures… they have to eat. Just like you and me."

She paused. "I should also note that a wight has another

way to sustain itself. If he'd drained you of a level, that would also give him energy."

Peabo nodded. It all made sense. It was crazy, but it still made sense.

"Thank you," he said.

Nicole smiled. "There's no need to thank me. I love that you want to learn. Now—help me search this place."

There wasn't much to search, unless Peabo wanted to poke through dead carcasses, which he very much didn't. But in the light of Nicole's incandescent glow, he soon spotted a metallic gleam in a pile of leaves. Moving closer, he saw what it was. A gold ring.

Remembering Nicole's warning about curses, he didn't touch it. "Nicole?" he said. "I've found something."

She joined him and crouched before the ring. Without touching it, she held her hand above it, and the ring began to glow. After a long moment she picked it up and studied it more closely. Peabo supposed it was just an ordinary ring, and went back to poking through piles of refuse with a stick.

He was just about to give up when he uncovered a partially rolled scrap of parchment. He tugged it out of the filth it was half-buried in, then unrolled it. There was wispy writing on the paper, but somehow he couldn't read it. Not because he didn't know the language, but because somehow his eyes refused to focus on the letters. Everything was blurred, and looking at the script gave him a headache.

"This is a patriarch's ring," Nicole said behind him.

Peabo turned. "What's a patriarch?"

She smiled. "I keep forgetting how little you know. A patriarch is a high-level member of the clergy. Out here in the middle of nowhere, you'd only be exposed to monks—they're just low-level acolytes. In the city, you'll find priests who are more likely a level three or four. Patriarchs are higher than that."

Peabo frowned. "I understand what levels mean when it comes to someone like me. Stronger. Faster. Better. But I got the impression that monks, or I guess clergy in general, they don't fight—"

"That isn't true," said Nicole. "They most certainly do fight. But… sorry, I didn't mean to interrupt you. Go on, you were saying?"

Peabo's eyes widened. It was the first time she'd noticed that she was always doing that to him. "It's okay. I was just going to say, I didn't realize monks had levels. But I guess it makes sense, if he has healing energy, like you."

"Ah, yes. Advancing in levels enables weavers to do things they weren't capable of doing before. Including," she said, hitching her thumb back toward the entrance of the lair, "reanimating the dead. If this wight used to be a patriarch, then it may well have had that ability."

"Would a patriarch also be able to paralyze me?"

"Easily." Nicole pointed at the scroll. "What's that you have there?"

Peabo handed it to her. "I don't know. I can't read it."

Nicole looked at the scroll and nodded. "It's got a level filter applied to it. I don't fully understand the mechanics behind these filters, but I know that people with lower levels can't deal with variable polarization. So if I want to write something private and don't want the courier to read it, I just use a variable polarization ink, and he'll never be able to make out what it says."

"Variable polarization," said Peabo. "So you mean the ink is actively changing its polarization. Wouldn't it need some power source to do that?"

Nicole looked at him and shook her head. "It amazes me that you understand cutting-edge research like variable polarization, yet you don't know the first thing about basic facts everyone knows."

Peabo flushed with pride. "Well, I can't say I understand what makes it variable, but I do understand polarization. It's where you can only see something at a certain angle, almost like you're looking through the slats of a window blind. So I would have to assume that variable polarization is where the ink is making that angle twist and turn so that it's almost impossible to get a straight view of what's written. And to do that shifting around, well… I figure it has to take energy to do that."

"Aye, it does. And that's why that ink tends to fade quickly. But at a certain level, maybe five or six, it depends, a person's vision improves sufficiently to be able to cope with those shifts in polarization. It's still not easy—reading an entire book chapter written with such an ink would probably give you a headache—but for a simple message, it's an effective way of maintaining some privacy."

"But you can read the scroll?" Peabo asked.

"Of course. And it's not good." She read aloud.

Stefan,

We've detected the appearance of the god's light. Come to the castle three hours past sundown, I'll meet you. A new plainswalker will be in the vicinity of the Desolate Plains.

I have a mission for you.

-D

"I'm guessing I'm the plainswalker they're referring to," Peabo said with a sigh. "But what is the god's light?"

Nicole shrugged. "I've never heard of anything called the god's light. But I have heard of Stefan." She held up the ring. "There's an inscription on this—that's how I know it belonged to a patriarch. A patriarch named Stefan. And there's the orange robe of a patriarch—"

"The wight was wearing a shredded orange robe! I'm guessing there's little doubt that Stefan was turned into that wight you just killed. But this Dee? Do you have any idea who that is? Or is that a common name?" Peabo paused. "And by the way, does everyone have only one name in this world?"

"One name usually suffices. If you're being formally introduced, you might be Peabo of the Desolate Plains. As to 'Dee,' that wasn't a name, it was just the first letter. So I have no idea who it might be." Nicole frowned. "But whoever they are, they tried to get this Stefan to do their bidding. My guess is, Stefan refused, so D killed him and turned him into a wight. Wights are driven by a compulsion given to them by their makers."

"That must have been some specific compulsion, because that thing didn't even give you a second look once it saw me."

"That's the thing that disturbs me the most. There's no doubt it was sent for you. I suppose that was its downfall, because in its single-minded desire to get to you, it exposed its back to me. That was a very lucky break for us, because I don't want to even think about facing a patriarch-turned-wight in a fair fight."

"Is it an easy thing to do?" Peabo asked. "Make a wight, I mean."

"It's extremely difficult. Beyond my abilities, that's for certain. Although the instructors at the Sage's Tower avoided certain aspects of necromancy, for obvious reasons."

Peabo was struck by a sudden realization. "Wait a minute. The letter we found after killing the skinwalker—that was also signed by someone named 'D'." He shivered in the musky dampness of the lair. "And now that I'm thinking about it, when that skinwalker saw me in the market, she tried to give me something to eat. Obviously I didn't take the bait, largely because by then she'd already freaked me out."

"Never take food from someone you don't trust." Nicole's eyes flashed a warning. "All I know is that someone has taken an interest in you, plainswalker. Which means there'll be more threats coming."

"So what do we do?" Peabo asked. "It seems like we need to track down whoever this D person is."

"Whoever is looking for you, they have the ability to

subvert a patriarch to their cause. That's beyond anything we'd find in these parts of the world. Maybe in Dvorak there is someone… I can't be certain."

"We can't just ignore this."

Nicole's lip curled into an evil grin. "Oh, trust me, I have no intention of ignoring this. We just need to enlist some help."

"Help?"

Nicole nodded. "We're going to Myrkheim."

CHAPTER ELEVEN

It was well past midnight when a dark figure stepped onto a balcony and looked to the south. The city was sleeping, as it should be, but his gaze sought a target that was well beyond the city. Somewhere to the south, something had happened. He felt it in his gut.

"Stefan has failed me," he growled with disgust. The skin-walker had not reported back, the patriarch was now truly dead, and what did that leave him with?

"At some point, a plainswalker will again appear in this world. Let me know when that happens, for he possesses something I need."

That conversation had happened a long time ago, yet the words were still fresh in his mind. It was unusual for anyone to speak to him in that manner.

"Nobody commands me," he muttered under his breath,

because every blade of grass and pebble on the street could be the king's eyes and ears.

At first, he had thought the king was wrong. He himself had taken care of the last plainswalker decades ago. That should have been it. Yet even from here, he'd heard the thunderclap, and every night since, he'd dreamt of a searing white light that tortured him unendingly. Just like thirty years ago.

The only way to end it was to take care of business.

He drew from his pocket a glass vial that glowed in a way only he could see. Its contents swirled, agitated at having been trapped for a time longer than he cared to count. With a quick squeeze, he shattered the glass, and there was a presence in the air.

The disembodied voice spoke to him telepathically. *"Master, what is your bidding?"*

"To the south, there's a plainswalker. Find him. Dispatch him. Once you've taken care of that, you're free to go."

A gust of wind blew past him, and the presence was gone.

The shadowy figure grinned.

"Enjoy your visitor, plainswalker."

Peabo trudged after Nicole as they walked south, skirting the edge of the Desolate Plains. "You said that the person who's after me is probably near Castle Dvorak, the big city on the island, and that's north. So can you explain to me why we're heading in the opposite direction?"

Nicole smiled. "Mostly because I like having you around and I don't want you dead. At least not quite yet."

"Gee, thanks." Peabo tilted an eyebrow in his best imitation of Spock. "If you could be a bit more informative… yup, that would be great."

She chuckled and pointed to a line of trees a quarter mile away. "We're heading for the safety of the southern forest. You, my friend, stick out like a sore thumb; I can't risk going all the way through the center of the island via the normal paths. Wherever you go, word will quickly spread."

"But shouldn't I be safe for at least a little while? Whoever sent that wight to kill me, they don't know it's dead yet. They shouldn't be sending anyone else after me for a while."

Nicole shook her head. "If they get word that you're still alive, you better believe they'll send someone else after you. Besides, the maker already knows the wight is dead—knew it from the instant it happened. Just as I can feel you through our connection, an animated corpse and the one who animated it have a connection. At least that's what I was taught."

Peabo wondered how that connection was maintained. The science he knew didn't apply here, but that didn't mean this world lacked sensible explanations. All of a sudden, despite everything else going on, he had a deep desire to go to school here, and learn about all of the stuff that he didn't even know he wanted to know.

A voice shouted from the edge of the forest. "Well, look at what the cat coughed up!"

Peabo looked to see a tiny man standing there, his arms crossed over his chest.

"Brodie!" he said with a smile.

"Who else would it be?" The dwarf sniffed loudly and nodded to Nicole. "Your lady buzzed me, so I hope you've got a good reason to call me up to the aboveworld again."

Peabo turned to Nicole. "So that's why you had us come this way. To see Brodie?"

"Of course."

"Wait a minute," said Peabo, looking back at Brodie. "How did you know we were coming? What do you mean, she 'buzzed' you?"

Nicole held up a gold ring. "I sent him a message through the ring he gave me when we first parted ways."

"May I see it?" Peabo asked. "The ring, I mean?"

With a shrug, Nicole handed it to him. But as he turned it over, examining every inch of it, he saw nothing unusual. It was just an ordinary ring.

He looked over at Brodie, who had dug out a matching ring. The dwarf tapped his own ring with his index finger.

Peabo felt the ring in his palm vibrate.

His eyes widened in excitement. "Whoa! When you tapped your ring, this one vibrated!"

"Aye, me boy. It's a communication ring. It's what it does." Brodie took the ring from Peabo's hand and tucked both rings into his pocket.

Peabo shook his head in amazement, then looked at the dwarf. "Well, I'm really glad to see you again. Although I'm not sure why we're all meeting here."

Nicole patted Peabo on the shoulder, then looked at Brodie.

"Of course we're meeting Brodie. How else are we going to get to Myrkheim?"

Brodie's bushy eyebrows furrowed. "Is that what this is about? If you think I'll just escort you down into my domain, you'd better have a very compelling reason."

"I do." Nicole draped her arm over Peabo's shoulder. "Our plainswalker has made himself a target for someone that we think is up near Castle Dvorak."

"What makes you think that?"

"Someone turned a patriarch into a wight and sent them after Peabo."

Brodie's eyes widened. "Indeed. Nobody in this part of the island could have done that. At least not those that live in the aboveworld. In fact, I'm somewhat dubious that there's anyone on the island who could do such a thing."

"Well, it was done, and I doubt that it's anyone out here in the farmlands. We need to get to the city, but we would prefer to do so without stumbling upon another assassin. I doubt whoever sent the wight would think to be watching the paths through Myrkheim."

Brodie frowned. "Well, I suppose that is a good reason. But before we make any decisions, let me see how you've been training up my lad. Peabo, lean down."

Peabo leaned over to let Brodie look at his swinging guild medallion, and as he did so, Peabo looked at his former mentor's medallion as well. He'd seen it before, of course, but back then he didn't know its significance, and he wouldn't have been able to read it if he did. Now that he understood the runes, he realized that the tiny man was much more than he seemed. Brodie was a ninth level at… something. That last rune was one he was unfamiliar with.

"Level three," Brodie muttered, then sighed. "Considering the short time you've been here, you're doing fine… but you aren't ready for the challenges ahead." He turned to Nicole. "Blood maiden, Myrkheim isn't for the inexperienced. A level three can't sign on to an adventuring troop to get you where you want to go."

"What does that mean?" Peabo asked. "I can't go through Myrkheim?"

"*We*," Nicole said curtly, frowning at Brodie.

"Hold on, kid. Let me think for a moment." Brodie scratched at his cheek. "I suppose some of my people might be heading in that direction and would consider hiring someone as low as level four—assuming of course you can acquire a recommendation from a qualified ranger. But at level three… never. It's simply too likely you'd get yourself killed or endanger the party. You'd get lost, or eaten, or you'll fall into a crevasse. No, you'll need to level up again before we can get you hired into an adventuring troop."

Peabo didn't like the sound of any of that. He turned to Nicole. "If Myrkheim is so dangerous, are you certain a trip overland wouldn't be a better idea?"

Nicole shrugged. "Nothing is certain. But whoever it is that wants you dead, they're clearly connected to someone powerful. The dangers of both routes are significant."

"Aye, the blood maiden has it right," said Brodie. "A patriarch is no lamb for the slaughter. I've crossed paths with a patriarch or two in my day. They're usually tough nuts to crack. And if what you're up against turned one and sent them after you... well, you've got more problems than your old friend Nolan ever had."

"Nolan?" Nicole asked.

"It's a man the boy and I knew. He was from the same world." Brodie looked up at Peabo. "I never told you how Nolan died, because I didn't want to worry you. But someone came after him, too. At first they sent a few normal bounty hunters. It was a very obvious thing, and Nolan was quite a skilled fighter for being a low level. He held his own when he was out and about. But soon after he left my care, he was poisoned."

"Poisoned? By whom?"

"It was one of the bounty hunters, and he'd clearly been trained as an assassin."

"How do you know?" Nicole's eyes widened as she looked back and forth between Brodie and Peabo.

"Someone had cleanly removed the skin from the left side of Nolan's face. There was no blood, which tells me that it was done only after my friend had been killed." Brodie frowned and his voice took on a somber tone. "I was the one who found him. He'd been renting a place from one of the Raiheim farmers, and when I entered the cabin, I tested everything. The pitcher of water was poisoned, the fruit in the basket was poisoned, and so were the remains of his last meal. Whoever did it, they took no chances. And I'm sure they took skin trophy as proof of the completed deed so they could get paid."

Peabo shuddered as he formed the mental image of Nolan with half of his face sliced off. Were these same people still on the lookout for someone like him? He glanced at the back of his hands, the unmistakable markings crawled up his wrist and continued under the sleeve of his tunic. He was literally a marked man.

"That settles it," said Nicole, glaring at Peabo. "You're not ever cooking *anything*. And I'll be tasting anything you eat before you eat it. I'm not losing you."

Peabo shook his head. "What good would that do? Then you'd die instead—and I don't want to lose *you*."

Brodie rolled his eyes. "Boy, don't you know she's immune to poisons? It's all part of that blood maiden hokum they do up at the Sage's Tower. It's unnatural, I say, but if Nolan had one of them by his side, or if he'd not left my side so hastily, maybe he'd still be alive."

"It's not *unnatural*," Nicole grumbled. "So, old man, are you going to escort us down, or do we need to find some other way?"

Peabo put his hand on Brodie's shoulder. "Please help us. I'll do what it takes—you know I will. If I need to prove it to you, then let's start now. Please."

The tiny man looked back and forth between them with a sour look. But finally he turned toward the forest.

"Bah," he growled. "Follow me before I change my mind."

Brodie led them past the chamber where Peabo had once lived, and into an underground world Peabo could never have imagined. He had thought that Myrkheim would be dark, cold, and damp, but as they trudged through passages leading ever deeper, it was anything but. While the upper levels were dim and smelled of freshly overturned soil, the lower levels were dry, clean, and somehow, bright.

"Shouldn't it be pitch black down here? Why does it seem like it's getting brighter?"

Without slowing his pace, Brodie motioned to the tunnel walls. "It's the fungus spores; they grow throughout Myrkheim. You've eaten plenty of the mushrooms they produce, but cooking them eliminates the glow. It's not bright enough to be good for reading, but it's never truly dark belowground."

They were crossing a large cavern when they had their first encounter with residents of Myrkheim. Eight dwarves wearing armor made from thickened plates of leather were coming from the other direction.

"Hallo!" said one of the dwarves, raising a hand in greeting. "Watcher, who are you bringing with you?"

Brodie clasped hands with the dwarf. "Not for you to worry about, Grant. What's with the young ones? Off for some training?"

"Aye, there's a report from one of the farmers that we've got a pair of ogres tearing things up in his field."

Peabo sensed the thoughts of the younger dwarves.

I wish Ranger Brodie were leading us. He's less likely to get us killed.

By the Nameless One, that's a plainswalker! He's huge. He's practically the size of an ogre!

I don't know if I'm ready for this. One ogre is bad enough, but two?

"Well, have fun, boys," said Brodie, waving and continuing on.

As soon as they were out of earshot of the group, Peabo asked, "Why was I able to hear the kids' thoughts, but not the group leader's?"

Brodie snorted. "You and your plainswalker tricks. You'll find that your mind-reading trick isn't very useful in Myrkheim. We're a working race, meaning we develop our children into proper adults—and level four is about when one gets control over the openness of one's mind."

Peabo wondered aloud, "I wonder why that is."

"Why what is?" Nicole asked.

"Why the ability to control what your mind transmits is linked to a level."

"Bah, that's just common sense." Brodie waved dismissively. "There are others who can read thoughts like you can—though not many. In Myrkheim, they often become teachers for the children. Children are foolish, and a teacher who can hear their scheming minds can correct them before they get into too much trouble."

Peabo chewed on this, and decided it made some degree of sense. The leveling system did seem to lend itself well to differentiating between childhood and adulthood.

As they moved deeper into a maze of interconnecting passages and caverns, Peabo said, "So, Ranger Brodie, where exactly are we going?"

Brodie snorted. "If I told you the name of the place, would it make any difference?"

"I suppose not, but—"

"Stop," Brodie said, holding out his hand.

They had entered yet another cavern, and at the far side was a group of creatures. Rats, much like the ones Peabo had killed in the aboveworld. He smiled and put his hand on the pommel of his sword.

Brodie saw the movement and nodded. "Peabo, take care of those scavengers. I want to see what you do."

Peabo felt a rush of adrenaline as he advanced quietly on the creatures. They were feasting on what looked like the body of another rat, and seemed oblivious to his approach.

Peabo raised his sword and sliced cleanly through the nearest rat, cutting it in half.

"Yes!" cheered a tinny voice from somewhere nearby.

The other three scavengers barely got a chance to react before Peabo dispatched them as well with three swift cuts.

"It's about time."

Peabo turned. "Who said that?"

"Said what?" said Nicole.

"Grab the essences, pea brain."

Confused, Peabo looked for the voice, but saw no one. The glowing essences from the kills drifted toward him, so he stepped forward and absorbed them.

"What the hell took you so long?"

Peabo shook his head to clear it. Was he losing his mind?

"Clean me off and sheathe me before you cut yourself."

Nicole approached with a wary look. "Peabo? Is something wrong?"

Peabo looked down at his sword, which was glowing ever so slightly. Had it always glowed like that?

"Well? Are you going to clean me or not?"

He looked up at Nicole. "Um… I think my sword is talking to me."

She raised her eyebrows, then smiled. "A sentient? Well, they do usually wake up on the first blooding with a new owner."

Whatever was going on, Nicole clearly didn't think it was as unusual as Peabo did. So as he pulled out his cleaning cloth and wiped down the sword, he said, "Sword, can you hear me?"

"I'm not deaf."

"Do you have a name?"

"Max, and you?"

"Nice sword," said Brodie. He turned to Nicole. "Where did he get it?"

"He spotted a skinwalker in the market, and we went and took care of it. The sword was either the skinwalker's or it belonged to the merchant it had killed. It's a level three."

Brodie nodded approvingly at Peabo. "Sentient swords are very rare. And that thing will grow with you."

"You mean as I level, it'll level?"

"Yes, though not at exactly the same time. The essences you gain will be shared with the sword. It actually slows your leveling a bit, but it's worth it."

Peabo was once again fascinated by the oddities of this world. "How does that work?"

"Now isn't the time for lessons, lad. Besides, I'm sure there'll be plenty of chances for you to discover more about your sword on your own. Come—let's keep moving."

Peabo still held the sword in his hand as they exited the cavern and entered another twisting passageway.

"Well, do you have a name?" the sword asked.

"Peabo," he whispered.

"What kind of name is that? Did your mother not like you?"

The thing was not only sentient, it was rude.

Peabo sheathed the sword, silencing it. It was hard enough dealing with new rules of science, much less a sword with an attitude.

CHAPTER TWELVE

At the enormous entrance to what Brodie had called the Metamorphic City, two twenty-foot-tall statues stood like sentinels. They depicted proud, stoutly built dwarves, each wielding two tremendous hammers. Beneath their gaze, hundreds of dwarves passed through into what appeared to be a massive city carved from the bedrock. Peabo couldn't believe that a place so big could exist underground.

"This place is huge!" he exclaimed.

"Bah," said Brodie. "This is merely the outpost level, where we stage trade goods going to and coming from the aboveworld. It's a mere village compared to the lower-level areas. Nolan told me stories of your Wild West, newly settled lands filled with dangerous engines—"

"Indians. There were Indians, not engines."

Brodie shrugged. "Either way, this is like that—a frontier level. The topmost section of Myrkheim."

A squad of dwarven soldiers marching in lockstep stopped in front of Peabo. Unlike the dwarves in the previous group, these men looked the part of a military unit. They meant business.

Their leader, who had a brace of daggers strapped across his chest and a pair of spiked maces holstered near his waist, took in the plainswalker and frowned. "What in all of the hells are you doing down here, plainswalker?"

Nicole answered. "Take it easy, soldier. We're with him." She hitched her thumb at Brodie.

The soldier turned to Brodie. "What says you, Watcher?"

"We're just arriving, and yes, they're both my guests."

With a loud harrumph, the squad leader shook his head. "Get them registered and tagged immediately. We don't need any accidents happening." And with that he and his squad marched away.

Brodie patted Peabo on the arm. "Don't worry, they're just one of the local patrols keeping things civilized. You're definitely not in the aboveworld anymore."

"He called you 'Watcher,'" said Peabo. "What does that mean?"

Brodie waved dismissively. "It's just an old title. It doesn't mean anything."

"He also said something about being tagged?"

"Aye. I have to register the two of you with the main hall's secretary. That'll get you a guest armband, so you're not mistaken for a stray ogre or other nasty."

Peabo noted that Nicole seemed completely at ease through all of this. "Have you been down here before?" he asked her.

"Absolutely. Though I visited through Igneous City, which is below the mainland."

As they walked down the main thoroughfare, lined with buildings that would have dwarfed the ones in the farming town where Peabo and Nicole had made their home, Peabo felt dozens of eyes staring at him. He was a freak in this place, a good two to three feet taller than everyone around him—other than Nicole.

He muttered to himself, "Now I know how Shaquille must feel."

"What?" Nicole leaned closer, putting her hand on his shoulder.

He shook his head. "It's nothing. I'm just very aware of how tall I am right now."

"You and me both. But it's okay. These people are a bit gruffer than the folks in the aboveworld, but they're solid and reliable once you've earned their trust."

"Aye, that we are," said Brodie. "And believe me, I wouldn't have brought you two down here if I had any concerns about your character." He motioned toward a building up ahead. "That's the registration office. Let's get you official and I'll show you around."

Peabo had to duck to get through a doorway labeled "Metamorphic Registrar – Outpost Level." A woman at a desk looked up, and her eyes widened. But then she saw Brodie, and grinned.

"Brodie! So good to see you! I suppose you're wanting to register these two?"

"Aye, darling, that's exactly what I need."

The woman stood. “Okay, you two. Follow me so I can get your images.”

“Images?” Peabo asked.

“You’ll see,” said Brodie. “Just do as she tells you.”

The woman took them into another room that housed a wooden box on a tripod. The woman fiddled with it, then grabbed a large flask, shook it up, and poured its contents into a wooden frame that she inserted into the device.

She pointed at Peabo. “Stand there. There’ll be a bright flash. Please don’t move.” She ducked under a cloth draped over the device.

With a bang, the room briefly lit up from a flash coming from off to Peabo’s right, and the smell of rotten eggs filled the air.

The woman peeked out from under the cloth. “Okay, face me now.”

Peabo did as he was told, and she shot him a thumbs-up. It was the first time he’d seen the gesture in this world, and he couldn’t help but smile as the device banged once again and the light flashed.

The woman pulled out the frame and repeated the process with Nicole. Then she took both frames and left the room.

“What exactly is she doing?” Peabo asked Brodie.

“I thought we’d covered that,” Brodie said. “She’s making an identification armband for the two of you. The rules down in Myrkheim are different than those in the aboveworld. You’ll need an official ID so everyone knows you’re down here for reasons that aren’t nefarious. We’ve got enough trouble with the other native denizens of Myrkheim that we don’t need extra grief from aboveworlders who don't have business down here."

"I don't see *you* wearing one."

"I'm not an aboveworlder, as should be pretty obvious. Dwarvenkind are native to Myrkheim."

The woman returned with two official-looking armbands, one for Peabo and one for Nicole. As she explained how to put them on and adjust the tightness, Peabo studied the armband he'd been handed. It had a likeness of him—two of them, one in profile—but they weren't photographs. They looked more like black-and-white negatives. You couldn't see any real facial features, but he supposed it was the best they could do.

His dad had been a photo buff, back before digital cameras were in vogue at home, so he'd learned about developing film, washing it, and fixing the image. This armband had the same funky chemical smell he remembered from his dad's hobby back in those days. The thought made him feel a bit more comfortable in this world; apparently not everything around here had to be so different. If they had primitive photography, what else might they have?

When they were done with the registrar, Brodie said he had to go see about getting Peabo assigned to some cleanup details, to prep him for hiring on to a travel expedition. In the meantime, the dwarf dropped off Peabo and Nicole at the Metamorphic Library. Apparently, until all the city's registrars had gotten copies of their paperwork, it was best they didn't wander around on their own.

Peabo scanned through a manual describing the creatures of this world. Occasionally he stumbled into a detailed illustration and as he flipped through the book, he noticed an image of a wight.

Since it was one of the few things he'd actually encountered, he stared critically at the image. The patriarch-turned-wight he'd encountered was definitely a bit juicier than what the drawing showed, but it did capture the eerie sense of awareness as it stared at him from the book.

Flipping to the next page, he skimmed the text and as he continued reading, his eyes grew wider with a sense of disbelief. "Am I reading this correctly?" Peabo whispered to Nicole, pointing at the monster manual. "Dragons are real?"

She nodded. "Of course. There's all sorts of them in the mountains over on the mainland, and a few that live in Myrkheim as well. The green ones are a nasty business. They belch poison. I take it they don't have dragons where you're from?"

Peabo shook his head. "No, but we have lots of stories about them, which is weird. This book says some of them are over forty feet long. How long is a foot?"

Nicole held up her hands in front of her to approximate the distance.

"That's another thing that's weird," Peabo said. "How is it that your 'foot' is the same length we use back on my world? Where I come from, there's a whole weird history as to how we came up with that measurement."

"Nothing weird about it to me," said Nicole. "A foot is one and half hand-lengths." She held up her hand. "From the heel of an adult's palm to the end of the middle finger."

"But we have big hands," Peabo said. "Do dwarves have the same size hands? I guess I never really looked at Brodie's."

"They do," said Nicole. "Which is probably why the hand-length, historically, was the basis of all our measurements. Any normal adult has the same sized hands, including bulky oversized plainswalkers." She winked. "But over the years, someone decided that they needed something a bit bigger, and instead of hands they used feet. Just know a foot is half again as long as a hand-length."

Peabo eyeballed his hand, and decided it was about eight inches long, which meant a foot was indeed twelve inches, just as it was back home.

"Aha!" Nicole pointed at a passage in the book she was reading. "It says here that there's a rare necromantic spell that would allow an advanced healer to raise a wight. But whoever raised that patriarch had to be at least level ten, likely higher. A high priest."

"That's bad, isn't it?" Peabo said.

Nicole shrugged. "Well, it's good to know what we're dealing with. But the spell used to do such a thing..." She shuddered. "I don't even want to think about it."

Peabo frowned. "Why do you look like you're about to throw up?"

"I'm just thinking about the kind of person who would even think to cast this type of spell. When someone is weaving one of the forces, especially for healers, it's something that comes from within. It's why I don't like to use my powers very often. Healing is fine, but when someone who is capable of weaving—"

Peabo cut in. "Sorry, just to be sure I'm following—weaving is when someone is using a spell, right?"

"Yes. It's when someone who can manipulate either the interior or exterior forces uses their ability. It's similar to how someone uses thread on a loom to create cloth. When I'm healing someone, I'm imagining how the skin stitches together, how the muscle fibers stretch and reform, everything. It requires almost a form of meditation to guide my focus. And let me tell you, there's something about it that's addicting. Using the powers makes you want to use them more. It can become an obsession of sorts. And after I healed you—I hadn't used my power in ages—the dreams came back that night."

"Dreams?"

"The dreams are a side effect. At the tower, they taught us that the dreams are a gift and a way of scrying new ways of using the forces at our disposal. They aren't bad, if you're a healer. But the thought of the nightmares that would follow a necromantic spell—one with a pure focus on death… they *have* to twist someone's mind, if it wasn't twisted already. And in fact, that's often what happens with people who go to that path."

"They turn evil?"

Nicole shrugged. "Not *evil*, but… well, maybe that's an apt description. I think of it as they go crazy. Swimming day and night in such thoughts…" She shuddered again. "No thanks."

Peabo was about to ask another question, but he was interrupted by Brodie's voice behind him.

"Peabo, are you ready to get to work?"

A matronly librarian shushed him and gave him a death stare.

Brodie rolled his eyes and spoke in a lower voice. "I've got you on an advanced cleanup detail with one of the senior classes. Hopefully that'll get you the experience you need."

"Thank you, Brodie." Peabo tapped the book he'd been

studying. "By the way, is there a way for me to check this out of the library? I'd like to finish studying it."

"What's got your interest?" Brodie leaned over and examined the book cover. "Ah, the basic monster manual. I have a copy of that back in my place from when I was in school. I'll go dig it up. But you need to get moving. Your detail starts in about twenty minutes."

"Twenty minutes? What supplies do I need? Books? Paper? Something to write with?"

"Books?" Brodie snorted. "Just bring your weapon."

"Listen here, girlie." Brodie glared up at Nicole, his brogue as thick as Peabo had ever heard it. "Our boy isn't exactly needing your help. He'll be with a full senior class of young dwarves, all led by a ranger who's at least level eight." He nodded toward the rest of the class, already gathering for the assignment nearby.

Nicole put her hands on her hips. "I don't care. I want to be around in case there's anything unexpected or—"

"Or your boy gets a booboo," Brodie groused. He turned to Peabo. "Boy, can you call her off? I told you these blood maidens are nothing but headaches. I swear she sounds like a mother who isn't ready to have her child weaned."

Peabo put his hand on Nicole's shoulder, and for the first time, pulled her into a hug. "It'll be okay," he whispered. "Let me do this by myself."

Nicole muttered into his chest, "But you don't yet know what's out there, or the dangers to look out for, or—"

"It'll be okay." He tightened his grip around her shoulders. She was freaking out, in her own subdued and gruff way, and it was sort of adorable. "Listen, it's about as safe as it'll get right now. And besides, let me have a little bit of dignity in front of the kids. They don't have *their* mothers fretting over them."

She pushed off his chest and smacked him on his arm. "I'm not acting like your mother!" Her cheeks reddened, and her expression softened. "Okay, maybe I am a little, but—"

"Bah, there's no but!" Brodie motioned to Peabo to move on. "Get to the class. I'll take care of this confused mother hen."

The air was strong with the smell of ammonia as Peabo and a dozen other students trudged through the dark caves. Bats chittered in the darkness above them, and their dung was everywhere. Peabo hoped there was a place to dunk himself after they were done, because he was going to stink when this day was over.

"Oy, plainswalker!" called the ranger leading the group. "I know the aboveworlders have trouble in the dark. Are you able to see okay?"

"I can see fine," Peabo said. Those same glowing mushrooms grew here as abundantly as they did everywhere else in Myrkheim.

"Good." The ranger came to a stop. "Class, look ahead and tell me what you see."

"Nothing," said one student.

"Dung," said another.

But as Peabo focused on the wide path ahead of them, he noticed something rising from the floor far in the distance. "Are those giant mushrooms?"

One of the dwarves gasped. "Oh, I see it. Shriekers!"

"Shriekers?" said Peabo.

The ranger looked up at him. "Plainswalker, I understand this is your first time in Myrkheim, but I expect that by the end of the week, you'll have gone through the monster manual and familiarized yourself with at least the first five levels of creatures." Shaking his head, he pointed to a dwarf in the back of the group. "Karel, tell the plainswalker what you know about shriekers."

The dwarf puffed out his chest. "They're mostly unintelligent fungi that move from dung heap to dung heap. They're called shriekers because if you get close to one or you bring a torch within sight of one, they'll start emitting a horrendous shrieking sound. The only way to deal with them is to chop them up."

"And what's the danger associated with them?" the ranger asked.

"Nothing, really," said another dwarf. "They're just mushrooms."

Immediately, three students shot their hands up. The ranger pointed at one of them.

"They're not dangerous in and of themselves, but there are some really nasty things that love to eat them, so if a shrieker sets off his greeting, you might get some unwanted visitors."

"Correct." The ranger turned back to Peabo. "Plainswalker, here's your challenge. Run over to those shriekers and use that sword of yours to dispatch them before they let out a sound. You'll need to be quick."

Peabo drew his sword. He loved having a challenge.

"It's about damn time you used me. What's up, pea brain? Who are we killing?"

Peabo silently wished the sword would shut up.

"Fat chance of that happening. So, we have shriekers? Let's do this. Just don't drop me and we'll be good. Come on. Let's get some, soldier."

Peabo paused. The damned sword was reading his mind.

But he shook his head and focused on the task assigned to him. After testing the grip of his boots on the guano-covered ground, he sprinted toward the mushrooms as fast as he could.

It wasn't fast enough. As soon as he got within ten feet of the first five-foot-tall mushroom, it let loose with an ear-piercing shriek.

Peabo sliced through the large brown cap, the sword cutting cleanly all the way through to the stem, and with a second swing, he felled it.

"Get some!"

Three other mushrooms were now screaming bloody murder. He chopped away at them as well, and before he knew it he was surrounded by piles of chopped-up shrieker.

[Image: XXXimage2.png]

He absorbed the four essences from the mushrooms as the class joined him at his position.

"Pretty good, plainswalker," said the ranger with a smile. "I'm pleased to see you know how to use that weapon."

"I'm sorry about the noise. I didn't get to them fast enough."

The class chuckled, and the ranger waved dismissively.

"Those things will *always* yell before you reach them. I just wanted to see how you move."

"Oh." Peabo felt foolish, but many of his classmates tossed him thumbs-up signs and he supposed he'd just gone through a very mild hazing. He flashed back to his days in the Special Forces and to the kind of stuff they'd all pulled on new guys. Sending a guy off for a bucket of rotor wash for the helicopter, making a guy spend a few hours looking for a box of grid squares, or telling a guy he needed to go fill out his ID-10-T form.

"Now that we know the plainswalker isn't a cake-eating aboveworlder like we feared," said the ranger, "let's get to our patrol."

The patrol went on for hours. They killed several dozen rats each, a bunch more of those shrieking mushrooms, and something called an anhkheg, which looked like a ten-foot-long praying mantis. Peabo was relieved when the ranger finally announced the patrol was nearing its end.

"All right, boys," he said, "we're almost done with the circuit. One pass through the northern farming quadrant and we're done for today."

They approached a large cavern, and for the twentieth time that day the ranger said, "What do we do when we're about to enter a new part of the cave system?"

The young dwarves all responded in unison. "Look up, down, and all around."

It was the same philosophy Peabo had learned in the Army. Keep your head on a swivel and always maintain situational awareness.

As he scanned the area ahead, he was overwhelmed by the musky smell of mushroom. The cavern was filled with all varieties, planted in rows across acres of tilled soil. At least none of them were shriekers.

One of the students pointed upward, and Peabo followed his finger to a pair of stalactites growing from the rock. Peabo couldn't see what was notable about them, but the ranger pulled out a sling and shot a small rock up at them. It struck one of the stalactites, sending it plummeting into the floor barely ten feet ahead of the group.

Peabo was about to remark how lucky it was they weren't standing under that thing, when the stalactite came to life, revealing a gaping maw filled with razor-sharp teeth. He reflexively drew his sword, stepped forward, and slashed at the rock. The sword bit through its thick flesh and blood spurted from the wound.

"Get some!" the sword screamed in his head.

Suddenly Peabo was yanked backward and landed on his butt. The other stalactite came crashing down from the ceiling, onto the very spot where he'd been standing a split second earlier.

"Fool, plainswalker!" the ranger yelled. "Did you not see the other damned piercer up above?"

Peabo certainly felt foolish as he realized his mistake. But he hopped back onto his feet and finished off the stalactite he'd attacked while a couple of students took care of the other.

When the piercers were put down, the ranger stepped in front of him and poked him as high on the chest as he could reach. "You *will* study the damned monster manual, and you *will* be prepared tomorrow. I owe a report to Ranger Brodie, and I assure you he'll hear about this. I don't need you dying while I'm leading a group, you hear me?"

"Sir, yes, sir."

Peabo felt like an idiot.

The ranger turned to the rest of the class. "Let that be a lesson to all of you! A split second is all it took. One of you could have been dead… and from a stupid piercer, of all things." He snapped his fingers. "Now, onward. Let's move it!"

As the class marched forward, Peabo knew what he had in store for him once the patrol was complete. Lots of studying—and plenty of grief from Nicole.

When they'd returned to the spot where they'd met that morning, the students were dismissed. All except Peabo.

"Plainswalker," said the ranger, "I need to speak to you."

Peabo walked over to the ranger. Hoping to head off the chewing-out he feared was coming, he said, "Thanks again for agreeing to have me on. I've learned a lot just today."

"I'm glad to hear it, plainswalker. And I'm confident you'll be learning even more when you get home tonight. That monster manual will not be reading itself, you hear me?"

"Yes, sir. I'll study it right away."

With a grim expression the dwarf looked him up and down.

Finally he nodded. "Very well. Tell the Watcher I'll be sending him my report. I expect you to know your stuff when you arrive tomorrow. Are we understood?"

"Sir, yes, sir." Peabo was starting to get that military vibe from the short man. He'd make a good drill sergeant back home… if he were taller.

When the ranger dismissed him, Peabo began his walk back to Brodie's place. He wondered if Brodie would let him see whatever report the ranger put together about him. But he didn't need to see the report to know many of the things he'd screwed up on: the mistake with the piercer was the most obvious one, but there were other times where he'd been a bit too eager to jump into the fray, and he sensed he'd gotten in the way of his classmates more than once.

In the Army, when you go out on patrol with a bunch of guys, there's almost never a time where you're involved in hand-to-hand combat. If you're doing that, you've screwed up. But things were different here. There were no guns, no bullets. Combat was in your face, sword and attacker within feet of each other. It had a very different feel, especially when sharing combat space with a bunch of other guys doing the same thing.

That was where Peabo's martial arts and military training merged. He understood fighting with a team from his time in the Army; and he understood close-combat fighting, including with swords, from his training in karate. It was just a matter of putting the two together.

He was feeling pretty good about his progress, and thinking about a long night of studying ahead of him, when a breeze blew over him, and the hairs on the back of his neck stood on end. He barely had time to wonder where the wind had come from when he was struck on the side of the head with what felt like a sledgehammer.

His heart racing, stars filling his vision, he drew his sword.

"We've been hit!" Max yelled in his head. *"Let me at that bastard! I'll show him what he gets for doing that!"*

Peabo spun around, looking for his attacker. But there was no one there.

"Where the hell is he? I didn't just get hit out of thin air—"

A blur appeared directly in front of him, and something smashed into his face—hard. Peabo heard the sickening crunch of his nose, and felt the warmth of the blood pouring down his chin.

He swung at the blur, and his sword connected with something. Whatever he struck, it made a keening noise, almost like a teapot whistle.

"What the hell is that thing?" Max groused. *"Are we being attacked by the Predator? He's flanking to the left!"*

Now that Peabo knew what to watch for, he caught the blur once again, and he swung the sword with all his might. He felt it dig deep into something, though he still couldn't see what. And then with a crack like the zap of electricity, a gust of wind exploded outward, pushing him back.

And then there was nothing.

No blur, no body, no blood other than his own.

"Max," said Peabo. "You get anything from our bag of wind?"

"Nah, it's gone. I think you killed it, whatever it was."

Peabo heard footsteps, and saw Nicole running toward him. "Peabo!" she cried.

He groaned, knowing how he must look right about now. When he wiped his face, his hand came back sticky with his own blood.

Nicole had already drawn her own sword. "What's happening? I felt you panicking and raced over to—"

"I didn't *panic*," Peabo growled. A gash on his cheek burned like hell, and he cleared his throat and spit out a huge glob of bloody phlegm. "I got attacked by something, but it's dead now. Or—" He thought about that. There had been no essence, so it couldn't have been dead. "Or… I guess it ran away."

Nicole looked around, then sheathed her katana and brought her glowing hands up to Peabo's face. "Stand still while I work on this." She squeezed his cheek, and the heat from the gash bloomed even hotter. "Tell me what happened."

While he explained, she worked her magic, and by the time he was done, so was she. He was still a bloody mess, but he was pain-free.

"Do you have any clue what that thing could have been?" he asked.

Nicole's expression was grim. "It sounds like an invisible stalker. They're not part of this world, so you can't really kill them here, where we are. I believe, however, that you might have killed its ability to be on this plane of existence. And no, I'm not going to try to explain that. You have a lot of studying to do before we even start on that topic."

"Are invisible, not-really-of-this-world stalkers just a normal part of life around here?" Peabo asked with a frown.

"No. In fact I've never encountered one before; I've just read about them."

"I guess that makes me the lucky one."

Nicole ignored the comment. "From now on, I'm picking you up when your patrol is over. You will *not* be walking around on your own. I don't know how this creature got here, or how it found you, but one thing is pretty clear: someone doesn't want you to exist."

Choosing the only table in the tavern built for aboveworlders, Peabo and Nicole took their seats, enveloped by the noise of dozens of conversations. A dwarven waitress came up to their table, made a point of looking at their armbands, and then smiled.

"How may I help you?"

Nicole immediately said, "Two beers, and what are your specials for today?"

The waitress looked young, with a clear, unwrinkled complexion. She was paler than most Myrkheimers, who normally had a swarthy skin tone. "We have barrier fungus stew, a sour apple crisp, a fire radish salad, and an above-worlder special that you might like: rat tenderloin in a cream sauce, baked in a pastry shell."

"I'll have the rat tenderloin," said Nicole. "That sounds delicious."

The waitress scribbled the order on a notepad and looked at Peabo. "And you, sir?"

The idea of more rat turned Peabo's stomach. "Is the fungus stew spicy?"

"Not by Myrkheimer standards, but an aboveworlder might find it to be spicy. The rat dish isn't spicy at all, if that's a concern."

"No, that's okay. I'll take the barrier fungus stew."

The waitress stared at Peabo for a long awkward moment, and then blushed. "I'm sorry, I don't mean to be rude. Are you a plainswalker?"

"Is that a problem?" Peabo asked.

"Oh, not at all, I-I'm sorry," she stammered. "I'm just pleased to see a real one in Metamorphic. I've read about plainswalkers in school, but never thought I'd get to meet one."

As the waitress walked off with their order, Peabo turned to Nicole. "That was weird."

She shrugged. "Not really. Your race is something of an enigma. There are many stories about plainswalkers, but almost none have been seen in ages." Nicole looked around, then leaned forward and whispered, "That's what has me worried. As I told you before, you stick out like a sore thumb. We may not want to have another meal in public—so enjoy this one."

The waitress returned with their drinks and food, and quickly departed for another table.

Peabo sniffed at his stew. Its warm, savory smell made his mouth water. But before Peabo could even try it, Nicole pulled the bowl away from him, dipped her spoon in, and tasted it first.

"Uh, if you wanted to try it…"

She then grabbed his beer, took a long sip, swirled it in her mouth, and swallowed. Only then did she push his food and drink back over to him. "There's no poison," she said. "And it's pretty good. Eat it before it gets cold."

"Thank you," Peabo said. He hoped it really was true that as a blood maiden, she was immune to poison.

The stew was indeed good. In fact, it was delicious. But Peabo had trouble enjoying it. With his mind on thoughts of invisible stalkers and possible poisoning, he wondered what else could be coming his way.

CHAPTER THIRTEEN

After three weeks in Myrkheim, Peabo was feeling fairly comfortable in the subterranean world—and the dwarves seemed to have grown used to his hulking presence wandering through the city. But Nicole had become a nervous wreck after news came down from the aboveworld that agents from Dvorak were looking for the "missing" plainswalker. It was only a matter of time before they figured out where he was, which meant he needed to hurry on his way. As a result, he'd begun pulling two patrols a day.

And when he wasn't patrolling, he was studying. After he'd memorized the monster manual front to back, Brodie had piled onto his nightstand all variety of books regarding history, including how the Nameless One had defeated all of the other deities and demigods to dominate the one church remaining in this world. He also spent a great deal of time in the library, which was where he was today, flipping through a thick tome titled *Metallurgical Studies of the Arcane.* He paused to read through a section in a chapter about the imbuing of essences.

The forging of a weapon of metal requires no more skill than that of a practiced smith, yet when an enhanced weapon is desired, one that can grow with its owner, a weaving must take place.

By application of an essence, a conductor can augment the results of the forging process. There is no guarantee that the binding of essence to metal will be successful, but the likelihood of success increases with the strength of the essence. Do not hope for much when attempting to bind an essence from a low-level creature.

Essence-enhanced items are rare and highly prized due to the difficult nature of their creation and their long-term utility.

Peabo still understood little of this weaving stuff, but Nicole had explained that there were weavers who, instead of using energy from within as she did, instead manipulated the energies outside themselves—such as the energy from an essence. These weavers were called *conductors*. Peabo hadn't yet met one, but in his mind he imagined a conductor would look very much like a Gandalf type of character, a wizard who could cast lightning bolts at things, something that he'd love to witness one day. He wished Nicole were around right now to explain more about what he was reading.

He paused in his skimming once more to read a passage on "sentience."

A sword imbued with an essence will evolve as its owner evolves. In so doing, the object will exhibit attributes that mimic a personality. The personality will be a confluence of several factors: attributes of the owner, attributes of the conductor who bound the essence to the sword, and attributes of the creature from whom the essence came.

It should be noted that all essences are shared between the enhanced object and its owner, and once they have leveled, the object is permanently bound to its owner. Only upon death can another use it without deleterious consequences.

Deleterious consequences? Luckily for him, whoever had previously owned Max had died, so he didn't suffer any consequences, but he wondered what would the sword do to someone else who picked it up? Shock them?

Peabo sighed. Yet another question for Nicole.

Nicole watched as Peabo scooped up some bat dung from a bucket and plopped it into a separate container. "What are you doing with that stuff?"

He began pouring boiling water into the container. "I'm purifying the potassium nitrate… or at least what I think might be potassium nitrate."

"You're speaking those Aingish words again. I have no idea what you said."

"English. And… wait." Peabo watched as the steaming water formed a disgusting soup that slowly dripped into a tray below the container. "I'm filtering what I think is a chemical that might be pretty useful. Evidently nobody around here has heard of incendiary devices, unless of course it's the kind you've talked about." He wiggled his fingers at her. "You know, that weaving nonsense."

"It's not nonsense. Just because you've never seen it…"

"I know, I know." Peabo continued to watch the foul concoction drip down, creating an ever-larger pool of clear liquid in the tray.

"You aren't going to drink that, are you?" Nicole said with a grimace.

Peabo laughed. "No… this is just a test. Patience."

For the next thirty minutes he made more of his filtered bat dung soup. He then boiled the filtered liquid until the water had evaporated, leaving behind white crystals.

Then he turned to Nicole, who had stayed to observe the entire process. "Can you get me some sugar?" he asked.

"You are *not* eating that," she said. "And I assure you that *I* am not."

Peabo made a patting motion in the air. "I swear to you, none of this is going anywhere near my mouth or yours. Please, while I finish this can you get me just a spoonful of sugar?"

"Fine."

Nicole rummaged around in Brodie's cooking supplies and returned with a container of sugar. "Here's the sugar. In exchange, I'd like an explanation of what you think you're accomplishing. And don't use your otherworldly vocabulary, just stick to Common if you wouldn't mind."

Peabo explained as he crushed the white bat soup crystals with a mortar and pestle, then set the heavy mortar onto the portable flame and began mixing a small measure of sugar into it.

"I noticed all of the bat droppings everywhere and I saw that your farmers were using it for fertilizer. Historically, so did our farmers, which made me think that the chemistry between my world and this one might be very similar. So, there are a few tricks I know from my world that could be very useful if they work here. That's what this is about."

She furrowed her brow. "What kind of tricks?"

Wearing a thick glove, Peabo grabbed the mortar and poured the heated mixture onto a metal tray. The crystals and sugar combination had partially melted, so that it now had the consistency of softened wax.

"The first thing I wanted to test is really simple. If this works the way I think it will, it'll create a bunch of smoke—"

"Listen here," growled Brodie, entering the home at that moment. "You'll not be filling my home with smoke. If you're going to be doing something that might stink or do harm, do it outside."

Peabo shrugged and picked up the metal tray with the cooling thumb-sized lump at its center. "Can one of you bring a striker?" he asked.

"Aye." Brodie pulled a handheld flint and steel from his pocket. "You can use mine."

The three of them went outside, where Peabo set down and molded the still-hot mound around a wick. Then he gestured to Brodie, who handed him the striker.

Peabo motioned everyone away. "This should be perfectly safe, but just in case, let's step back. If it does what I think it will, it won't smell all that great."

Peabo shielded the lump with one hand, squeezed several times on the striker, and sent a torrent of sparks falling onto the wick. The moment the wick caught fire, he hurriedly stepped away.

Within three seconds of the flame getting close to the substance, a spark flashed and gray noxious smoke billowed upward.

"It works!" Peabo cried.

Brodie yelled through the smoke, "It makes smoke. Why is this a good thing?"

Peabo smiled. "This is just the beginning, trust me."

Peabo had never imagined himself getting used to living underground in a cave, but Brodie's four-room home on the outskirts of Metamorphic City was very comfortable. He and Nicole shared one room, Brodie had his own bedroom, and there was a common eating and living area. There was even an actual latrine with running water underneath. It was luxurious compared to the forward operating bases he'd experienced in Afghanistan.

Nicole took on the cooking for the three of them, and it was always something new. Breakfast today consisted of the ever-present mushrooms, but this time there was a casserole made from some root vegetables, and Peabo was pleased to see something that looked like a steak. He was afraid it was actually a mushroom until he took a bite and its savory juices practically exploded on his tongue. This was real meat. And not smoked rat, either.

Nicole smiled at him. "You'd think I didn't feed you by the way you're wolfing that down."

Brodie was also chowing down. "The boy knows a good piece of purple worm, properly cooked, when he gets it."

Peabo stopped mid-chew. He'd seen a picture of the beast in the monster manual. It was a giant earthworm with a poison stinger.

"I'm eating purple worm?" he said.

"Aye. The lads down in level three encountered a huge beastie almost sixty feet long. Tasty, isn't it?"

Peabo tried to push away the idea that he was eating a worm. He'd eaten worse. Once, on a hop to Sicily, he and a bunch of his Special Forces buddies had on a dare eaten *casu marzu*—a sheep's-milk cheese filled with live maggots. It was horrid. This was far less disgusting in concept—and in taste… well, there was no comparison. This tasted wonderful.

"Mark me down as a big fan of purple worm," he said.

Nicole pointed her fork at him. "Did you go to the testing center, like I asked?"

"I did. For twenty gold royals they strapped me to a machine, put something around my head, and after two minutes of clicks, they said 'ninety-five percent.' I'm guessing that means I'm almost ready to level?"

"It does." Nicole turned to Brodie. "Do you think one more day?"

"Aye, or two." The dwarf hitched his thumb to Peabo's waist. "Don't forget, the sword gets its share as well."

"It's taking too long," said Nicole. "I spotted two above-worlders in the city yesterday. Neither of them were registered."

Brodie waved the comment away. "If they're here for any length of time, they'll be registered or they'll be picked up by a patrol. I wouldn't be so worried. The boy is safe."

Nicole scowled. "He stands out, Brodie. And damn him, but he likes to talk to people."

"What's wrong with that?" Peabo asked, annoyed.

"She does have a point, plainswalker," said Brodie. "You're a bit too outgoing for your own good. I know that's just who you are, but my advice is, when you know you have an assassin looking for you, keep a low profile."

"How am I supposed to keep a low profile when I'm surrounded by dwarves? I'm twice everyone's size down here, and my skin looks like one of my parents made it with a tree. It doesn't matter whether I talk to anyone or not. As Nicole has told me repeatedly, I stand out."

Nicole frowned, thinking. "Brodie, does the city have an alchemist?"

Brodie shook his head. "I know where you're going with this, and no. Nobody around here performs that sort of thing. There's usually no reason."

"What thing?" Peabo asked.

"The maiden's thinking about a skin-changing potion."

"What's that?"

"It's a potion most often used by assassins who want to change themselves into utter blackness for a night kill. The whites of the eyes, the skin, even the teeth are all dyed from the inside out. It's quite effective. And quite expensive. At least a few hundred gold royals."

Nicole nodded. "I was thinking that with the right formulation, we can change you, at least temporarily, into something that looks a bit less like a plainswalker. You'd be able to at least pass for a large aboveworlder."

"It doesn't matter," said Brodie, "since there are no such alchemists in Metamorphic City. There might be some in the Dvorak Castle environs though, once you get there, if there still be a need for it."

"Did you find a group heading north?" Nicole asked him.

"No," Brodie said with a sigh. "Unfortunately, most of the adventuring groups are preoccupied at the lower levels guarding the construction of the new interconnect system. Nothing for at least a month."

"A *month*? We don't have—"

Brodie held up his hand. "Maiden, I may regret this, but… I can lead you two where you need to go." He wagged his thick finger at Peabo. "But you still *absolutely* need to get to level four before we set even one foot into one of the interconnect levels. We'll be going by stealth, and I don't need your mind broadcasting our presence everywhere."

"My mind?"

"The ability to cloak one's thoughts from the attention of others is a feature of graduating from child to adult in the adventurer's ranks," Nicole explained.

"Aye, that typically happens at level four, and at least for most people, it's an automatically learned ability. It'll just be there."

"Well," said Peabo, "thank you for escorting us. I appreciate it."

Nicole stood. "And I'm going to go pack our bags. We're leaving the *moment* you get back from patrol." She poked Peabo in the chest. "Get that level *today*."

As she turned and walked to their sleeping quarters, Brodie shot him a crooked smile. "Better get going, my friend. Who knows what she'll do to you if you're still lazing around when she's done."

Wearing a ranger's cloak and ducking in the shadows, Nicole followed the aboveworlder through the city of Metamorphic. This man and his partner were the same ones she'd seen yesterday, and neither was wearing the armband of a registered aboveworlder. But now the two men had split up, and she had opted to follow the larger one.

On occasion he tried to question passersby, but the standoffish dwarves more often than not brushed past him as if he wasn't even there, and the few who did pause only exchanged a few words with the man before moving on.

Nicole hung back and did her best to remain out of sight. But even twenty feet away, she smelled the guy; he stank of urine and alcohol. Still, his gait was steady and practiced, and she'd known many a practiced fighter who was deadly whether they were sober or almost blind drunk.

As the man entered the crowds of the market, she took the opportunity to get closer, and she managed to hear snatches of the man's conversation with a merchant.

"Tall aboveworlder…"

"…haven't seen…"

"Plainswalker?"

The dwarf merchant nodded.

Nicole put her blowgun to her lips and launched an almost invisible dart. The man slapped his neck and spun around, frantically looking for his assailant. But before three heartbeats had passed, the strong sedative in the glass injector had taken over, and Nicole caught the man as he collapsed.

The merchant's eyes were wide with concern, but Nicole calmed him. "No worries," she said. "My husband, he has fainting spells sometimes. I'll take care of him."

"Y-you need help?"

Nicole lifted the stranger up in a fireman's carry and shook her head. "I've got it, thanks."

Staggering under her load, she ducked out of the square and moved swiftly down a passage that ran along a cliff-like precipice. She dropped the man like a sack of potatoes, not off the cliff, but next to it. Then she knelt next to him and grimaced at his rank odor. She grabbed him by his greasy hair and delved into his unprotected mind.

"Why are you here?"

As she buried herself in the man's thoughts, she barely controlled her gag reflex. Flashes of the man's memories popped up in her head. Images of former victims.

He was a rapist. An assassin. A thief. And a searcher. The coppery scent of blood was everywhere in his history. How many people had he already killed? And why? What was his purpose?

He'd recently been in the town of Dvorak, where he met with a man cloaked in shadows—a man who hired him. Nicole couldn't identify who the dark man was, but this smelly bastard was clearly terrified of him.

And then the cloaked man spoke, and his tone made Nicole's blood run cold.

"Plainswalker."

Nicole gasped for air and shivered with revulsion as she yanked herself out of the man's mind. There was now no doubt what this man's mission was.

Peabo.

With a heave, she sent the man tumbling off the cliff,

crashing to the ground thirty feet below. Rats ventured forth from a nearby nest and began feasting on his broken body.

Nicole rose to her feet and headed back to the marketplace. "One down, one to go."

Peabo motioned for quiet as he crept toward the entrance of the cave, sword in hand. The ranger was by his side, and the rest of the class trailed behind. There'd been a report that three ogres had been spotted on the outpost level outside Metamorphic City. Their oversized tracks led to a natural opening along the craggy edge of a cavern. And now, from somewhere inside the dark, looming entrance, came the splintering sound of something wooden being broken.

"We store some supplies in that cave," the ranger whispered. "There's no exit. But we won't have the room to fight them in there. Let's wait them out."

"What if I figure out a way to get them to come out?"

The ranger shook his head. "Too dangerous. They could be —wait, what are you doing?"

Peabo sheathed his sword and pulled out a fist-sized brownish-yellow rock with a long black wick sticking out of it. He'd been waiting for an excuse to try it out. He'd never used anything this primitive in Kandahar or in any of his training, but the idea that he was bringing part of his Army training to use in this place made him smile.

"There's no reason to let them destroy what's in there," he

said. “I’ll flush them out. Just be ready for them to come running.”

Using a striker, he lit the fuse and hurled the smoke bomb into the cave. Immediately a bellow erupted from within, and seconds later, smoke began pouring from the cave’s entrance.

Peabo drew his sword

“Alrighty then!” it said. *“Let’s get some!”*

The monster manual had said ogres were about nine feet tall and very strong. But the first creature to stagger blindly out of the cave was easily eleven feet tall.

Peabo didn't hesitate; he slashed heavily from left to right against the back of the creature's knee, separating the tendons with a sharp series of snaps. The behemoth collapsed on his useless leg, and Peabo rammed the tip of his sword into the ogre's now-exposed neck. Blood fountained from the wound.

The ogre slammed a fist into Peabo's chest, sending him flying backward, the breath knocked out of him.

That was when the other ogres came stumbling out, a bit smaller than the first but still huge. With a yell, the class charged them. Peabo tried to launch himself back into action, but he hadn't even caught his breath before all three ogres were dead. The fight was over almost as soon as it started.

The ranger gave Peabo an uncharacteristic smile. "My boy, that's some trick you played. What was it?"

Peabo rubbed at a sore spot just to the left of his breastbone; he wondered if the ogre had managed to crack a rib. "It's sort of hard to explain."

"Well, whatever it was, I like it. And that first beastie you hobbled, it has to be one of the biggest I've ever seen in the upper levels." The ranger smacked Peabo's arm. "You okay, plainswalker?"

"I'm fine," Peabo lied. His chest was really bothering him. The monster manual hadn't been lying—those things were strong as hell.

"Oh, take some Motrin and change your socks, you big baby," said the sword.

Shut up, Max, Peabo thought back. The damned thing had somehow dug through his memories and latched on to the personality of Max Decker, his drill sergeant from boot camp. The guy had been a real asshole—but in a good way.

Peabo walked over to the body of the ogre that he'd downed. It probably weighed eight hundred pounds, maybe more. The creature's one dying smack had nearly knocked him senseless. He was lucky he wasn't hit twice.

A large ball of essence bubbled up from the corpse and drifted toward him. Peabo tapped at it with his sword, and as it shot up the length of his blade, he felt time stop. All movement halted, and the world became deathly quiet.

His mind reeled. Nothing around him had changed, but *he* had; it was like a door had opened in his head. He had no words to describe the tingling sensation that flooded his senses other than… euphoria.

He had just leveled up.

"Oh, yeah! Now that's what I'm talking about, pea brain!"

The sword had leveled up as well.

The pain in Peabo's chest flared and vanished. And then the world started again. The noise of the others, their movement, everything was back the way it was.

The ranger looked him in the eye and nodded approvingly. "Congratulations. You're now an adult."

"How'd you know?" Peabo asked.

The dwarf winked. "I've witnessed thousands of kids graduating into adulthood, and the signs are always the same. You think you're any different?"

"I don't know. I guess not."

The ranger chuckled and announced to the class, "Today we're going to cut the circuit a bit short so we can deliver the plainswalker to the Watcher."

Peabo had mixed feelings about leaving the group. He knew there was a lot more to learn down here, but if Nicole was right, and there were people hunting for him, the best defense was a good offense.

It was time to move on.

CHAPTER FOURTEEN

Peabo found it hard to say goodbye to Metamorphic City. He'd come to like the gruff, independent people who lived there, and the underground city had provided relative comfort, certainly when compared to the days that followed their departure. He, Nicole, and Brodie rested little as they traveled through a maze of tunnels and passages that skirted past the main thoroughfare of Myrkheim's interconnect level—called such because it had passages to pretty much anywhere the dwarves needed to go.

They found a small cave to make camp, and Peabo sat against the wall and chewed on a piece of heavily spiced dried mushroom. They couldn't heat anything without giving away their location. Nicole sat beside him and leaned her shoulder against his.

"Are you as lost down here as I am?" he asked her.

She patted his knee. "I could probably find my way out, but

that's only because I've been through here a few times. You've got to be a dwarf to really get around down here."

"Aye," said Brodie, sitting nearby. "You can spin us Myrkheimers around and around and we can naturally tell you which way things are. It's just something we're born with. It's also why we like it down here more than up there." He pointed a finger upward. "And the idea of not having a proper ceiling above you… it just isn't natural."

"How much farther is it to Dvorak?" Peabo asked.

Brodie aimed his finger up and to his right. "It's about a day's travel in that direction. We have another day on the interconnect level, and once we're under Dvorak, it's just an hour or so to get to the outpost level and the forest exit just outside the castle."

"How many cities are there in Myrkheim?"

"I think it's twenty?" Nicole responded. "Isn't that right?"

"Aye, maiden. That would be the truth of it. How far into Myrkheim have you been?"

"Just level five," Nicole said in a hushed tone. "I can't really say what I was doing, but it was definitely a sight to see. We ended up leaving pretty quickly with a pack of umber hulks chasing after us."

Brodie chuckled. "I've been hearing that them beasts have been traveling in larger packs lately. It used to be you might encounter those only in lower levels, and rarely more than one or two at a time."

Peabo frowned. "Do the lower levels tend to have higher-level monsters lurking about?"

"There's none that'll tell a dragon where it can be going, but generally speaking, it gets more challenging the deeper into Myrkheim you are," Brodie said. "And there's entire nests and villages of unmentionable creatures if you go down deep enough. But the cities of Myrkheim are also much grander at the lower levels. You've only seen a mere outpost. And of course, the patrols are much more fun further down. You won't see children clearing the area like you did up here. At the lowest levels, you'd have to be at least a level eight or nine to even be considered for the patrols. Believe you me, we have some interesting things living down in the depths of this world."

The group fell silent, and soon Nicole and Brodie found their sleeping positions, using their packs like pillows. Peabo was taking the first watch.

But there was something on his mind.

"Brodie, what does—"

"Shh, he's already asleep," whispered Nicole. "What's your question?"

"I was just wondering. A bunch of the soldiers called him a Watcher, or maybe *the* Watcher. I'm curious what it means."

"I'm not sure. I've heard that title before. It's an ancient one that I didn't think was being used anymore. I know it has something to do with the Nameless One."

"You mean he's a priest of some kind? The dwarf kids seemed to think of Brodie as some kind of ranger, which I thought was like a senior soldier."

"Bah," said Brodie, without opening his eyes. "You two

don't know how to shut your yaps, do you? A ranger isn't just some soldier, and I'm not a damned priest. Watcher is just an old title. It doesn't mean anything. Now let me get some sleep."

Nicole patted Peabo's knee and closed her eyes, but Peabo leaned his head back against the wall and wondered what Brodie wasn't telling him.

"How long would it take to get to Dvorak from Metamorphic if we weren't constantly taking these detours?" Peabo asked.

"I've fast-marched it in thirty-six hours before," Brodie said as he led them through another winding passage. "But if we took the fast routes we'd risk a serious confrontation, and we don't have the numbers for that."

"What kind of confrontations?"

"Last time I was down here," Nicole said, "we ended up having to deal with a group of nearly three dozen orcs."

"How many people were in your group?" Brodie asked.

"Only five, but Zenethar was guiding us. Do you know him?"

Brodie chuckled. "That old trickster. What is he nowadays, a level fourteen conductor?"

"Fifteen."

Peabo's eyes widened. He didn't even realize the levels went that high. Orcs had been mentioned in the monster manual as "pig-like" humanoids, which had caught his attention, as it implied they did have pigs somewhere in this world —and if they had pigs, they had to have bacon. A plateful of bacon would definitely sit well with him right about now.

"I'm almost afraid to ask," he said, "but how could five people deal with that many orcs?"

"Imagine you're a wandering troop of orcs, looking for trouble," said Nicole. "You spot a small group of above-worlders and a single dwarf. You charge, and suddenly you find yourself falling upward… where you're impaled by stalactites in the ceiling."

"Brilliant!" Brodie said with a laugh.

"Falling upward?" Peabo said.

Nicole draped her arm over Peabo's shoulder. "If you're a high enough level conductor, you can manipulate all variety of forces, even gravity."

Peabo imagined gravity suddenly reversing itself. "What would happen if he had done that in the aboveworld?"

A sly grin appeared on Nicole's face. "I suppose anything that goes up, eventually must come down."

Brodie turned to Nicole and raised an eyebrow as if to say, *Is that what they taught you in that damned Sage's Tower?*

"There's limits to the power," Nicole continued. "I read that the effect only lasts around a second or so. So the highest fall would be just about twenty feet. It worked in our encounter because we were in a low-ceilinged cavern."

"A twenty-foot fall would still be enough to break some bones, I'd think."

"It would, but impaling them on stalactites is far better," Nicole said with a gleam in her eye. "But again, we just took advantage of the situation facing us. Low ceiling, stalactites above, and lucky for us, the orcs were stupid enough to be gathered together in a tight formation. The gravity effect only covers a limited area."

"Aye," said Brodie. "Tactics are important in our trade, and orcs aren't particularly good at them. But I'm sure you're familiar with such, plainswalker, seeing as you were a professional warrior in your world."

Nicole looked at Peabo in surprise. "You were? I know you have fighting skills and were familiar with the use of a sword, but I got the impression that it was just an interest of yours. They have a warrior's guild where you're from?"

Peabo shrugged. Somehow, he'd failed to mention anything to Nicole about his Special Forces background. "I suppose you could call what I was involved in very much like a warrior's guild. Although I'm not yet sure how much of that experience helps in this world."

"Nonsense," Brodie barked. "The patrol ranger told me what you did with that smoke stone. You downed an ogre chieftain by yourself at level three. That's almost unheard of. Boy, don't sell yourself short. All of your experience, whether gained here or in your other life, it's part of who you are. It all helps."

The tunnel they were traveling along opened out into a large cavern. Brodie nodded in satisfaction.

"Here we are. Just ahead is the passage that leads up to Sedimentary City. And from there, it's a quick slog to the aboveworld just outside of Dvorak Castle."

Peabo remembered the ranger's advice. *"Look up, down,*

and all around any time you're entering a new area. You can never tell what might be hiding in the shadows to get you." He panned his gaze all around. It was a particularly large cavern, the far wall a good quarter mile away, and to the left and right, the walls were almost beyond his sight altogether.

"A quick sprint to the other side of the cavern," said Brodie, "and it's the fourth small cave entrance from the left. Just follow me."

The dwarf took off like a race car. Nicole easily ran alongside him, but there was no way Peabo could keep up with their pace. He was definitely the tortoise in this group.

The entire far wall was pockmarked with cave entrances. How in the world Brodie knew which cave went where was beyond Peabo's understanding. But Brodie ran directly to one of them, then he and Nicole stopped and waited for the plainswalker to catch up.

Peabo was sprinting so as not to be too embarrassed by the speed of the others, but as he approached, he slowed—and one foot slipped out from under him on the loose gravel. He ended up sliding on his butt the last ten feet, and stopped right under Brodie's glowering visage.

"You're faster than you look," Peabo said sheepishly.

A growl sounded from somewhere nearby, and Peabo scrambled to his feet just as an eight-foot-tall monstrosity appeared from one of the other cave entrances. Peabo had seen a picture of a creature like this one in the monster manual—an *otyugh*. It was like a hide-covered ball of writhing muscle, with four thick legs, a giant three-foot-wide mouth, and several octopus-like tentacles.

"Don't get hit by the tentacles!" Brodie yelled as he rushed the creature, a longsword in each hand. "They carry diseases!"

One of the tentacles shot out at the dwarf with whip-like speed, but Brodie ducked and lopped off the tentacle with two quick slashes. A greenish liquid sprayed from the stump.

Another tentacle came for Peabo, but Nicole stepped in front of him and chopped it off, leaving a four-foot-long section of writhing tentacle landing with a thump at his feet.

Peabo drew his sword and attacked.

"What the goddamn hell is that?" the sword shouted in his head.

But Peabo was too involved in the fight to reply. As he chopped off one tentacle, he parried an attack from another and ducked the green ichor that spewed everywhere. Brodie was fighting like a whirlwind, drawing most of the creature's attention, and Peabo seized an opening to slash at the bulbous creature's thick hide.

"Aw, yeah. Guts and glory!" the sword yelled as it sliced through the hide and bit into something hard.

Peabo hopped back and was about to take another swing when Nicole leaped on top of the creature and buried her katana to its hilt. The attack sent a shiver through the creature, its stubs waving frantically. Then it convulsed, rolled slightly to its left, and stopped moving. A large glowing essence bubbled up from within the creature's body, floated toward him, and was quickly absorbed as he tapped the blob of energy with his sword.

Nicole leapt off nimbly, and Brodie saluted the above-worlders with one of his swords. "Well done."

Nicole hurried over to Peabo and ran her hands over his arms, chest, and legs.

"What are you doing?" Peabo asked, feeling uncomfortable.

"Just checking for any splashes. Brodie's right: that thing is full of diseases."

Brodie grinned and shook his head, then cautiously approached the cave entrance that the otyugh had exited from. Peabo felt a slight rumbling in the ground.

“What—”

“Shh!” said Brodie, motioning for silence. He backed away from the cave, grabbed Peabo by the sleeve, and pulled him away, with Nicole following.

“What’s going on?” Peabo whispered.

“Lad, trust me. You don’t want anything to do with whatever is in that cave.”

Instead they entered the cave Brodie had chosen to begin with, which proved to be a passage that sloped upward. As they climbed, Peabo thought back to what he knew of otyughs from the monster manual. The creatures were known to live in symbiosis with other creatures. Bigger creatures.

“What exactly was in that cave with the otyugh?” he asked.

Brodie, who’d taken the lead, ignored the question, but Nicole whispered, “My guess is it was a green dragon. They’re sometimes found underground near outpost levels, so they have easy access to the aboveworld if need be.”

“A dragon? Whoa. I’d give anything to see a dragon in real life.”

Brodie snorted. “Trust me, you want no part of that thing. Before we start looking for whoever’s after you, I’m going to have to have a talk with the Sedimentary City guard and let them know we’ve got a dragon that’s entirely too close to the city.”

“Did you just say ‘we’?” Peabo asked. “I thought you were only volunteering to lead us to Dvorak safely. Are you staying with us on our quest?”

“Bah. What kind of Watcher would I be if I let you go off up there and get yourself killed?”

"I thought you said that's just an old title that doesn't mean anything."

Brodie scowled. "Shut up, plainswalker."

CHAPTER FIFTEEN

Peabo stared at his reflection in a mirror on the wall of the security office in Sedimentary City. It was the clearest image of himself he'd seen since coming to this world, and the man who stared back sent chills through him.

Is that really me?

He looked similar to the other aboveworlders. His facial features were a bit broader than others, perhaps, but befitting a brutish fighter, and his mostly brown skin wasn't unusual in this world. What *was* unusual were the darkened striations on his face and body. It was as if a lightning pattern had been tattooed across his face.

They were the mark of a plainswalker.

And that was his problem. Even though hardly anyone had ever laid eyes on a plainswalker, they all knew about the skin markings. And they were so distinct that, to any assassin looking for him, they were a dead giveaway. He might as well have had a horn growing out of his forehead.

Which was why Brodie had snuck them into this building and hid him in this office while the dwarf had gone to the aboveworld to retrieve something that would solve this very problem. Now Brodie was back, potion in hand, and it was time to undertake the transformation.

"Come on, boy, let's get this over with," Brodie groused.

Peabo took the leather flask from him, unstoppered it, and sniffed at what was inside. That was a mistake. He nearly dropped the potion as the horrid smell hit him.

"What the hell is *in* this?" he said.

"What are you complaining about?" said Brodie. "It's a skin-changing potion, not a fruity drink."

Nicole sniffed at the potion as well, then shrugged. "I've smelled worse. Though I should have warned you not to smell it. The alchemists in the Sage's Tower told us never to sniff the potions. Only the Nameless One knows what in the world they put in there, but they always smell worse than they taste. Just hold your nose and drink it as quickly as you can."

Peabo took a few deep breaths to psyche himself up… and then he chugged the potion. It took all of his focus to power through the nasty stuff, and the moment he was done, he shuddered with revulsion. "That stuff had *chunks* in it!"

Brodie shrugged. "So?"

Peabo felt a heat in his stomach almost immediately. It spread upward into his chest and down along his legs.

Nicole handed him a cloth. "You'll need this."

"Why—" He cut himself off as he began sweating

profusely from every pore on his body. “Holy crap, this stuff is giving me hot flashes.”

He removed his shirt, which was soaked, and wiped himself down with the cloth. He’d never sweated so much in his life. His skin was on fire, almost as if he’d had boiling water splashed on him.

And just at the moment he thought it couldn’t get any worse, a cold wave washed over him. He’d heard the term “bone-breaking cold” before, and had never understood what it meant. He did now. He was shivering so hard, it felt like his body was going to fly apart.

But after what seemed like a lifetime, the cold slowly dissipated.

Nicole directed him to look in the mirror, and he did.

The markings on his face were gone.

“Holy crap. It worked.”

“Aye,” Brodie responded.

Peabo looked at his arms and chest. Nothing there either. No striations, no markings whatsoever.

Nicole ran her fingers along his jawline. “I don’t like it. I miss your old face.”

He clasped her hand and gave it a quick kiss. “You said it’ll start wearing off in a couple weeks. I’ll be back.”

Brodie tossed him a long brown robe. “Put that on.”

Peabo held it up. “Why do I have to wear this?”

“Because your face may not give your identity away anymore, but your build is still bulkier than most above-worlders. Besides, since we’re looking for a patriarch, a monk's robe will make it easier for you to be asking questions without raising suspicion."

Peabo put on the robe, but strapped his belt over the outside so he had access to his sword. Testing his ability to move in the garment, he moved his arms back and forth, then drew the sword, which immediately remarked, *"A goddamn monk? You're no monk, you're a warrior. Let me see that warrior's scowl!"*

"Shut up, Max."

Peabo slammed the precocious sword back into its scabbard and looked at his companions. "So, do I look the part of an aboveworlder?"

Nicole nodded. "I'm afraid so." She sounded disappointed.

Brodie opened the door to the office. "We're ready then. Let's go find out what happened to this Stefan of yours."

They emerged from belowground directly into the middle of a forest. Peabo breathed in deeply, filling his lungs with fresh air. He'd been underground for nearly a month, and though he'd come to enjoy living with the dwarves, there was something about being outdoors that he had missed.

He looked back and watched as a giant tree ripped its roots out of the forest floor and shifted over to seal the cave from which they'd just exited.

"Brodie," he said, "one day you're going to have to explain this whole tree thing to me. In my world, trees don't move."

A creaking sounded in the boughs of the nearest trees, as if a strong wind was rushing through the upper parts of the forest. But Peabo didn't feel any wind.

"You hear that, plainswalker?" said Brodie. "They're laughing at you."

The ranger headed toward a faint forest trail and motioned for the others to follow. Peabo hung back for a moment and hesitantly patted the trunk of the tree guarding the cave. "Sorry if I was rude."

He was just about to turn away when the tree's bark shifted under his hand and a pair of eyes blinked at him. With a yelp, Peabo scrambled backward, and Nicole howled with laughter.

Peabo pointed at the tree. "That thing is… it's… I don't know what it is!"

"Stop playing with the trees and let's go," Nicole said. She grabbed his arm and pulled him along the trail.

"It had eyes! Are they all like that? Alive? Or, I mean, intelligent?" he whispered.

Nicole shook her head. "Now is not the time to talk about things any three-year-old should know. We've got to go to the chapel of the Nameless One and start unraveling why people want you dead."

Peabo stared with amazement when he saw what a real city looked like in this world. They'd left the forest behind and had been walking along the side of a road for nearly an hour, and now they were at last entering the outskirts of the city of Dvorak.

His only experience of civilization in the aboveworld was the farming town of Raiheim, and this place presented a distinct contrast. Gone were the one- to two-story wooden buildings, and in their place were stone edifices stretching up into the sky, some nearly a hundred feet tall. If Raiheim was some town in suburbia, this place was New York City. In fact, this place reminded him of pictures he'd seen of how New York City looked back in the late 1800s. Lots of buildings, narrow side streets that were just wide enough to accommodate wagons, and hundreds of people bustling about.

And the smell was so different here than back in Raiheim. Back in the farming community, manure and sweat were pretty much the predominant scents of the land. But here, the smell was of pine and flowers. Hanging above every doorway were garlands of blooming ivy, and there were few wagons in sight.

Running down the center of the city was an extra-wide main thoroughfare, and at its end stood an immense building whose footprint alone had to occupy a dozen acres of land, with vast green fields surrounding it. The sight reminded Peabo of the British estate on the show *Downton Abbey*. America certainly didn't build places like this, nor did the parts of Afghanistan he'd wandered through.

"Is that Dvorak Castle?" he asked.

"Aye, but that's not our destination."

Brodie pulled two robes from his pack, one brown and one red. He put the red one on himself, and gave the brown one to Nicole.

"Jeez," said Peabo, "you look like a cardinal in that thing."

"A what?" asked Brodie.

Nicole put her hand on Peabo's shoulder. "He's a high priest of the Nameless One."

"He's what?" Peabo said it louder than he'd intended. He frowned at Brodie. "How is it that she knows this and I don't? And didn't you say you *aren't* a priest?"

Brodie shrugged. "Of course I'm not a priest. Would a priest wear a high priest's robe?" Then he started walking again.

"Gee, thanks a lot," Peabo called after him.

As Nicole and Peabo followed, she spoke in Peabo's mind. *"Don't let him upset you. He and I talked a while back about strategy while you were on patrol, and that's when I learned the specifics about his service. I'm sorry, I should have told you, but it slipped my mind."*

Peabo just scowled. *How the hell does she project thoughts into my head anyway? I have to learn that trick.*

Nicole gasped. "You just did it!"

"I did what?"

"I heard what you said just now," she projected. *"About learning that trick. It's a feature of the pairing we have. I guess you were too low level to be able to do it before."*

"Whoa, really? Can you hear me right now?" Peabo thought back at her.

"Yes. I can."

He'd never seen her smile so broadly before, and the smile was contagious. His mind raced with the possibilities.

"Is there a limit to how far we can be from each other and do this?" he asked.

"About as far as you'd normally be able to hear our voices.

In the Sage's Tower, they explained that what we're doing is projecting an aspect of our energies from one person to another. But to be able to receive and transmit, you need to be on the same wavelength. Does that make sense?"

"It makes perfect sense," Peabo replied, enjoying this mental communication. *"It's like a secure communications channel. This world has much that's similar to where I come from, but the twist on the sciences is all about how energy is transferred."*

Ahead of them, the dwarf came to a stop in front of a two-story building with a tall spire. When Peabo and Nicole caught up, he spoke to Peabo in a soft voice.

"Do you remember back in Myrkheim when I told you your back story?"

Peabo remembered. "You said that if anyone asks, I'm from Koryl, an obscure village on the mainland that most people even on the mainland have never heard of. I've come to Myrkheim to pay my respects to you before heading to a visit with the patriarch."

"Very good." Brodie nodded his approval, then turned to Nicole. "You're a student of mine and nobody will question your accompanying us. Other than that, both of you... just follow my lead."

The front door opened, and a man in a black robe walked out. When his gaze landed on Brodie, the man's eyes widened.

Brodie spoke in a loud voice. "Good morning, servant of the Nameless One."

The man looked shaken as he bowed slightly to Brodie. "G-good morning, High Priest. I didn't know we were going to be getting a visit from anyone today."

"That's because I wasn't planning on coming to Dvorak today, but here I am." Brodie hitched his thumb toward the two hooded figures behind him. "I have a missionary who seeks an audience with Patriarch Stefan."

"Oh!" The black-robed man's face drained of color, and he looked unsteady on his feet. "High Priest, please forgive me, but I haven't seen the patriarch in a long while. Maybe the senior priest can help. I'm just a junior priest, new to the—"

"Go, then," Brodie interrupted, motioned toward the church's front door. "Lead us to someone who can help. I don't think any of us want to unnecessarily lengthen this missionary's quest."

"Y-yes, sir."

As the priest rushed back into the church, Brodie gave Peabo and Nicole a wink. "I wonder where Patriarch Stefan could possibly be."

The inside of the church was beautifully constructed, with finely chiseled stone and carved wood everywhere. Even the pews gleamed brightly, and the entire place smelled pleasantly of pine resin and warm spices. High on the walls, colorful stained-glass windows depicted events that Peabo didn't recognize, but as the sun shone through them, they splayed colorful light across the empty pews.

The junior priest led them to the private chambers of Senior

Priest Vasil, in the back of the church. But the senior priest, like the junior, said he hadn't seen Stefan in two months.

Brodie glowered upward at the priest, who was easily a good three feet taller than he was. "Are you seriously telling me that you have no idea where Patriarch Stefan is, nor when he'll return?"

Vasil sighed. "I'm afraid so, High Priest. The patriarch kept his own counsel and rarely confided in me." He wrung his hands. "In all honesty, I'm worried. It's not like him to leave on such a long trip without some instructions to us on the care of the flock."

"Are extended trips common for Patriarch Stefan?"

Vasil tilted his head. "Common? No. He has gone on a few pilgrimages to the mainland, but I wouldn't say it's common. And like I said, he always leaves instructions. And now, with the arrival of a missionary from the mainland," he nodded toward Peabo, "one he'd asked to meet him at Dvorak, my worries increase. Our patriarch is many things, but he's not inconsiderate of other people's time."

"Does the patriarch have living quarters in this building?" Brodie asked.

"He does." Vasil opened a drawer in his desk and pulled out a key. "Did you want to inspect his quarters?"

Peabo was surprised there was no argument about privacy. In the military, there was no such thing, and apparently the same applied here. Either that, or Brodie's rank in the church outweighed any hesitation the senior priest might have had.

"Yes," said Brodie. "The missionary has confided in me the nature of his visit with the patriarch. We need to look through the man's possessions and see if something was left behind." He extended his hand toward the door. "After you, Vasil."

As the senior priest led them across the church to another wing, Peabo couldn't help but think the man moved like a fighter. He'd wager this guy had been on both the receiving and delivering end of many a punch in his day.

The priest unlocked the door to the patriarch's room and handed Brodie the key. "I will be in my office. When you are done, if you could return the key, I'll lock up."

Vasil walked back down the hall, and Brodie waited until he was out of sight before opening the door. "One second," he said to Peabo and Nicole. "Let me take a slight precaution."

He took a few steps back from the door and rolled up his sleeves. A glow moved slowly down his arms, and a buzzing, staticky noise sounded all around him.

"What is that noise?" Peabo asked, only to realize that he couldn't hear his own voice. He was sure he'd spoken, but he hadn't made a sound.

"Brodie is making sure we aren't overheard," Nicole said in his head. She smiled reassuringly.

Brodie's arms were now glowing from his elbows to the tips of his fingers. Then he touched his palms to each other, and the glow drained from his arms and formed a glowing dot hanging in midair. The static continued.

"What did you just do?" Peabo asked. Or tried to. Again, his voice made no sound.

Brodie pointed at his ears and shook his head. Then he led them into the patriarch's bedroom and locked the door behind them. The glowing dot remained outside, but the static could be heard in here as well. Brodie beckoned them forward into the middle of the room, and finally the static vanished.

Peabo breathed a sigh of relief.

Now that they could talk again, Nicole explained. "Brodie set an area of silence around the entrance to the room, for privacy."

"Aye. Now let's get cracking on seeing what this man was about."

"Wait, I want to understand how that static trick works."

Brodie glowered at him. "Lad, we don't have time for lessons right now. That spell of mine will only last for a short time. Get moving." He moved to a desk in the corner and began searching through it.

Nicole spoke in Peabo's head as she peered under the patriarch's mattress. *"I'll explain while we search. But don't just stand there. Help look. Tell us if you find anything that gives even a hint as to why someone would instruct Stefan to kill you."*

Peabo began rifling through the man's dresser drawers, and Nicole continued.

"In this world, sound travels in a pattern. Think of it like an invisible wave, a steady and repeating undulating snake. What Brodie did was extend some power into the air to counteract those invisible waves, effectively squashing them flat. If they're flat, then whatever sound is there will be muted. At least, that's how it was explained to me during my training."

The more Peabo learned about this world and its intricacies, the more he wanted to know. What she'd just described was the same technology he'd used for years in the field. The headgear he'd once worn was built on the same kind of sound-dampening technology. It just required special electronics, whereas here… well, here something different was required.

"Either of you finding anything?" Brodie asked.

"Not yet," said Nicole.

"Me neither," said Peabo. "Wait—hold on."

He'd just opened the bottom drawer of the dresser, revealing a small pile of treasure. Several bars of gold and silver, along with something that caught his attention: a metallic box the size of a loaf of bread. Engraved on it were symbols that looked like little lightning bolts. He reached for it —and with a resounding crack, he found himself sitting on the floor with Nicole chuckling and healing his burnt fingertips.

"What the hell just happened?"

Brodie continued rummaging through the patriarch's desk. "Sorry, my boy. That was one of the prelate's courier boxes. Those things are spelled against thieves."

Nicole shifted her attention back to the room and continued searching.

Peabo looked at his fingertips. Other than a few blackened scorch marks, he was fine—no pain or blisters. He thought to Nicole, *"Thank you for the heal. Can you explain what that box is for?"*

"When the prelate needs to send something to the heads of the churches, he uses one of those boxes. The prelate puts something in his box and it appears in this one. I've seen one at the Sage's Tower, but I've never seen it used. Don't ask me how it works, because I have no idea and couldn't even begin to guess."

They searched the rest of the room and came up empty. Finally Brodie stepped back and sighed. "I hate to say it, but I think I'll need to call for some intervention."

Nicole's eyes widened. "You mean commune with the Nameless One?"

"Aye. It's been quite a long time since he and I had a one-on-one. I hope this isn't pushing my luck."

"What do you mean?" asked Peabo. "Are you saying you can talk to God… and he'll answer?"

Brodie chuckled. "Let's hope so."

The dwarf grabbed a clear flask of sand from the desk and sat cross-legged on the floor. Nicole followed suit, and she motioned for Peabo to do the same. It took everything he had not to ask more questions. He knew that now was not the time to pepper the pugnacious dwarf with distractions.

Brodie poured the sand out onto the floor, spreading it evenly to form a rectangle one foot wide and twice as long. He drew two circles in the sand, and just above each circle he drew a different rune, one signifying "yes" and the other "no." Brodie then closed his eyes, and his body began to glow with a preternatural white aura.

Peabo felt the hairs on the back of his neck stand on end. Was this some kind of strange Ouija board?

Brodie opened his eyes, and his voice sounded strained as he asked, "Is Patriarch Stefan dead?"

A mark magically appeared in the circle labeled with a "yes."

Peabo couldn't believe what he'd just witnessed. *How can that be possible?*

Nicole spoke in his head. *"It's a very high-level ability. I can't do it, and even Brodie is struggling. But he's getting a response from the Nameless One himself."*

Brodie leaned forward and smoothed away the mark within the circle. Then he straightened up and asked another question.

"Was he sent to kill the living plainswalker?"

Peabo felt a tingling in the air, almost like the static cling of clothes coming out of a dryer, and then the invisible finger again made a mark in the "yes" circle.

Brodie took in a shuddering breath and cleared the mark from the sand once more. Beads of sweat appeared on his forehead.

"Was Patriarch Stefan sent on his mission to kill the living plainswalker by someone who is from Dvorak?"

Peabo glanced over at Nicole. Her eyes were wide as saucers.

The invisible finger made a mark in both the "yes" and "no" circles.

What does that mean?

Nicole thought at him, *"I have no idea."*

Brodie's face was red with strain as he cleared the responses away. Whatever he was doing, it was clearly taking a toll.

"Was the order given to Patriarch Stefan to kill the living plainswalker on behalf of someone on the mainland?"

A mark appeared in the "no" circle.

"Was the order to kill the living plainswalker given by someone residing in Dvorak Castle?"

The answer was yes.

Peabo's jaw dropped with that revelation. Who in that castle would even know he existed, and why?

Brodie's eyes were bloodshot and he looked like he was about to pass out. Peabo sent a thought to Nicole: *"Is Brodie okay?"*

She nodded, but her expression was grim.

Brodie pulled in a deep breath and let it out slowly. "Was Lord Dvorak the one who—"

The sand exploded in a shower of grit, and Nicole had to lunge to catch Brodie's unconscious body as he toppled forward.

As Peabo blinked the sand out of his eyes, Nicole laid Brodie on his back and moved her hands, which were now glowing, along his neck. After a moment Brodie coughed, sat up, and groaned.

He pressed the heels of his hands against his temples. "Oy, I'm not doing that again for a *very* long time."

Nicole scooted closer, her hands still glowing. "Let me help."

Brodie motioned her away and staggered to his feet. "No, girl, none of that will help. I just need time. Both to recover, and to process what we've learned." He looked at Peabo. "What did *you* learn, lad?"

"Well," said Peabo, "we now know that someone local sent the patriarch after me. And then you started to ask about Lord Dvorak. Was what happened after that… was that some kind of an answer?"

Brodie chuckled and shook his head. "No, that was just a loss of connection. When communing with the spirit world, the more specific the question gets, and the more drained I am, the more likely it is that I'll lose the connection to the Nameless One."

Peabo imagined having a phone conversation with God and losing the signal. Was that truly what he'd just witnessed? The concept was laughable, but he'd seen it with his own eyes.

"I assume Lord Dvorak is the person living in that castle?" he asked.

Nicole nodded. "He's the top authority on the island. The only one he answers to is the king himself."

"And you think someone like that would want to kill me?" Peabo said, alarmed.

"We don't know that," Nicole said soothingly.

"But we know enough," said Brodie. "We don't know who sent the patriarch after you, but we know where they are. Dvorak Castle."

CHAPTER SIXTEEN

Sweat poured down Peabo's face as he lunged at the unseen opponent. With a fluid motion, he turned and snapped a front kick that begged for a real target.

Even after coming to this world, he'd continued working on his katas—exercises to help him focus on his martial arts forms. They were different now, in this new body. He'd spent nearly thirty years in the body he'd been born in, and had been practicing martial arts for twenty of those; now he had to adjust to a different center of mass, and the flexibility wasn't quite where it used to be. Still, as he flowed from one attack to another, muscle memory kicked in. Slight changes in timing were all that he needed for this much bulkier form.

"You look like you're having fun."

Peabo saw Nicole watching him. "I figured you had Brodie in hand, so I was working on my forms."

Nicole looked around the clearing. "It's almost like this place was meant for a sparring ring."

Peabo looked around as well, then frowned. "I swear those trees have moved since I got here. There was more space before."

"They wanted to watch," Nicole said. She took on a boxer's stance. "Shall we see how you're doing?"

Peabo grinned, but he also remembered how she'd kicked his ass all over that grassy hill where they'd first lived. "I suppose if you break anything, you'll be able to fix it."

Without warning, Nicole aimed a kick directly at the side of his knee. He hopped back, just barely avoiding the strike. She growled and pressed her attack with a rapid flurry of punches and kicks. Peabo was instantly on the defensive.

But then she overextended one of her lunge punches and he took advantage of the brief opening to execute a spinning heel kick. She just barely hopped out of range.

Again she pressed her attack, and again he was backpedaling, focusing only on not getting hit. Her speed was too much of an advantage, and it took everything Peabo had not to get slammed.

He paid particular attention to her feet, always a clear indication of what an opponent is going to do. And as the fight progressed, he noticed flaws in her technique. Little things that would be openings, if she'd only repeat them.

And then she did.

She launched a vicious sidekick, and he sidestepped it, caught one of her feet in a leg sweep, knocked her off balance, and followed it up with a flying sidekick of his own. She blocked it, but just barely, and she staggered from the impact.

She had speed, but he had power and momentum.

Now he was the one on the attack. He forced her backward with a series of punches and kicks, which she blocked effectively. He pushed harder, focusing only on offense. He was running on pure instinct as he mixed kicks with punches and sweeps, all with the goal of knocking her off balance.

And then, with a surge of speed that he hadn't seen from her before, Nicole dropped to the ground and swept his legs out from under him. Before he knew it, she was on top of him, legs straddling him, hands pinning his wrists to the forest floor.

She laughed. "You've gotten much better than when we first met."

Peabo pushed her upper body up into the air, but her legs tightened around his waist and hooked behind his legs.

"Shall we continue?" he said.

She hopped off of him and shook her head. "I can't fight for as long as you can. I don't have your kind of stamina."

"Seriously?" Peabo wiped the grass from his clothes, feeling disappointed. "We *have* to do that again. I need someone who can really push me."

"Why don't you ask Brodie? I've never fought a dwarf, but I've heard they can stay in the fight much longer than most." Nicole gave Peabo a quick hug. "I'm really happy to see that you're taking this combat seriously. I'm a pretty good fighter, but I advise you to learn from a variety of people—you'll learn a lot more that way. After we're done here in Dvorak, I know some places on the mainland that we can go to get you training with some of the best fighters in the world. I think you'd really blossom."

"Oy, enough of this blossoming talk," said Brodie, stepping through the trees, which seemed to have gathered into an even tighter circle now. He looked up at the boughs and grumbled, "Are you all so hard up for entertainment that *this* is what gets your attention?"

Peabo grinned. "I guess you're feeling better."

"I am, and I'm tired of waiting around." Brodie snapped his fingers. "Let's get going. We've got research to do."

Peabo watched from across the street as Nicole approached one of Dvorak's merchants and began chatting with him. Almost immediately the man took on a dour expression, shook his head, and pointed down the road.

Peabo looked down at Brodie, who was also watching. "I think the honey isn't catching any honeybees."

"You've got that right." Brodie's nose scrunched up as if he'd smelled something foul. "What in the world did this patriarch do that has so many people afraid to speak about him?"

"Or even *think* about him," Peabo said. "Whenever I bring up the patriarch with someone, their minds go blank."

"Pfft! If this Stefan has somehow put a block on people's ability to *think* straight about him, then it's pointless. But let's let the maiden do her job. She's a trained influencer and seductress; one of these people will eventually talk about him."

"Nicole a seductress? Are you serious?"

Brodie scowled. “You’re not a child, and don’t make me start thinking you’re a dimwit. She’s an attractive woman who spent the better part of her life being trained in all of the assassin’s arts, including how to get close to someone. I’m sure you understand what that means.”

Peabo pressed his lips together. Although he’d long ago gotten over seeing Nicole naked, and even sleeping in the same bed with her, he had trouble seeing the gruff and no-nonsense woman being soft and girly. He’d never seen that side of her. Maybe seduction meant something different in this world.

The merchant couldn’t help but notice the tall young woman who approached his stand and flashed him a warm smile. Her long blonde hair, worn freely, framed an attractive pouty face with crystal-blue eyes. This woman had to be new in town, because she would have drawn his attention just by walking down the street, especially with the way her hips swayed back and forth.

As she looked over his earthenware pots, she licked her full lips. When she spoke, it was with a husky tone. “How long have you been in Dvorak?” She leaned forward to examine one of his pots, giving him a full view of her own wares.

“Uh, a-all my life, miss. Can I help you with something?”

The woman straightened, and he forced his gaze upward, trying desperately to keep his eyes on her face.

She smiled as if knowing where his eyes had been, then breathed in deeply, letting her chest push harder against the cloth that was just barely keeping things in their place. "I'm new to this town. I just came here from the mainland and I was wondering if you'd been to the church lately."

He nodded vigorously. "Every week, miss. I do go regularly."

"I was told by my priest to seek out the patriarch when I arrived. Do you know where I might find him?"

A chill raced up the merchant's spine. "I know nothing about him." This was true. He'd never exchanged a word with the head of the church in Dvorak. The man was too intimidating. "But Senior Priest Vasil is a very nice man." He pointed to the south. "If you're seeking the church it's in that direction."

The woman pouted and stuck the tip of her finger between her teeth before slowly dragging it down her neck and between her breasts. The merchant couldn't keep his eyes from following where that fingertip led him.

Suddenly the woman grabbed his hand and cupped it between her own. "Please. I have something I really need the patriarch to know." She pulled his hand closer to her, pulling him slightly off-balance as she whispered, "I'd be ever so grateful if you had any idea how I could find the man. I assume you're here all day, every day?"

He felt his cheeks warm, and a bead of sweat trickled down the side of his face. "Y-yes... but..." His hand was practically between her breasts, and his mind raced in an unwholesome direction. He closed his eyes for a second and pictured his wife and three kids at home. But he wasn't doing anything wrong; this woman was simply asking for help.

He blinked the confusion from his mind, pulled back his

hand, and spoke quietly. "I can't say anything about the patriarch. He's a powerful man, and I'm just a merchant. I don't know where he is anyway; I've not seen him at church in at least a month, maybe two. But if you want to find him, go talk to his mother. If she's still alive. They were close, that much I know."

The woman smiled. "Where does the patriarch's mother live?"

The merchant felt a warning tickle the back of his neck as if some instinct was telling him he shouldn't say anything. Who was this girl asking these questions, anyway?

He pulled in a deep breath, looked from side to side, and whispered, "She has a small cabin near where the holy stream comes down from the mountain. Years ago, I was fishing and walked farther upstream than I normally would, and I spotted the patriarch visiting with her at her cabin. That's all I know. I would tell you more if I could."

"Thank you," said the woman, and she turned and walked away.

The merchant looked down at his stand and saw that she'd left behind a gold royal. He pocketed the small bar of gold, then looked up. The woman had already disappeared.

He should have warned her that the patriarch's mother was rumored to be a witch.

Peabo smelled the smoke from a campfire before he saw anything. There was something else in the air, too, and it raised goose bumps all over his body.

"Something's wrong," he said. "Can you feel that?"

Brodie shook his head. "No. What do you feel?"

He drew his sword and Max groused in his head, *"What the hell, Pea brain. Don't start getting all blubbery on me just because you're feeling weird."*

Ignoring the sword, Peabo breathed in deeply and inhaled the scent of pine. He looked up at the trees. *What am I sensing?*

A gust of wind groaned through the boughs above.

"Oh crap, the trees have got that right. Retreat greenhorn, you ain't ready for none of this! Advance to the rear you idiot!"

Brodie and Nicole both looked at him in surprise. "Did you just ask the trees something?" Nicole asked.

Peabo's heart skipped a beat as Max freaked out of something and he shifted his attention to his companions. "What?"

"The trees just gave us a warning. They said, 'Tell the plainswalker he must not be seen by the witch woman.'"

Peabo's mouth fell open as Max mentally berated him. *"I told you to retreat, you sorry bald-headed twinkle-toed communist puke!"*

The boughs groaned again, and a giant pine behind Brodie shifted slightly. Then its bark cracked open, revealing a passage that descended into the ground.

Brodie motioned frantically toward the dark passage, and Nicole hissed in Peabo's mind, *"Go inside, the trees will hide you! Hurry, she's coming!"*

Peabo scrambled into the passage. The entrance sealed

itself shut behind him, leaving him in utter darkness. But a voice from outside penetrated the darkness. A woman's voice.

"What are you two doing here?"

Brodie responded. "I'd heard tell that Patriarch Stefan had been seen here. I'm looking for him."

"And who are you to be looking for my son?"

The woman didn't sound old enough to be the patriarch's mother. There was a power behind her voice; it resonated with confidence.

"I am Brodie, a high priest of the Nameless One. This is my acolyte."

"Neither of you are wearing your vestments, but… I sense the truth in your statement. Though it carries some falsehoods as well."

Peabo wondered how the woman could so easily sense that. The trees had called her a witch woman. A weaver of some kind?

"Why are you here?" said the woman. Her voice was louder now, almost as if she stood right next to him.

"I was sent to find Patriarch Stefan. None have seen him in two months, and the local priests are worried."

"I'm afraid you're going to be disappointed. I haven't spoken to my son in at least three turns of the season, maybe longer."

"I'm sorry to hear that," said Nicole. "I wish that weren't so." Her voice was soothing and calm. "Please, take this as an offering. I know it's meager, but it's what I could find."

There was silence for a full fifteen seconds, then the woman laughed with surprising intensity. "Toffees! Of all things in this world, you bring me the one thing my son would always bring for me."

"Oh, I'm sorry. I didn't know—"

"Nonsense, child, it is a gift I appreciate. What else can I do for you?"

"Madam, do you know anything of Patriarch Stefan's usual travels? Possibly somewhere he might go when needing seclusion?"

The woman paused before responding. Then: "I smell something in the air that isn't right. It smells of lightning."

"Oh crap, get ready... this broad's gonna eat you for dinner and use me as a toothpick. How the hell—"

Peabo slammed the sword back into its scabbard.

"Maybe a storm is coming?" Brodie suggested casually.

Peabo thought of the lightning pattern markings on his body. Or at least they used to be on his body. Could this woman actually *smell* him?

"Maybe." The woman sighed. "Honestly, I do miss my boy. It has been a long time since things were right between us. I warned him that his elevation to patriarch would bring attention from Lord Dvorak—and that's something nobody in their right mind would want. Sadly, things happened exactly as I predicted they would. Dvorak turned my boy from his path. I'm sure of it."

"How do you know?" Brodie asked.

"I don't 'know' in the conventional sense, High Priest of the Nameless One. But I have my ways. Ancient ways that you'd never understand. I can't sense my boy, and I haven't for a long time. I'm sorry, but I can't help you any further. I wish for you to leave this place. Do not be here when I return."

She must have departed, for after that all fell still. Peabo waited, and a few minutes later the exit appeared once more, and he scrambled up to the forest floor.

"Don't say a word," Nicole said in his head, and without any further discussion they made a beeline for Dvorak City.

Peabo sat in the Dvorak library, reading whatever he could find on this Lord Dvorak. The librarian had been particularly helpful in locating some old tomes that spoke of the lord's reign, the longest the island had ever had. Nicole was with him, doing research on the castle's history, while Brodie took care of some business elsewhere.

As Peabo read about the rule of the Dvorak family, some blanks in his understanding of new world civics were filled in. There was some kind of royal family on the mainland, and they'd ruled the world as far back as history went. The hierarchy was something like English royalty, with a king, and lords, and mayors and such. Taxes were paid, and peace was kept by the king's men.

Nicole's voice broke into his thoughts. *"Find anything interesting on Lord Dvorak?"*

He sent his thoughts to her. *"Yes, but it's hard to know what would be interesting to* you. *There's been like sixty generations of Dvoraks ruling the island. Some of these books talk about their accomplishments—like taming parts of the wild, or treaties with the people in Myrkheim—but there's very little specific about the individual rulers. Like, I can't even tell what their names are. I assume Dvorak is the family name, but—"*

"What do you mean by family name?" Nicole asked.

"You know, like a last name? One name the whole family shares?"

Nicole looked confused. *"I don't think we have that concept here. If you want to share your name with your child, you name him Peabo the younger. You're formally known as Peabo of the Desolate Plains. And each of the lords is known as Dvorak."*

Peabo knew that last names were a relatively modern convention back on Earth, too. He'd seen early English churches with the priest names engraved from the 900s, and back then, many of them had only a single name.

He pointed at the page he'd been looking at, which featured portraits of much of the Dvorak line. *"These people look inbred."*

Nicole gazed at the pictures. *"What do you mean?"*

"Well, I know they're related and all, but still, it's weird how similar they all look. I mean sure, the third one has a scar on his cheek, the fifth one looks like he's eaten every pastry in the city, and so on, but if you look at the most recent Dvorak and the earliest... they look almost like brothers."

Nicole shrugged. *"I suppose the Dvorak genes breed true. Sometimes a man will only produce male offspring. Or children with dark eyes. I've even heard tell that there was one family who for generations had skin that had a blue hue to it. It can happen."*

Peabo pointed toward the sheets of parchment in front of her. They looked like blueprints. *"How about you? What's that you're looking at?"*

"Plans for Dvorak Castle. Unfortunately, everything I'm finding is either about the outer grounds or the new wing that was added about a century ago. Nothing about the main structure."

He put his lips to her ear and whispered, "It feels strange looking at each other and not talking."

She furrowed her brow. *"Don't do that. It's safest for us to speak this way. There are those who could hear us from afar."*

"You mean like the witch woman? I swear, I think she could almost smell me."

"She probably could. Witches are a type of conductor."

"Was she high level?"

"I think so, but I'm not sure. That reminds me. The warning you received from the trees—how did you do that? You spoke to them, didn't you?"

Peabo shrugged. *"All I did was the same as I'm doing now with you. I just thought at them, and I guess they heard."*

Nicole's eyebrows went up. *"I didn't think that was possible. What you and I do is unique to the bond we share. Even Brodie can't hear our conversations."*

"Speaking of Brodie, what exactly is he planning, and why does he have you researching the castle? Does he intend for us to storm the castle, and to what end?"

"Honestly, I wouldn't put it past him. There's something very strange going on in this city. You've seen how people react when we bring up Stefan; even in death, the patriarch has

everyone spooked. It's probably good that he's dead, but I'm wondering about what his mother said. She believes Lord Dvorak turned her son away from his path. What if it was Lord Dvorak who turned him into a wight? If it was, we have a much bigger problem than a rogue patriarch." Nicole interlaced her fingers with his beneath the table. *"If a lord of the kingdom wants you dead, then there's very little we can do within the law to prevent that. It's within their rights to sentence death upon whomever they wish."*

Peabo gave her an evil grin. *"If that's the case, I may just have to become an outlaw."*

"*We,*" Nicole replied. *"There is no 'I' when it comes to us.* We *may have to become outlaws when this is all said and done."*

CHAPTER SEVENTEEN

As Peabo and his companions walked north on the main avenue, Dvorak Castle directly ahead, he felt that same tingling sensation he used to feel just before jumping out of a plane or breaching a building. He breathed in deeply and slowly exhaled.

"Rumor on the street is they don't like clergy at the castle," he said to Brodie.

"A rumor, you say?" The dwarf grinned. "Well, there's only one way to dispel a rumor."

Nicole spoke in Peabo's head. *"I can feel your heart racing. Calm down. We're only going to confirm a few things."*

They entered the castle grounds and passed another half mile through well-manicured fields and gardens before arriving at the entrance to the massive castle. A half dozen soldiers stood guard in head-to-foot armor—some kind of form-fitting chain mail that looked like something Peabo might have seen in a museum about the Middle Ages.

One of the guards took two steps forward. "Halt, sir. What business do you have here?"

Brodie spoke in a loud and clear voice. "I'm a high priest of the Nameless One, and I have business with Lord Dvorak."

The guard frowned and glanced at Peabo and Nicole. "And they are?"

"One is my acolyte; the other is a missionary from the mainland. We seek an audience with Lord Dvorak. This should have been cleared already."

"It was?" Peabo thought at Nicole.

"Hush," she replied.

The guard's frown deepened. "Please wait." He turned to one of the other guards, and they spoke in hushed whispers. Peabo tried to read their thoughts, but failed. These men were presumably level four or higher, which had proved to be where people were able to block his ability to peek into their minds.

After a few moments, the guard faced Brodie again. "I'm sorry, High Priest, Lord Dvorak is not in the castle at the moment. I believe he's gone hunting. I'm sure it is a disappointment—"

"Then let me schedule a time with him when he'll be back. When do you expect him?"

"I'm sorry, I don't know exactly when he will return. It will almost certainly be at least a week. Either way, it's the seneschal who arranges such things, and he's taken ill and has gone to the mainland for treatment."

Brodie puffed out his chest indignantly. "Why not seek the

clergy in town? They surely could heal whatever ails the lord's seneschal."

The guard shrugged. "It is not my business to question the decisions of my betters."

Brodie spoke firmly. "Speaking of betters, do you understand that I'm a high priest, and *my* superior sent me here? The same superior who is the head of the church of the Nameless One. And you're telling me that I cannot set up a time to meet with Lord Dvorak at all?"

The guard looked uncomfortable. "I'm very sorry, High Priest. Neither I nor Lord Dvorak mean any disrespect to you, to your superior, or to the church. I just cannot help you right now. Maybe in a month. I expect things will be better then. If you're staying in town, I can arrange to notify you as soon as an appointment with our Lord Dvorak can be arranged."

"I'll be at the church," Brodie said gruffly, then turned and walked away.

Nicole and Peabo rushed to keep pace, and fell in alongside him. When they were well out of earshot of the guards, Peabo whispered, "That didn't go well."

But Brodie grinned. "Didn't it though? You never break into a home before seeing if the door is unlocked. Now we know."

Peabo looked over at Nicole. *"Did he just say we're breaking in? Into that fortress?"*

Nicole shrugged. *"Seems like the next logical step."*

"What kind of clergy condones that behavior?"

She raised an eyebrow. *"One that doesn't take no for an answer."*

It was late evening, and Peabo and his companions were gathered around a table with several priests in a residence owned by the church. Brodie and Nicole were drinking beer, as were the priests, but Peabo opted to just sit back and watch. He'd been dealing with a headache all day, and didn't want to push his luck by adding beer to the mix.

"I can feel your pain," Nicole projected. *"You want me to try and heal it again?"*

Peabo shook his head. *"That didn't help before. It must be tension or something."*

Brodie stood and rapped his knuckles on the table, then waited for silence before speaking. "Brothers, you're all sworn to uphold the oaths of your office in the church, so even in here, we're speaking as men of the Nameless One. No barriers, no judgment, and complete confidence. Are we agreed?"

The priests nodded and voiced their affirmation.

"Good." Brodie hitched his thumb toward Nicole and Peabo. "We spent the day in town trying to get more information about our missing patriarch and his relationship, if any, with Lord Dvorak. Brothers, something is amiss in this town. Why does everyone fear speaking of Patriarch Stefan?"

The priests exchanged glances, and then the senior priest spoke. "High Priest—"

"Vasil, in this room, let's skip the honorifics. The name is Brodie."

The man nodded. "Very well, Brodie. People in this town know of Stefan's reputation from before he entered the priesthood. In particular, they know of his mother, a witch of some significance whose hatred for the church is well documented. I've personally investigated several claims that the woman was sacrificing animals in rituals designed to reawaken one of the Dark Ones."

Peabo gave Nicole a questioning look.

"Remember," she thought at him, *"I told you that eons ago there was a great battle and the Nameless One is the last of his kind? Well, there's an entire pantheon of ancient deities and demigods, it's just that most of them are evil. The Dark Ones are twins from that pantheon. They're among the worst."*

"Was anything ever done about her?" Brodie asked Vasil.

Vasil shook his head. "The woman is smart. She covers her tracks. I've never found enough evidence to take action."

"Forget the evidence, what did you think? Was she dabbling in the dark arts?"

Vasil frowned. "I'd hate to be wrong about such a serious matter, but… well, I can't dismiss the possibility."

Nicole leaned forward. "So Stefan's mother has a bad reputation, and that makes the son suspect as well?"

"Sadly, yes, though it shouldn't," said Vasil. "I've worked with the man for over a decade, and he has always been a paragon of virtue and trustworthiness. But in the view of the public, his mother's reputation nevertheless taints all the good the man did. It's really a shame."

Brodie turned to a middle-aged priest who'd been staring at the tabletop with a troubled expression. "Pavel, what say you about Stefan?"

The priest still didn't look up. "I hate to speak ill of anyone, especially if we fear that harm may have befallen them. And maybe it was simply the mantle of being the patriarch that affected him so, but… ever since Stefan became the leader among equals, I felt that he closed himself off from the rest of us. He was always dutiful in his observances with the flock, the rituals, and prayer, but… he did change. There was a time when Stefan told uproariously funny jokes in this very room, but that was a very long time ago. In fact it's been a long time since I've even seen the man smile."

Another priest chimed in. "I saw a similar behavior change. Like Pavel, I assumed it was due to the stresses of responsibility."

Brodie frowned. "Well, let's put Stefan in our nightly prayers for the next month. But I would also like to learn more about Lord Dvorak. The word on the street says he's a gentle ruler, but that he doesn't care for the church. Anyone have anything to say about that?"

A white-haired priest answered in a voice that was thin and reedy with age. "I'm the oldest one here, and I've been acquainted with almost everyone around this table for decades. I've seen many things in this town change over the years, but the one thing that has remained a constant throughout my ninety years of existence has been Lord Dvorak. From the grandfather, to the father, and now to the current Lord Dvorak, I've watched them all. Not only that, but as a junior priest I spoke to my elders, and they told me of earlier lords that preceded my time. And throughout all these Lord Dvoraks, one truth has remained: not one of them has ever set foot in our church."

Brodie nodded. "That doesn't necessarily mean Lord Dvorak has anything against the church. Perhaps he simply doesn't believe."

"Still, is it not curious that he doesn't want to get involved with the community?" the old priest countered. "Lord Dvorak is a kindly ruler—truly benevolent. But like his forebears, he is distant, and rarely if ever seen during the day. In my ninety years, I've been within twenty feet of one of the lords only four times. Once as a child, twice in my middle age and once not so long ago."

Another priest spoke. "I've heard rumor that Lord Dvorak suffers from an inherited condition that makes him sensitive to many of the daytime pollens. At night, when the flowers and trees are resting, such a sensitivity is certainly easier to deal with."

"Has anyone seen Lord Dvorak's children?" Brodie asked. "His wife?" He looked again at the old priest. "Yanko, have you ever seen any of Lord Dvorak's family?"

The old man shook his head. "I have never seen anyone but a circle of guards with the lord. However, the one time when I saw Lord Dvorak's grandfather, back when I was a child, I recall that he thanked a flower merchant for having sent flowers for his wife's birthday. Like I said, all of the Lord Dvoraks have been pleasant enough, for a lord of the kingdom. Just rarely seen."

Peabo frowned. Four sightings of three generations in the span of ninety years? There was definitely something strange about this Dvorak family.

Lying next to Peabo in bed, Nicole could feel his tension. He was having a dream, and she suspected it was a nightmare.

She reached across the bed and gently laid her glowing hand on the back of his neck. She'd tried massaging it, healing it, even applying a healing balm to it, yet the ache was still there, just out of reach of her healing powers.

As she pressed herself closer to him, she kept her hand on his neck, closed her eyes, and tried to sense his dream.

Her darkness became his.

His darkness became hers.

He was in a forest.

He was talking with the trees, warning them about something. The low bellow of the boughs above, the tree-speak, drifted down to him, yet Peabo couldn't understand it. It frustrated him.

And then Nicole smelled something.

Burning wood.

A forest fire.

Peabo raced forward, sending his thoughts to the trees. Telling them to flee.

Nicole ran her free hand along the side of his chest and whispered soothingly, "It's okay. It's just a dream."

Suddenly the dream world was aflame. Reds, yellows, oranges, and blues flooded her senses, the colors writhing together, separating, and then exploding into a bright coruscating fountain of energy.

Peabo sat bolt upright in bed, wide-eyed and panicked.

Nicole sat up with him. "It's okay. You were only dreaming." She wrapped him in a protective embrace and pulled him back down. "It's okay. I'm here with you. Get some sleep. Tomorrow's going to be a long day."

Peabo stood by in the office of the church as Brodie drew a map of Dvorak Castle according to the description currently being given to him by an old woman, a former maid who'd worked in the castle for many years.

"Oh yes, I remember it like it was yesterday when the new banisters were installed," she continued. "It was glorious to behold such workmanship. And they did it so quickly. I was but a young thing at the time, but it fascinated me so."

Brodie gestured to the sketch he'd made of the second level. "Dear Hanna, do you recall where Lord Dvorak's bedroom was located?"

"I do!"

The frail woman sounded so excited to help, it put a smile on Peabo's face.

She pointed at the sketch with a shaking finger. "It was exactly fifty paces from the beginning of the corridor to the doorway of Lord Dvorak's bedroom and office suite. I counted the paces because the corridor was so long. You know, in my later years, Lord Dvorak had one of the workmen make me a cart with wheels so it was easier for me to take my cleaning supplies from room to room." She put her hands against her cheeks. "My, he was so kind. And such a handsome man.

Every turn of the season, he would personally give each of us a season's bonus, never forgetting even the lowest of us."

Peabo cleared his throat. "Miss Hanna—"

"Oh dear, no." The woman put her gnarled hand on his arm. "It's just Hanna for the likes of me. I'm just so pleased I can help the church with their gift to Lord Dvorak. It's a beautiful thing you all are doing."

"But it's a secret," Brodie reminded her.

The old woman's eyes widened. "Oh, of course. I would never say a thing."

Peabo gave the woman's hand a gentle squeeze. "Hanna, did you ever see Lord Dvorak with his wife?"

Hanna shook her head. "No. She didn't live in the castle. It was said that she lived somewhere nearby. You know," she smiled a toothless smile, "the rumor among the maids—although this was probably wishful thinking—was that one of the elder Lord Dvoraks had married a castle maid, and so it had become a tradition of sorts with each subsequent lord. Just silly talk, of course. I was married and didn't rumormonger, but I heard the gossip all the same. The girls believe that the maid who married Lord Dvorak was always given her own place to stay, so as to keep their secret safe."

Brodie showed her both of his drawings, one of each level. "What do you think, Hanna? Am I missing anything here?"

The old woman leaned forward, her nose no more than a foot from the paper. Then she made a smacking sound with her lips and nodded. "High Priest, you have a second calling as an artist. Somehow you managed to get what I was thinking and put it on paper. Yes, this all looks quite correct." She looked at him and grinned. "Of course, things could have changed in the last fifteen years since I worked there, but I think it's unlikely."

Brodie slid a gold royal across the table to the old woman. "Please accept this from me, personally. Promise me that you'll buy some good food and have a very nice meal with it."

The old woman shook her head. "Oh, I can't accept this. It brought me real pleasure to just sit and talk about the old days. I don't need—"

"Please." Brodie put the gold royal in her hand and closed her fingers around it. "Don't hurt my feelings. It would mean a lot to me if you take this and spend it on yourself. Promise me you'll do that."

Tears appeared at the corners of the old woman's eyes. "Bless you." She turned to Peabo. "Bless you as well. I'll never forget this day when I got to sit and chat with a high priest of the Nameless One and a real honest-to-goodness plainswalker."

A chill raced through Peabo's body. It took every ounce of control for him not to react to the woman's words. His skin markings were hidden; how did she know he was a plainswalker?

Brodie escorted the woman from the room, and when he returned, he had a cloth in one hand. "Lean down so I can reach your face."

Peabo bent over, and the dwarf wiped his cheek with the white cloth. When he pulled it away, it had a black streak on it.

"Hanna's eyes may not be as sharp as they used to be, but it's telling that she saw a black smudge on you and put two and two together," Brodie said. "We can't afford overconfidence, and that means we need to put this plan together and execute it quickly."

The door opened, and Nicole walked in.

"Well?" said Brodie. "Did you get the information?"

She nodded and took a seat. "None of the guilds in town know of anyone over level seven in the area, except possibly the witch, who isn't part of the guild system. But—do you know who *else* isn't a part of the guild system?"

"Who?" said Peabo.

Nicole and Brodie spoke at the same time. "Lord Dvorak."

"So," said Peabo, "the only people around here strong enough to turn Stefan into a wight... were the witch and the lord."

"And I refuse to believe his own mother turned Stefan into a wight," said Brodie. "That leaves only Lord Dvorak."

"But everyone seems to think he's a good person," Peabo protested.

"Are you forgetting the signature?" said Nicole. "The 'D' who signed the letter to Stefan? And don't forget about the skinwalker's victim, who received a similarly signed letter."

Brodie nodded. "Sometimes the obvious is obvious for a reason. Either way, when we eliminate the other possibilities, we only have one target left."

"Okay... okay, you're right. Then what's the plan?" Peabo lowered his voice. "You're not thinking we're going to kill—"

"No!" said the dwarf. "What kind of person do you think I am? The plan is to gather information. Learn more about who this man is and what connection, if any, he has to Stefan. And then, if we have reason to, I can call on my superior with what we find. But we will do all this in a manner that adheres to the king's laws."

"Okay. When are we planning on doing this?"

"First thing in the morning," said Brodie. "I have an alchemist delivering some things tonight that should help. Now," he said, tapping on his maps, "let's talk specifics. We're going to make this quick and precise."

CHAPTER EIGHTEEN

Peabo used a wooden block to tamp down the black powder he'd just poured into a hollow half-sphere of metal. He then blew gently on the edges, making sure there was no stray dust.

"What are you doing up so early?" Nicole said with a yawn, climbing out of bed to look over his shoulder.

"Brodie said he had a plan, but as a soldier, I was always trained to have an alternate plan if things go sideways."

"And what is this? Another of your smoke stones?"

"Not exactly. I've reformulated the powder I made back in Myrkheim." Peabo carefully screwed a second half-sphere onto the first, resulting in a sphere about the size of a baseball. A black wick came out on one side, and at the end of the wick was a tiny flint-and-steel clamp he'd picked up earlier in the Myrkheim market.

"What does it do?" Nicole asked.

"Let me clean up and I'll show you."

Peabo swept any hint of dust away from his work area, set aside the two spheres he'd made so far, then pulled out a spare wick with a clamp.

"This string is doped with the black powder, so all you need to do is give that clamp a quick squeeze, and we're done." He handed her the string and clamp. "Go ahead and try it."

Nicole squeezed the metal clamp, and with a click, the string started sparking like a Fourth of July sparkler. She quickly dropped it.

"Okay, that's a better firestarter, I guess. And what does the other part do? The metal ball?"

"I haven't tested them yet, but they should explode."

Nicole looked confused.

"You know, *explode*? Like… blow apart?" Peabo said. It dawned on him that he didn't know the word for *explode* in Common. Maybe they didn't even have a word for it. "Um… it will burst very quickly, causing a great deal of damage."

Nicole nodded, but he could tell she didn't quite get it. Peabo didn't try to explain further; she'd understand once she saw one work. *If* it worked, that was. His chemistry background told him that the ingredients he'd used *should* burn, and in a confined space like the metal sphere, that reaction *should* feed on itself, making it very quick—and, hopefully, that *should* make it explosive. But there were a lot of shoulds in that equation.

Nicole began changing clothes. "Brodie asked for us to wear light clothing. None of the robes."

Peabo paused to take in the beautiful shape of the woman who'd become part sister, part wife, part friend.

"If you keep staring at me like that," she said, "I'm going to ask you to give *me* a show as well."

Peabo felt his cheeks get warm. "Do you know what Brodie's plan is? How are we going to get past all those guards?"

Nicole shook her head. "I have no idea. We'll find out pretty soon—if you hurry up and get dressed."

It was still very early in the morning when the three of them stopped just outside of Castle Dvorak, hidden within the forest that bordered the property.

Brodie pointed to Peabo. "I need you to just listen, lad—we don't have time for questions. I'm going to give you a very quick lesson on the planes of existence."

"Plains as in—"

"Which word of 'don't have time for questions' didn't you understand?" Brodie snapped. "You, me, the maiden, we're all on what we call the material plane. We think we see and hear everything, but what we're seeing and hearing isn't actually a *complete* picture of what's there. There are other things as well —such as ghosts, which exist both on this plane as well as another. And sometimes lightning sends not fire, which we're used to, but a shimmering orb of energy very much like the essences we absorb into our bodies. That too exists in multiple planes of existence.

"These planes are not all alike. Essences come from a positive plane, where energy is generated and leaks into our plane.

Wights, though they're mostly creatures of this world, have parts that exist in a negative plane, where energy is absorbed or stolen from others.

"The reason I'm even explaining any of this is because I don't think we have a chance of entering the castle within this plane."

"You mean we're going to—"

"No questions!" Brodie snapped. He opened a pouch at his waist, revealing nearly a dozen stoppered vials of amber liquid. "These vials allow someone to phase into the ethereal plane. The ethereal plane isn't *truly* a different plane—it's closely connected to our world, as well as to some other planes. But when we use these, it'll shift our bodies into a state that…"

He paused. "Let me take a step back. This might be very hard for you to imagine, but simply take it on faith that this is so. Our bodies are made of tiny parts that you cannot see, and these parts are made of smaller and smaller parts. At the smallest level, these parts are like a clock. They vibrate with a particular rhythm."

Peabo didn't allow the smile he was feeling to reach his face, but to his delight, Brodie was explaining to him the basic concepts of a science he was already familiar with—molecules, atoms, and even the vibrations of subatomic particles.

"When we enter the ethereal plane, we change the pace at which these tiny parts vibrate. To anyone looking at us in this world, we'll seem to have vanished, but really we're just vibrating at a different frequency that no one can see." He pointed at Peabo's sword. "I'm sure you've waved around that sword of yours, or one like it, enough times to realize that when something moves at a particular rate, it almost becomes invisible, yes?"

Peabo remembered how the blades of his oscillating fan back home would disappear when on high. He nodded.

Brodie continued. "Good. Yet because the three of us will be using the same potions, all the tiniest parts of our bodies will be vibrating at the same frequency, and we'll still be able to see each other, even speak with each other. Do you understand?"

Again, Peabo nodded silently.

"Okay, *now* you may ask a question," said Brodie.

Peabo knew the grumpy dwarf would likely only allow one or maybe two questions. "I assume when we're in this ethereal state, we can't touch anything?"

Brodie nodded.

"Then how are we supposed to open a desk drawer, or pick up a piece of parchment to look for a clue as to what Dvorak's up to?"

Brodie grinned. "Very good question. This potion will only last about ten minutes. Once we've applied it, we race directly through the front door—because not only can we not touch things, we can pass right through them—and go straight to Lord Dvorak's bedroom; according to Hanna, he has a private office in there. Once we're inside, we wait for the potion to wear off, then explore and collect what we need. When we're ready to leave, we reapply the potions and exit."

Peabo thought about this. It was a good plan. He looked at Brodie. "Believe it or not, I don't have any other questions."

"Thank the Nameless One for that." Brodie handed out the

vials. "Slather some of this over your body, clothes, hair, face, everything that's exposed, and then drink the rest. Hurry now —let's get this over with."

The world looked hazy as Peabo ran toward the castle. Except it wasn't exactly running… it was more like rollerblading with a lot of floating going on. When he tried running in the conventional sense, he only managed to bury his feet a few inches into the ground. But after a few awkward seconds, he got the hang of it. The ground wasn't solid, but it had a different density than the air. By using slow oblique motions to push lightly off the ground, he managed to drive himself in the direction he wanted.

As Brodie had promised, they swished past the guards without notice, passed right through the front door, and entered the opulence of Castle Dvorak. It was exactly as the old maid had described it. They skated their way to the staircase, took duck-like steps to climb, passed another bevy of guards on the second floor, and walked directly through the door to Lord Dvorak's chamber.

Passing through a solid door was a particularly strange sensation. Peabo could feel that the door was there, but it didn't serve as a barrier to movement. The molecules of his body simply drifted between the wood fibers, like sand through a sieve.

They looked around to be sure the room was unoccupied, as they had been told it would be. Wherever Lord Dvorak had gone, he had not yet returned. Brodie then pulled a glowing satchel from his pack. The satchel, unlike everything else in this hazy semi-real world, looked solid and real.

"We won't have time to read everything," the dwarf said, "so just take whatever papers you can and put them in this. It'll store more than you think."

His voice sounded distant and slightly off-pitch.

They waited quietly for a few minutes, and then in an instant the world snapped back to normal. Everything that had been hazy was now once more crystal clear and solid. They quickly set to work. After all, they were behind enemy lines, and didn't want to be here any longer than they had to.

As Peabo moved to search the dresser, Brodie stood at the desk and swept everything in sight into his satchel.

"What do you think Lord Dvorak will do when he realizes lots of his stuff is missing?" Peabo asked Nicole.

She smiled. *"Probably lose his mind."*

It took only about five minutes to clear the room of everything that might be useful. It was the slowest and fastest five minutes of Peabo's life. When they were done, Brodie sealed the satchel and put it back in his pack. Then he walked over beside the bed, pulled a glowing fist-sized rock from his belt, crushed the rock in his hands, and sprinkled the glowing dust onto the stone floor.

"Tell me what you know of Lord Dvorak," he whispered.

Peabo heard and felt the vibration of speech coming from the floor. The voice was very low, but understandable.

"Lord Dvorak has never set foot on me."

Brodie's expression turned grim. "Stones, tell me what you know of the Lord Dvorak's use of this room."

The floor by the bed vibrated for a moment as if humming to itself.

"Lord Dvorak spends much time at his desk and beyond his desk. That is all he does within my presence."

Peabo turned back to the desk and frowned. There was no "beyond the desk." The large and ornately carved wooden desk was set against a stone wall.

"Where is Lord Dvorak now?" Brodie asked.

"Beyond his desk."

At that moment a metallic click sounded from the direction of the desk itself.

Brodie was suddenly covered in a shimmering white haze. "You two stay behind me," he hissed. He tossed a bag toward the bedroom door, and as it landed, sharp metal shards spilled across the entranceway.

Nicole was also glowing. *"Be ready for anything,"* she said in Peabo's mind.

Peabo drew his sword, and Max immediately spoke up.

It's about damn time, pea brain. What have we got?"

Brodie sniffed the air, grimaced, and muttered a single word.

"Undead."

Peabo felt a surge of panic. His companions were much higher levels than he was, and they looked very worried.

The desk, which had to weigh hundreds of pounds, swiveled noiselessly, along with a section of the wall, to reveal a dark passage. And within the passage was a pair of bloodshot eyes. It was as if the darkness was cloaking all other detail but those eyes, and yet Peabo knew with certainty who he was looking at.

Lord Dvorak.

Peabo's every instinct told him to run. He didn't have to ask what he was staring at. He knew.

Lord Dvorak was a vampire.

In his head, he rattled off what he knew about vampires from the monster manual.

He's undead. To kill him, I need to chop off his head.

He can drain levels just by touching me.

He's a night dweller, and has to avoid direct sunlight.

He's going to be blazing fast, and stronger than he looks.

And there was one other fact Peabo knew about facing vampires, but it didn't come from the monster manual: *I'm not ready for this.*

The two sides stood eyeing each other for what seemed like forever, but likely was no more than a second. Then Dvorak spoke in what sounded to Peabo like a Russian accent.

"What makes you think thieves such as yourselves can enter my private quarters? Disturb my slumber? And not suffer consequences?" The man breathed in deeply and shouted, "Guards!"

Brodie made a quick motion toward the door, and the shards of sharpened metal began swirling in a vortex. The door opened, and the first guard to step through screamed as he was shredded into a bloody mess.

Dvorak lunged, and to Peabo, everything seemed to move in slow motion.

Nicole slammed her katana into Dvorak's outstretched arms. The weapon shattered on impact, and the vampire slapped Nicole viciously out of his way. She let out a shriek that pained Peabo to his core.

He slashed with all his might at the blur that was the ruler of the castle, and the sword screamed *"Get some!"* as it struck one of the vampire's arms, slicing it off at the elbow.

Suddenly, Peabo was blasted off his feet by a fiery explosion. Brodie had just brought a literal pillar of fire onto Lord Dvorak.

The vampire let out an ear-splitting cry of "Plainswalker!" And then, moving with impossible speed, he fled back into the secret passage.

With a surge of adrenaline, Peabo raced after him. But the passage led only to a stone sarcophagus, its heavy lid slowly sliding closed. Without thinking, Peabo squeezed the clamp on his makeshift grenade and lobbed it toward the stone coffin. The metal sphere clanked as it bounced off the edge of the sarcophagus and fell into the narrowing crack just before the lid could close all the way.

An instant later he was blasted back by the shock wave of an explosion that rivaled anything he'd seen from a modern grenade.

Peabo's ears were ringing, but he was unharmed. He looked up to see Brodie racing into the passage, and Peabo breathed a sigh of relief when he saw Nicole at the dwarf's side, alive and well.

The yelling of guards sounded from Lord Dvorak's bedroom. Peabo squeezed the clamp on his last grenade and tossed it back down the corridor. The resulting explosion shook the walls and brought down the bedroom ceiling, sealing Peabo and his companions inside the secret passage, cloaking them in darkness.

Then a light appeared above Brodie. The dwarf was standing where the sarcophagus used to be. It was no longer there, but the body of Lord Dvorak was. It was shredded, but intact.

Brodie murmured a prayer, then separated the vampire's head from its body.

The sound of muffled yelling came from the direction of the bedroom. Either the guards had survived the explosion, or more likely, more of them had arrived.

Brodie handed Peabo and Nicole more vials of the plane-shifting potion. "Quickly, apply that and drink the rest so we can flee. The guards will pick through that wreckage soon enough. I'll hold them back."

"No," said Peabo. "I can keep them away." He was just as shocked as his companions were when he said it, but he felt as if he knew exactly what to do.

He remembered talking to the trees, and the trees talking to him. They had said something about a fire. If he could only remember the details.

It was then that a giant blob of the vampire's essence drifted toward him. The moment he absorbed it, he was flooded with the euphoric rush of leveling.

And everything was clear.

An image of a forest fire appeared in his mind. The light from the fire split into multiple colors, as if being divided by a prism into its constituent wavelengths. But the result was more than a rainbow. Each of the colors spoke a different language. Existed on a different plane. And he could make them dance. Separate. Combine. And vanish.

Without understanding how, he focused all of his mental energy on the space between him and the wreckage outside the hidden passage. In the back of his mind, he was aware of the guards rapidly forming a path through the destruction, but it was the light pouring through that widening hole that was his only care. Peabo imagined that light as the waves he knew they really were. He stretched that light across the passage and weaved all of the wavelengths together into a reflective mesh.

As he worked, Nicole rubbed the potion on him. *"Whatever you think you're doing, hurry,"* she thought at him.

There was now a shimmer in the air, where Peabo had placed the mesh. His head throbbed with the effort, and he wasn't even sure if what he was doing was working; he was running on pure instinct.

At that moment, two bloodied soldiers, swords at the ready, pushed through. Though they stood no more than a few yards away from the three intruders, they stared blankly. They couldn't see past Peabo's mesh.

"Bah! Where the hell did they go?"

The lead soldier spit on the ground, and he and his companion departed back through the hole.

Peabo and Nicole drank what was left of their potions, and in moments, they had escaped the castle.

CHAPTER NINETEEN

Nicole woke with a start, her heart racing and her palms sweating. She and Peabo were in bed, her back to his front, with his arm draped over her. His hand was cupping one of her breasts in a way that, were he awake, would no doubt embarrass him greatly. As always, she sensed Peabo's anxiety, but for once she knew what it was about. For the first time since Jakub was alive, she'd seen images of her partner's dreams while *she* slept.

Her throat thickened with emotion at the thought of the man she had intended to be with for the rest of her life. Jakub had been the fourth son of a rich merchant who was in some way related to the king, yet he had rejected a life of ease and privilege, opting instead for one of adventure. He was the prince who lived life as a pauper and did what he felt was right, always.

It was because of this that the head of the Sage's Tower had partnered her with him. Their pairing was done with the hope of keeping him out of trouble. She tempered his wild nature without stifling it. And it didn't take long for her to do what she'd been trained never to do, for both her own sake and his: she fell in love with the man she was partnered with.

When he died, her will to live died alongside him. Nothing would ever be the same, and his family felt that she'd failed them all. She thought more than once about killing herself, but didn't have the courage. It seemed a fitting end when she was dragged halfway across the world, to a place nobody would know of her, and put up for sale like chattel in some rural backwater. And when the only price she fetched was a humiliating pittance, she saw that as a sign… and decided then and there that she'd find a way to end her life.

Until the new man turned out to be even more confused and upset than she was. Maybe that was what made it possible for her to continue.

Because the new man… he needed her. Just like Jakub had.

And Peabo *still* needed her.

She pressed closer to him and focused on his dream.

He was struggling with something in a forest. It seemed like a typical nonsensical dream, but it had the feeling of something more. It had something to do with a light and colors. Whether it was a rainbow-colored bridge, or colored lines, or even a painting, it was impossible for her to tell, yet in the dream, Peabo was distraught over it.

"The light from prisms can kill or heal," Peabo muttered in his sleep.

In the dream, a glowing ball of scintillating light grew and grew. He focused on it until it overwhelmed him, then he shivered and said in a sorrowful tone, “I can’t control it.”

And the scene exploded into yet another one that Nicole couldn’t make any sense of.

Peabo had been complaining about headaches, and it was no wonder he was having them if his sleep was haunted with these recurring images. And she was in no condition to help, not after what had happened at the castle. With but a touch, the vampire known as Lord Dvorak had drained her of two levels, and she’d been ill and exhausted ever since. Brodie said that the prelate was creating something to help restore her, but that she would still need a long recovery before life would regain any semblance of normality.

She didn’t have time for that. She needed to be there for Peabo. She was determined to find the strength to recover quickly, for his sake.

Peabo muttered something about darkness.

She sent her thoughts to him. *“It’s okay, it’s just a dream…”*

He tightened his embrace, and the darkness of the night claimed them both.

“Are you sure you’re okay?” Peabo asked, putting a blanket over Nicole.

She reached up and cupped his chin. “I’ll be fine. That’s the first time I’ve ever been drained of a level, much less two. I don’t recommend it.”

He wished she'd never had to experience anything like that. Though it had been a week since their confrontation with Lord Dvorak, she still hadn't fully recovered. Her skin looked pale, and she slept most of each day.

"But the prelate's restoration worked, didn't it?"

"It did. I'm back to level seven. But honestly, it made me feel even worse. I've read that level restorations are a shock to the system, and now that I've experienced one, I can confirm the truth of that claim. I feel like I've been run over by a wagon filled with boulders."

Peabo leaned over and kissed her cheek. "I'll watch over you for as long as you need to get better. While the castle guards comb the town for the thieves they never saw, it's better that we lie low anyway. We'll be out of the way in the church's safe house."

"Speaking of that, did you and Brodie figure out what exactly it was that you did to get the guards not to see us?"

Peabo shrugged. "We've talked about it a lot, but… no. As I've said, it just came to me. And I haven't been able to repeat it. To be honest, I'm not exactly sure what even came over me, but at that moment I was so sure I knew what I was doing."

"Lucky for us you did. It's what ended up saving us."

Peabo wiped a stray hair from her face. She looked so unwell. She might be back to level seven, but she was somehow less vital… less like Nicole.

"Get some rest," he said.

She closed her eyes, and almost immediately the tension drained from her face and her head lolled to the side. She was asleep.

Peabo watched her chest rise and fall. He knew that something had changed between them, at least for him. From the moment he saw her fall unconscious to the floor in Dvorak's chambers, he'd known how he felt. It didn't have anything to do with whatever hocus-pocus nonsense was involved in the whole pairing ritual. His feelings were his own, not a result of some crazy charm.

As he straightened and stepped away, his vision blurred and a wave of nausea washed over him. The room tilted, and he had to lean against the nightstand to keep from losing his balance. The headache and its associated symptoms were getting worse each day. Maybe it was some kind of infection? Ear infections did all sorts of crazy things back home.

But if it were something so trivial, he'd have expected Nicole's attempts at healing to have succeeded. He was afraid it was something more.

He pulled in a deep breath and let it out slowly. That cleared his head and reduced the nausea. Letting go of the nightstand, he walked unsteadily out of the bedroom.

He needed Brodie's help.

"Nicole's tried to heal the headache," Peabo explained to Brodie. "She even tried to massage the tension away. But so far, none of it has helped."

He was seated on a hard wooden chair in the church's guest office, with Brodie standing before him, studying him with a pensive expression.

"I'm not about to start giving you a massage, plainswalker, if that's what you're angling for," Brodie grumped. He reached out, his hands glowing, and placed them on either side of Peabo's head. "Exactly when did this start?"

Peabo wiped a few beads of sweat from his face. Whatever Brodie was doing, it was making his skin tingle, and not in a good way. "I've had them off and on for a long time, but nothing like this. I guess it really got worse after what happened at the castle."

Brodie gave him a severe look whose message was very clear: *Don't talk about what happened.* There were rumors on the streets of an incident at the castle, and Brodie didn't want any stray talk to be picked up by prying ears who might connect the three of them to what had happened.

He lowered his hands and took a step back. "Unfortunately, I can't sense an injury in you—which means there's nothing that I can heal." He frowned. "The maiden spoke to me of your nightmares. Have you always had them, or are they new? Or perhaps, have they changed recently?"

"I didn't have nightmares before coming to this world," Peabo replied. "But Nicole has told me I've had bad dreams about my family I left behind. I don't remember those dreams, but apparently I was having them right after we were first paired."

Brodie waved dismissively. "You had those same dreams back when you lived with me, too, right after you came out of the Desolate Plains. I'm talking about much more recent than that. Something that might coincide with the headaches."

Peabo leaned back in his chair and struggled to remember

anything of his most recent dreams. "I guess you'd have to ask Nicole," he said. "I don't tend to remember my dreams. All I can bring to mind are images of a forest, something to do with sunlight, maybe colors? And darkness as well."

Brodie began raking his fingers through his beard. "Interesting. This almost sounds like weaving fatigue."

"What's weaving fatigue?"

"It's something we usually see only in children. Those who have the ability to weave the forces, whether internal or external, tend to accidentally stumble onto their abilities at a young age. It can often be alarming for the parents—especially out here in the countryside," Brodie added with a chuckle. "They'll race into the church worried their six-year-old is a demon—simply because they spotted her with glowing hands, trying to make the dairy cow feel better. So it's not surprising that many children hide their abilities. They realize they can do something no one else can, and they fear it will get them called names by their friends, shunned by their family, or worse. But hiding an ability doesn't make it go away; it's still there, unused, and building pressure on their system. And the resulting symptoms aren't so much different from yours. Headaches, nausea, strange dreams. And no amount of healing will help."

"So you think that maybe I'm repressing some type of weaving ability?"

Brodie shrugged. "It's possible. I mean, we don't know exactly what you did during the incident of which we'll not speak. In fact, I have utterly no idea how such a thing was done. Still, I think the next step is to get you tested, see if there's something to this idea."

"Tested? Like at the fighters' guild?"

Brodie scoffed. "A fighters' guild is not exactly the epitome of weaving knowledge in this world. What you need is a weavers' guild. Unfortunately, there isn't enough demand for such a group in these parts. The closest thing we have is the church."

"So you'll test me? And then what? If I'm suffering from this weaving fatigue, is there something you can do to make it go away?"

"One thing at a time," Brodie said. "Let's do the test first."

Brodie took Peabo to a building adjacent to the church, where another priest, Viktor, was to perform the test. As Brodie stood off to one side, watching quietly, Viktor sat Peabo down and asked him about his symptoms. The priest was tall and thin, with an angular face, but his expression was warm, with laugh lines around his eyes, and he listened intently as Peabo spoke.

"Very interesting," he said when Peabo was done. "It could indeed be a case of weaving fatigue."

"Is that common?" Peabo asked. "How often do you evaluate people for this?"

The priest made a so-so hand gesture. "Every couple months someone will be brought in. The symptoms aren't usually as bad as you're describing, however." He looked thoughtful. "I wonder if that's because of your age. Mostly we only see this in young children, you know. One time a mother even brought in an infant to see me. It seems that when the mother was breastfeeding, and her milk was running low, the baby's hands glowed and pressed on the mother's breast. The frightened mother quickly weaned the child, but after that the child wouldn't sleep—just cried all night. My guess is he was repressing his talent and this was causing a headache, but the poor boy had no way to communicate it other than to cry."

Viktor rubbed his hands together. "Well, let's not keep you waiting." He stepped over to a counter, where he retrieved a metal hoop and a roll of what looked like aluminum foil. He sliced off a length of the foil, then began folding it over the edges of the hoop, making what looked like a foil tube with the circumference of a basketball.

"What exactly is that for?" Peabo asked uneasily.

Viktor smiled. "Excellent question. This foil is very thinly hammered iron." He tilted his head in Brodie's direction. "It comes from the smiths of Myrkheim, since they seem to be the only ones who are reliably able to make the metal thin enough for this test. If you're truly repressing weaving abilities, there'll be an imbalance around your head which will give off a type of energy. It'll either attract the foil or repel it—"

"Like a magnet?" Peabo asked.

Viktor nodded. "Exactly so."

As the priest crimped the last bit of the foil along the hoop, Peabo thought about all the little things Nicole had taught him about how weaving worked, and how energy was transmitted in this world. Given what he knew, it actually didn't surprise him that there'd be human magnetism involved at some point. If the normal state was an undetectable amount of magnetism, then a test to measure an imbalance made all the sense in the world.

The priest stood in front of him and held up his testing device. The foil was so thin it fluttered in the air. It reminded Peabo of the edible gold leaf he'd seen decorate a fancy dessert one time, long ago.

"Please stay still as I lower the hoop," Viktor said. "This is the largest hoop I have, but it's still going to be a tight fit for you, and we don't want to tear the foil by you brushing against it."

Peabo nodded once, then stayed completely still.

The priest stepped forward, held the tube over Peabo's head, and began to lower it. "Good. Now, if the foil curves inward or bulges outward, we'll know that—"

Peabo heard a metallic tearing, and Viktor gasped and stepped back.

"Well, that settles that," said the priest.

Brodie burst out with laughter. "Holy balls of the Nameless One! I wasn't expecting that!"

Peabo looked at the priest's device, and saw that the foil had been shredded in multiple places. "What happened?" he asked.

Viktor was looking at the device with a bewildered expression. "Normally, the effect is very minor—that's why we use such thin foil, so we can detect the effect. But your imbalance is severe—strong enough to completely blow out the test foil." He looked Peabo in the eye. "Plainswalker, you've got a problem."

Brodie came over and patted Peabo on the shoulder. "Don't

worry, my friend. The good news is we know that what's going on in your head is real. Now we've just got to figure out what we can do about it."

"What *can* we do about it?" Peabo asked.

Brodie folded his arms across his chest. "You have two options. One is to train the ability, use it, and relieve the pressure before your head pops right off your neck. The other is to continue to repress the ability, but manage the symptoms. The skills will eventually fade from lack of use, almost like an atrophied muscle, and in turn, the symptoms go away as well. But I believe your symptoms are much too severe for such an approach. Would you agree, Viktor?"

The tall priest nodded. "I agree. It's very rare for anyone to exhibit such an imbalance. I've personally never heard of it—"

"Oh, I have." Brodie smiled. "In that instance, suppressing the skill wasn't possible. Training had to begin."

"Did training work for him?"

"It was a girl, and yes. She's quite a talented conductor of the force, and I believe she's one of the few aboveworlders who's ever even been below the fifth level of Myrkheim."

Peabo looked back and forth between Brodie and Viktor. "So that's the solution? I start training as a healer?"

"Oh, absolutely not." Viktor chuckled. "Your way definitely lies with the conductor side of weaving."

Just when Peabo thought he was getting the hang of this bizarre world, a twist had to be sent his way. He wiggled his fingers at the two priests. "Wait. You're saying I'm a wizard?"

Brodie's expression turned sour. "Honestly, I'm not sure what you are. I've never encountered a conductor who didn't exhibit some of the normal sparks, flames, and other disasters that are part and parcel of that discipline." He looked at Viktor. "Have you?"

The priest shook his head. "I haven't, High Priest."

"What about—" Peabo stopped himself. He was about to mention what he'd done at the castle, but he decided that OPSEC was king, just like in the Army. With Dvorak guards out looking for people to hang, operations security—not to mention Brodie—demanded he keep his mouth shut about what happened. Viktor seemed like a nice guy, but Peabo didn't know if he could be trusted, and besides, the priest had no need to know.

Still, it seemed Brodie already knew what Peabo had been about to say. "Peabo, what you did wasn't something I'm familiar with. We need to consult with a proper weaving guild about that. I'll talk with the prelate and see what he suggests."

They thanked the priest for his time, and stepped outside. Peabo swayed a bit and still hadn't shaken off either the nausea or the pain. But in one way, he felt better—because whatever it was he was going through, he was getting closer to an answer.

He heard the front door to the cabin open, and he left the bedroom to find Brodie walking in out of the rain.

"Well?" Peabo asked. "Did you get the translations?"

"Aye, my boy, that I have." Brodie patted his pack and laid it on the table. "It took a while for me to find a conductor who had the ability to unravel all of that crazy gibberish our friend in the castle had scribbled, and even that conductor said it was unlike anything he'd ever encountered. Unfortunately, even with all of that crazy gibberish scribbling the man had done, it wasn't the treasure trove of information we had hoped."

"You didn't find anything useful? No connection to Stefan?"

"Well, yes and no. Sit, and let me show you what we have."

Brodie sat across from him and pulled some papers from his pack. "Most of it was diary entries about items of governance. Interesting tidbits about the king, or rumors from the mainland. The records go all the way back to the original Lord Dvorak. Which, as it turns out, is also the current Lord Dvorak. It seems there has only ever been one. As to how he became what he was, we don't know. He never mentions anything in his notes."

He pulled several sheets from the pile and pushed them over to Peabo—a set of originals and a set of translations. The originals were on ancient parchment that was deteriorating due to age.

"I've collected a few key passages that I think we were looking for. What did you call it, 'the smoking gun'? Anyway, I'll let you read it."

Peabo looked first at the original. It was nothing but geometric shapes, fragments of letters, and dots. Then he read the translation.

Day 1939

I've been trapped here for more planetary revolutions

around this yellow star than I care to think about, and I still don't know how I ended up here.

The last thing I remember was dropping the ship to sub-light speeds and suddenly finding myself skirting past a primordial black hole. The damned thing was on none of the star charts, and before I could do anything, the ship was torn apart by tidal forces.

And then I woke up here. In this strange primitive world. The first few seasons I wasted time and energy in trying to figure out how to get back to my life. I don't belong in this primitive hellhole, but I'm over that now.

"Does that make any sense to you?" Brodie asked.

Peabo nodded. "I can't believe it, but I think Dvorak was like me, someone who came here from another world." A world, from the sound of it, that was much more advanced than his own.

He continued to read.

Day 2105

At some point, a man has to make the best of a terrible situation.

The people here are primitive, but they have endearing qualities that make me not want to kill them all.

Day 2202

The physics of this world are clearly different, and it makes me wonder if somehow I managed to survive the crossing over through what we'd always thought was a singularity at the center of a black hole.

Have I landed in one of the alternate universes that we'd detected, but never figured out how to reach?

It's the only explanation I have.

Regardless, I've given up on trying to find a way back and instead am quickly learning how the sciences work in this strange, backwards world.

Day 13032

This body I now possess—it is beginning to ache. I have no idea what the lifespan of these creatures is, but I fear that time may be running out for me. If I'm ever going to get home, I need to come up with a solution soon.

Day 14508

I've met the king of this land, and I'm concerned.

After my years of research on the physics of this world, and after all of the work I've done to elevate myself and hone this weak body into the most it can be, I now realize that I'm nothing.

This king... he confirmed what I've always considered to be native superstitions. These creatures believe in divinities that manifested themselves on this world and evidently vanished in a giant war. Like most things from primitives, you can't believe such stories, but after meeting this king, I wonder.

I can't quite tell whether the king is simply powerful beyond anything I've experienced so far, or if he's not even mortal. But the things he did before my own eyes... I didn't think they were possible, even with the technology at home.

Since I've made my home in seclusion on this island, the king asked me for a favor. I'm afraid of what might happen if I don't do what he asks. It seems wrong, but after what he showed me, I can't tell what he's capable of.

How quaint—to think that I'm starting to believe in a higher power other than my own.

But given this king's power, why does he need me to keep an eye out for one particular primitive? Is that the key to his power? Does this primitive make him more powerful?

I have no idea what powers this plainswalker might have, but I'll be damned if I'll give the king access.

Peabo looked up from the paper. "Holy crap, that's more than just a smoking gun. I guess we did the right thing, didn't we?"

"Without a doubt." Brodie slid the papers back into the pack.

Peabo drummed his fingers on the table. "What do you make of the stuff he said about the king?"

Brodie sniffed. "I think that if the king is looking for a plainswalker, you might want to consider keeping your disguise for longer than we'd originally planned."

"How long?"

"A lifetime might be a good start." He raised a hand to

forestall any objection. "I'm serious. We've stopped Dvorak... but it seems to me that it's the king who really wanted you. And if he's as powerful as the vampire believed, that's not a good thing." Brodie wagged his finger at Peabo. "Besides, if you thought the vampire was difficult... well, you've never been to the mainland. There are those there who could erase us from existence with practically no effort whatsoever. So yes, my counsel to you is to keep a low profile."

Peabo sighed. "I suppose I need two things."

"And what are they?"

"More of those skin-changing potions, and a plan for what to do with the rest of my life."

"The potions are easy. In fact, I'll go ahead and get a supply of them." Brodie looked Peabo in the eye. "As for what to do with the rest of your life... I have some thoughts on that."

CHAPTER TWENTY

Peabo shifted restlessly in his sleep as his mind traveled to another time, another place, to a world he'd never seen before, yet one that seemed vaguely familiar. He was in the middle of a crowd of people, and they were all staring at the glowing hologram displaying various news feeds coming in from all over the continent.

The anxiety of the crowd was palpable as a news reporter spoke. *"It's now official; the peace talks have failed. The representatives from the twins' coalition have declared—"*

The signal blinked off, and people in the crowd began yelling at where the image had been, many of them shaking their fists.

What was going on? Where was he, and what kind of place had a hologram displaying the news on a public street?

A woman tugged at Peabo's elbow. "Jolie," she said, "I got

the word. He's providing us a shelter. Let's go before it's too late."

Peabo wanted to stay, to see if the signal came back on, but he found himself pushing through the crowd and sped after the woman, who kept looking back at him to make sure he was following. When they were clear of the crowd, they ran, covering nearly a mile before arriving at the outer walls of the city.

Outside the walls was nothing but a desolate plain. But two dozen women were gathered there, apparently waiting anxiously for something. Peabo and his companion joined them.

Suddenly, one of the women pointed upward. The clouds had parted, and a giant dome-like structure broke through, plummeting to the ground.

"The shelter! Just as promised!" said the woman at Peabo's elbow. "We'll only have a minute before it seals itself."

The sound of the object's approach grew louder and louder as it rapidly descended. Then Peabo felt the hairs on the back of his neck stand on end, and the structure slowed before touching down with a ground-shuddering thump. It was so heavy that it sank nearly a foot into the rocky surface of the plains.

It was a flat-bottomed geodesic dome, maybe twenty feet tall at its center, with a circumference of at least two hundred feet. As soon as it had settled, a door yawned open, and the entire group, including Peabo and his companion, raced for the entrance.

As he passed through the opening, Peabo marveled at the dome's thickness. The outer walls were over two feet thick.

The door closed behind them, but before it closed all the way, he heard people outside yelling. A riot? But then the door clicked shut, silencing the sounds from the outside world.

His companion leaned toward him. "Jolie, isn't this the sign you mentioned?"

The woman was crying. "It is," he said to her. "It's almost over."

But it wasn't his voice. Nor were these his words. It was a woman's voice, speaking her own words. Only then did it dawn on him that he must be experiencing someone else's dream. Or was it a memory?

"A place for people like us… it's hard to imagine." The crying woman covered her face. Peabo looked around and saw that nearly all the women were now crying.

The ground shuddered, and Peabo heard the boom of what had to be a gigantic explosion. And then another. And another. Despite the thickness of the outer walls, the dome shook as the explosions continued, each one seemingly closer. Soon they were occurring with the frequency of popcorn popping in the microwave.

There was no way the outside world could survive.

One of the women in front of him fell to her knees and clasped her hands in a sign of prayer. "It's finally come to it," she said. "The gods, they're at war."

Peabo shot upright into a sitting position, awake and in his bed. Nicole was asleep next to him. His heart was racing, and sweat covered his body.

Blinking the sleep from his eyes, he stared off into the darkness of the bedroom. What had he been dreaming about? Whatever it was, it had already faded; all he sensed now were the fading wisps of a nightmare.

He felt just like he was back at a forward operating base in Afghanistan. Those quiet nights were some of the scariest times he'd had during any of his deployments. The quiet just before storm. Was that what he'd been dreaming about?

He tasted blood, and wiped his face.

Damn it.

Swinging his legs out of bed, he looked for a hand towel. His nose was bleeding.

Isabella held her mother's hand as they walked through the market. It was the middle of the afternoon, and her head ached terribly. Normally she would have taken a nap after lunch, but the dream from the night before still haunted her, and she was afraid that a nap would wake the monsters again. Mommy had told her that she'd forget all about the dream when it was daytime, but she hadn't. Even though the sun was shining brightly, the lady from the dream was still in her head, whispering things. The lady had promised to protect her from the monsters, and even give her toys and candy if she did what she asked, but it was too much. Mommy would be furious if she did any of the things the lady in her head was asking her to do. And besides, she wasn't allowed outside of the cabin by herself — she was only six, and there were bad people in town.

As Mommy talked with the fruit merchant, Isabella spotted a dwarf walking through the streets. She knew he was from Myrkheim; the dwarves all came from the world below.

The lady in her head whispered something, and without knowing why she did so, Isabella ran toward the dwarf as fast as her feet could carry her, yelling, "Plainswalker! Plainswalker! I need the plainswalker!"

Just before she could reach the dwarf, her mother scooped her up and carried her away, scolding her for running in the streets.

The lady in her head was angry, but it didn't matter. Mommy couldn't hear the lady, and she certainly wouldn't listen to Isabella.

As they moved hurriedly away, Isabella looked over Mommy's shoulder at the dwarf, who was watching her with a serious expression.

It was pre-dawn, and Peabo and Brodie had just finished their business with the alchemist. They now had a supply of skin-changing potions that should be good for several months.

It had been almost ten days since the incident at the castle. The word on the street was that there were thieves in town, and everyone was on the lookout for strangers, but there were no rumors about Lord Dvorak. As far as anyone knew, he was still alive, cloistered away in his castle.

Hearing running footsteps, they both turned to find a little girl racing toward them, yelling, "Plainswalker! Plainswalker! I need the plainswalker!"

Peabo cringed as the girl's words echoed through the early-morning gloom.

The girl came to a stop right in front of them and stared wide-eyed at Brodie. She was dressed in nightclothes, barefoot, and had her hair up in pigtails.

Brodie smiled reassuringly at the girl. "You're the little girl who tried to talk to me yesterday. Why do you need to find a plainswalker?"

"The dream lady told me to—"

The girl suddenly tensed, her back arching as if she was being electrocuted. She shifted her gaze and looked up at Peabo with eyes that had turned completely white.

Peabo's jaw dropped. "What in the…"

The voice of a woman projected from the body of the girl.

"Greetings, plainswalker. I apologize for my method of contacting you. I wish I could meet you in person, but I can't. I'm stuck in a manner that you can't even begin to comprehend. I've been waiting for them to send another. I didn't think it would take untold millennia. This world needs our help, but I couldn't do it alone. I tried, and now I'm stuck between worlds.

"I need you to report to the Sage's Tower. They'll know what to do with you."

"Hold on," said Peabo. "Who and what are you?"

"We don't know each other, and I only have barely enough energy to break through the veil. Who and what I am, and who and what you are, will become clear once you're there. We

plainswalkers need partners, and I didn't accept that at the time. This world needs your help."

The glow faded from the girl's eyes, and she collapsed into Peabo's arms.

"Bella!" shouted a woman from somewhere nearby.

"Over here!" Peabo yelled, and the child's mother was there in seconds.

"Nameless One, no! What happened?" The mother reached for the child and Peabo handed her over.

Peabo worried about the child wandering the night by herself. Whoever it was that had reached out to him didn't seem to care that she had a child wandering in the dark looking for him. He shrugged. "I think she was sleepwalking. When she reached us she fell right asleep. You might consider keeping her in sight while she's sleep, for her own safety."

"I'm so sorry," said the mother. She too was wearing bedclothes and no shoes. "The rascal snuck out her window, which will certainly be barred from now on. And thank you for calling out. I might never have found her all the way here past the hill. I'm getting her back into bed."

As the woman walked away with her child, Peabo turned to Brodie. "What just happened?"

Brodie's gaze followed the woman and child as they vanished into the early-morning mist. "I've never seen such a thing before in my life. I've heard of foretellings, but not like that." He turned and began walking back toward their cabin. "Remember how we were discussing the next steps in your training?"

“Are you suggesting I need to go to the Sage’s Tower for that?”

“Maybe. But I’m not sure if that’s the wisest course of action, despite what we just witnessed. And even if it is, you don’t just walk up to the Sage’s Tower and enroll in training. Especially you.”

“Why especially me?”

Brodie looked at Peabo and frowned. “I still forget how little you know. Let me give you a bit of background. Other than the king’s castle, the Sage’s Tower is the oldest building still standing from the end of the First Age, and as such—”

“What’s the First Age?”

Brodie waved off the comment. “Forget I mentioned the First Age, it doesn’t matter. I merely mean to say there’s a lot of history, and extremely rigid rules, within those walls. The maiden could tell you all about that. Which leads me to my point. The Sage’s Tower has been, since its inception, a place only for women. They take in young girls for training in the weaving arts. And there’s no potion I know,” he gestured up and down at Peabo, “that would allow you to pass yourself as a young girl.”

“That does pose a problem,” Peabo said. “So what—”

He stopped himself as a sharp pain in his head doubled him over. He grabbed at his skull, then crouched and put his hands on the ground to keep from falling over, but the next thing he knew he was lying flat on his back, and Brodie was hovering over him with two glowing hands.

“Hold still. Your nose is bleeding.” As the dwarf held his glowing hands over the bridge of Peabo’s nose, he added,

"We'll consult with the prelate right away. I'd been reaching out to a weaving guild on the mainland, but given this morning's visit… I don't know. Perhaps the prelate can advise us on what to do."

Peabo watched as Brodie cleared off a small table in his borrowed office at the back of the church. Brodie had set up one of those zones of static that killed any noise so they wouldn't be overheard, and he'd also stationed Vasil, the senior priest, outside the office's locked door, to make sure nobody came near. The dwarf was determined that they not be disturbed.

When Brodie was ready, he sat at the table and spoke in a hushed tone. "What you're going to see is something you're not allowed to speak of to anyone. Any conversations with the prelate are to be considered confidential. As confidential as a conversation you might have with the Nameless One himself. You can't even talk with the maiden about this, do you understand?"

Peabo nodded solemnly. "I do."

Brodie withdrew a ring from a pocket and held it up. "This ring is similar to the one I lent to the maiden. It was conferred on me by the prelate when I became a high priest of the Nameless One. It is used for private conversations between myself and the prelate."

"How exactly do these communication rings work, anyway?"

Brodie chuckled and shook his head. “Always you with the questions about how things work. You will indeed make a very interesting weaver. A weaver of what, it remains to be seen. But if you must know, these rings are born in pairs, from the same casting and the same bar of gold. Even once they’re separated, they still share that connection, like siblings, so that when I tap or squeeze a pattern onto this ring, a similar tap or press will be felt as vibrations on its twin—which is on the prelate’s finger. We have developed a code so that each sequence of taps and squeezes spells out a word.”

“Is it something like this?” Peabo tapped a sequence on the table as he said, “Dot, dot, dot, then dash, dash, dash, and then dot, dot, dot. Each dot is a tap, and each dash I guess for the ring is a squeeze. Is it like that?”

Brodie’s eyes widened and he remained speechless for a few seconds. “You never cease to amaze me. That’s exactly correct. But now I’ll be using a feature of this ring that I’ve never used before. In fact, I didn’t even know it was possible until the prelate instructed me on its use for this meeting. Evidently this ring will allow us to also hear things. Hence the area of silence.” He glanced toward the door. “Which will dissipate soon, so we should get started. Are you ready?”

“I am.” Peabo wiped the sweat from his palms. He was surprised by how nervous he felt, like he was meeting with a general for the first time.

Brodie turned his ring to the side and showed him the markings on the outside of the band: two tiny X’s. He put his thumb and forefinger on the X’s, pressed, and held them there. After a time, the ring began to glow.

A man's voice projected from the ring itself.

"Brodie, as always, your timing is impeccable. Is our guest with us?"

"Yes, Prelate, the plainswalker is here."

Peabo leaned closer. "I'm here. It's good to hear your voice, sir."

A chuckle came from the ring. *"The boy is charming. Tell me, plainswalker, what is your name?"*

"Peabo, sir. I mean, Prelate."

"Well, Peabo, Brodie has filled me in on your situation. As I'm sure you understand now, we're treading on unfamiliar territory with you. Brodie has kept me informed on your health concerns as well as the results of your testing, and I agree that something needs to be done—urgently. And when Brodie told me about what happened this morning with that little girl, and the message she delivered, I did a little research on the Sage's Tower in the archives from the First Age."

There was that talk of the First Age again. Peabo needed a history lesson, but now was *not* the time.

"Brodie, did you know a woman designed the Sage's Tower?"

"No, Prelate. I didn't know that."

"And that's not even the interesting thing. Not only was she a woman... she was a plainswalker. The very first plainswalker founded the Sage's Tower. For some reason, I'd always assumed the plainswalker of legend had been a man, but evidently I was mistaken."

Brodie's eyes widened. Clearly this was as surprising to him as it was to Peabo.

The prelate continued. "As you know, the tower was intended for women's education in the weaving arts. But… I found a passage in one of the old records that spoke of an exception. Evidently the founder expected other plainswalkers to come—and to be educated there. That has never happened, but it was the founder's original intent.

"Unfortunately, that was in another age, and when I reached out to the headmistress of the Sage's Tower, she made it quite clear that no male students would be allowed within the tower walls, plainswalker or not… unless they passed a very specific test. She sent that test to me, and I hope it will make sense to you. It's a form of writing that you are required to interpret before being allowed entry. If you can read it, you will be admitted. If not, there is nothing more I can do."

"I will certainly try, sir."

"Good. Brodie, I just sent the test to the Dvorak location courier box."

The metal box that had previously been in Patriarch Stefan's room was now sitting on Brodie's desk. Still holding the ring in one hand, he placed his other palm, now glowing, onto the courier box. Peabo winced at the memory of the nasty zap he'd gotten from that thing, but for Brodie, the box merely made a metallic click, and opened.

Brodie pulled out a thin metal card, about the size of a credit card, and placed it in front of Peabo. Peabo picked it up and studied it. One side was black, with no discernible features. The other side had strange markings, but they were covered by a patina that made it look very old.

"Prelate," said Brodie, "I've handed the item to the plainswalker."

"Peabo, can you make sense of it?"

Peabo glanced at Brodie. "Can I get more light?"

Almost immediately the table began to give off an eerie white glow.

Peabo peered closely at the faint characters. His first reaction was that it looked like a CAPTCHA sequence—the kind of obfuscated text that was used to verify it was a human at the computer terminal.

"Sir," he said, "it looks like something from my old world. But the writing is somewhat obscured by some sort of rust or patina. Is it okay if I wipe it with a cloth?"

"The headmistress said this is a copy of the original, so I suppose there's no concern about damaging it."

Peabo was nevertheless very gentle as he wiped the surface of the card. And when he saw the letters underneath, his heart began to thud so loudly in his chest he wouldn't be surprised if the prelate could hear it.

The words were in English!

He sounded out the bits of partial words he could make out.

"Reporting in…"

"duty…"

"In"

"iron SLAG"

That wasn't right.

Peabo studied the words again. Suddenly his blood turned to ice, and his mind raced back to another world, another universe. It was his first day at a new job. He'd just stepped through a doorway, the door sliding up behind him with frightening speed, when a blinding light beamed directly onto him and a voice spoke: *"Mr. Smith, welcome to STAG."*

STAG. The Special Technologies Analysis Group. The outfit that had changed his life forever by sending him on this journey into another universe.

The room was beginning to spin.

He pulled in a deep breath and let it out slowly.

"Peabo," said Brodie, "are you okay? Can you read that thing?"

Peabo nodded. "I can."

"What does it say?" the prelate asked.

Peabo felt anger boil up from within him. He gritted his teeth and balled up his fists. He felt a vein throbbing in his neck.

Another breath… and he shook out his hands.

It says, "Reporting in for duty. I'm from STAG."

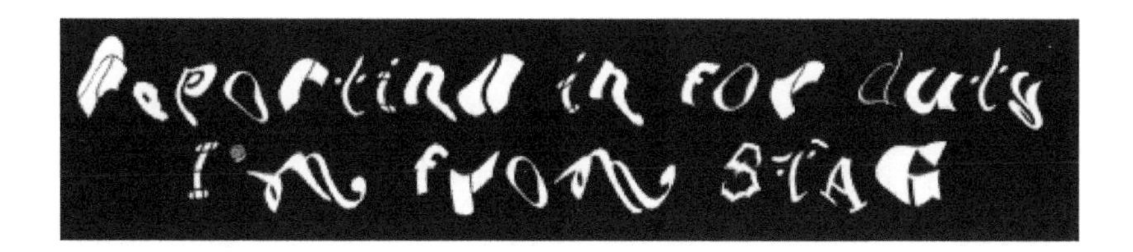

PREVIEW OF THE SAGE'S TOWER

Standing in a giant cavern deep in Myrkheim, Peabo watched as three platoons' worth of soldiers organized themselves in a manner that seemed very familiar. With his Special Forces background, he was used to working in small groups, but this brought him back to his infantry days when the entire company would get rousted to go on maneuvers. But there were two key differences between now and then: the majority of these soldiers were four feet tall or less, and there wasn't a firearm in sight.

Nicole, a tall blonde who could literally kick his ass from one end of this cavern to the next, came over and draped her arm over his shoulder. "Are you doing okay?"

Both the tone of her voice and her furrowed brow made it clear she was worried about him.

"I'm fine," he lied. "The headache isn't that bad right now."

"Liar." She never minced words. "You bled all over the pillows last night. You're nothing resembling fine." The blood maiden nodded with approval at the soldiers. "I think all of the prelate's escort has arrived."

"I don't understand what the big issue is. How many people do we *really* need to get to the mainland?"

Nicole gave him the look she reserved for when he'd said something particularly stupid, but she spoke with an uncharacteristically warm tone. "You've never made this trip, so you'll just have to trust me. With a group of this size, even the stupidest creepy-crawly will stay out of our way."

Brodie, the high priest of the Nameless One and their mutual friend, joined them. "You look like week-old garbage," he said, looking Peabo up and down.

"Gee, thanks." Peabo shook his head. Brodie was always griping. If he wasn't, Peabo would be worried about the old man. "Can you explain why we aren't just taking a boat to the mainland? You wouldn't need this many people for a boat ride."

The dwarf snorted and began repeatedly poking Peabo's chest with a thick finger. "First of all"—poke—"us Myrkheimers aren't fans of being up in the aboveworld more than we need to be. Second"—poke—"there's not a boat made that'll survive an attack by a kraken. Third"—poke—"I'm not risking my hide on the skills of some sea captain I don't know. Fourth—"

"Okay, stop poking me! I get the picture." Peabo rubbed at the sore spot where the priest had been finger-stabbing him.

"What's a kraken? I've memorized the monster manual from front to back, and there's no mention of it."

Brodie waved dismissively. "There's a second edition, but don't you worry about that yet. You're not ready for that."

Peabo was still a newbie in this world, and at moments like this he wished he could scour through everything Brodie knew so he'd have a clue about what was going on.

The sound of crunching gravel echoed throughout the cavern as a large wagon rolled into view at the entrance, pulled by three red-eyed creatures. They looked to Peabo like a cross between an ox and a Clydesdale, but these behemoths were about eight feet tall at the shoulder.

"Ah, there it is," said Brodie. "The transport has arrived."

"Why do we need that huge wagon?" Peabo said.

"It's for you," Brodie and Nicole said at the same time.

"Me? I don't need a special transport. I'll march with everyone else."

Nicole began rubbing his shoulders—which was what she always did when trying to calm him. "Peabo, I know you think you're fine, but you're not. It's a long underground journey across the island, under the ocean and to the mainland. I've seen you getting worse, and believe me when I say that you won't survive this march if you don't ride in that wagon."

As the wagon continued through the cavern, the soldiers stepped aside, creating a path that led directly to Peabo. It was clear that everyone had known the plan except for him.

He took a deep breath, let it out slowly, and tried to remain adult about this. Nicole was right. Even standing upright made him feel lightheaded, and the nausea that came with his damned headache was constant now. He was in crap condition. Marching alongside the others, he'd only slow everyone down.

The soldier at the head of the wagon, cracking a whip and flicking his reins, maneuvered the vehicle around so that its back faced Peabo. Two soldiers unlocked the back gate, and it yawned open on a set of well-oiled hinges.

"Plainswalker," one of the soldiers said, offering his hand. "Let me help you get on."

Peabo ignored the hand and climbed onto the wagon by himself. He was sick, but he could still step onto a wagon. Nicole hopped up beside him, and the soldiers closed the gate behind them.

Brodie cupped his hands to his mouth and announced to the assembled group, "In the Nameless One's service, let's get moving!" He then began rattling off orders like a competent captain might in the army. He assigned one platoon to take point, another to cover the rear, and the rest of the soldiers to serve as a protective barrier surrounding the wagon. They certainly weren't taking any chances.

With a cloth in her hand, Nicole dabbed at Peabo's upper lip.

"Damn it," Peabo groaned. He was bleeding again.

"It's okay." Nicole cupped his face with two glowing hands, and he felt something high up in his nose get hot as she tried healing him… again.

The wagon began to move, and Peabo sighed. This was going to be a long trip.

Waking from a fitful sleep, but keeping his eyes closed, Peabo sensed the rocking of the wagon traveling along the underground path through Myrkheim. He tried to find sleep once more, but couldn't; the voices of everyone around him were so damned loud. It was like a hammer pounding incessantly on his temples.

"I think there's another four hours before our next rest break."

"He doesn't look like a plainswalker. Where are his markings that I read about in seminary?"

"I wonder if the high priest realizes he's got a failed blood maiden sitting next to the plainswalker. The woman can't be trusted."

That was when Peabo realized he wasn't hearing conversations, he was hearing people's thoughts. Nobody would have said that about Nicole aloud, at least not within earshot of her. She'd probably kill them.

But, no, that couldn't be right. He shouldn't be able to hear their thoughts. He could peek into low-level minds, but these were seasoned soldiers, certainly past level four, the point at which the mind closes itself off from being spied on.

He started to sit up, only to realize he couldn't. He couldn't move at all, not even to open his eyes. And yet… he could see everything around him. He could see Nicole beside him, sitting cross-legged, staring down at the ring in her hand, but he wasn't seeing her from the wagon—he was seeing her from above. He was somehow hovering over the wagon, looking down, watching everything from that vantage point. He could even see his own body, still asleep.

He'd heard of out-of-body experiences back on Earth, and had never put any stock in it. Evidently, it wasn't all nonsense, for he was having such an experience right now.

Brodie was sitting across from Nicole, and they were having a silent conversation with their paired communication rings, tapping the equivalent of Morse code to each other. Though their messages were silent, he could hear their thoughts.

"I hope they've got an answer at the tower," thought Nicole, tapping the message to Brodie.

"You seem to lack confidence in the women of the tower, despite the prelate's recommendation that we take him there."

"Brodie, I lived there for a decade, and I know what goes on behind those walls. I wouldn't subject anyone I cared for to such a thing, ever."

The dwarf gave her a quizzical look. *"You care for him? I didn't think such a thing was allowed."*

"Shut up, Brodie. I'm still my own person, regardless of my vows. Do you think it's coincidental that all of this started right after the castle incident?"

"I think not. The essence he gained from Lord Dvorak must have been immense, and he leveled immediately. I'd wager that something up in his head was unlocked at level five, and he's missing some key training that we know nothing about."

"I'm worried for him."

"You should be. Is the sedative you gave him strong enough to last the trip?"

"Yes. I hated doing it, but he's stubborn, and he'll hurt himself without even realizing he's doing it."

A sedative, Peabo thought. So that's why he couldn't wake up.

Peabo realized that he could shift his point of view and his position just by just willing it. Sensing activity somewhere ahead, he glided forward, like a ghost flying across the train of soldiers. As he neared the point of their procession, he discovered there was some kind of assault taking place, though he had only caught the tail end of it. He watched as a dwarf soldier felled some sort of humanoid creature with a pig-like snout, nearly cleaving the creature's head off its shoulders in the process. There were already a half dozen other corpses on the ground.

Orcs. Peabo recognized them immediately from his studying of the monster manual. They were nothing like the orcs in the Lord of the Rings movies, but rather, pathetic scrawny things. Clearly they hadn't given the dwarven escort much reason to pause.

As the orcs were dragged to one side of the cavern and the procession continued, two of the soldiers stood over the corpses and muttered some prayers of dedication. Peabo listened in on their thoughts, and then on the thoughts of the other soldiers. These weren't just work-for-hire guild members; they were the prelate's men, the equivalent of some kind of papal guard—an elite unit, and proud of their service.

Suddenly Peabo snapped back into his body. He still

couldn't move or open his eyes, but he felt Nicole dabbing at his nose, and heard her crying. He sensed her fear. She was terrified he was going to die.

Brodie whispered beside him, "He's fighting the sedative. That's likely what's causing him to bleed. Scoot over—I'm going to put him into a deeper sleep."

Peabo felt Brodie's hand touch his forehead. A warmth enveloped him, and the world went dark.

Having woken up just as the wagon climbed up into the daylight, it took Peabo a few minutes for his eyes to adjust to the brightness. Breathing deeply, he detected the scent of the ocean somewhere nearby. He didn't need to ask, he sensed that they were now on the mainland.

Nicole glanced at him from across the back of the wagon and gave him a timid smile. "Are you feeling okay?"

His stomach rumbled, and before he could clear his thoughts to respond, Nicole scooted closer. She handed him a water skin and some dried meat. "You've been asleep for over a day. You need some energy."

Peabo bit off a chunk of the meat and began chewing. The jerky tasted like some kind of chicken, but it tasted like it had been spiced with an odd combination of spices that left his lips tingling and his tongue feeling a bit numb. "Where are we?"

"We're passing through Elmheim." Brodie said from the front of the wagon. "Just relax and we'll be there soon enough."

Peabo looked on with awe as the wagon wound its way through a city that made the Castle Dvorak area look like a humble village. Despite the medieval technology of this world, the buildings stretched up into the sky, their architecture all spires, pillars, and ornate masonry. It reminded him of the old buildings in Vatican City. In fact, it was strange how similar the construction was to Roman, baroque, and even Gothic styles, yet this world's architecture had its own unique flair, giving the city a familiar and an alien quality at the same time.

"What's got your interest?" Nicole asked.

"I'm just amazed at the buildings. They're all so much bigger than the ones back in Dvorak."

"How does it compare to where you're from?"

Peabo shrugged. "In our biggest cities, like New York, the buildings are taller, but they're less… I'm not sure how to say it. I guess these buildings are more intricate and more unique. A lot of the buildings where I'm from are very similar to each other. How old is this place?"

"Very old."

"How old?"

Nicole turned her head to the front of the wagon. "Brodie, do you know how old these buildings are?"

The dwarf, who was sitting next to the driver, pointed at a building with pillars and a triangular roof profile. It reminded Peabo of the Parthenon. "There was a land quake almost five hundred generations ago that leveled much of this province. The oldest buildings, like this one here, were constructed during the rebuild."

"And a generation is roughly how many years?"

Brodie shrugged. "Twenty or so."

Peabo did the math. That was almost ten thousand years. There weren't any buildings back home that were still standing after that many years. If he remembered his history lessons correctly, the pyramids were at best half that age.

Nicole grabbed his hand and held it between hers. Ever since he'd woken up about two hours ago, she'd been very touchy-feely, which was unlike her.

"Are you okay?" he thought at her.

She gave him a lopsided grin and projected her thoughts into his head. *"I'm fine, just worried about you. Are you feeling okay?"*

"I'm okay." And it was true. Other than a dull ache at the base of his neck and feeling sore from having slept on the wagon, he felt fine.

"There she be," Brodie announced as the wagon crested a rise and a series of towers loomed large ahead of them. "The Sage's Tower. The tower complex is even older than the other buildings here. It's among the few buildings in the province to have survived the land quake."

"How old does that make it?" Peabo asked.

"I can't really say. It's a construction from the First Age, so at least one hundred thousand turns of the season."

"How is that even possible?" Peabo asked.

The towers loomed higher as they approached. Together they resembled a castle, but without outer walls. There were five towers in all, one on each corner of a large square, with the tallest of the towers being in the center.

"The stones are resistant to wear, if that's what you're asking," Nicole explained. "You seem shocked by this."

"I am," Peabo admitted as the wagon rolled to a stop.

A group of about a dozen women exited the center tower, led by a tall blonde who radiated a white glow.

Nicole whispered in a shaky voice, "That's Ariandelle, the headmistress."

The women approached the wagon, Ariandelle leading the way. Suddenly Peabo's nose began bleeding. Nicole brushed at Peabo's face with a glowing hand.

"Nicole," said Ariandelle with a smile. "It is a surprise to see you. Weren't you paired with…"

A redheaded woman next to the headmistress whispered in the taller woman's ear, and Ariandelle looked sad for a moment before deliberately turning to face Peabo.

"Plainswalker. Yes, I can see who you really are. And despite all that you've been through to get here, your journey has only begun." She shook her head. "It's a good thing you've arrived in time. I see that the bleeding has already started. I can sense the pain within you."

The woman's voice had an airy, almost ethereal quality to it —much like her unnaturally glowing skin. Peabo felt the urge to reach out and poke her to verify that she was flesh and bone and not some kind of weird spirit.

She pulled out a metal card, about the size of a credit card, and held it out to him. "Please, read this aloud."

Peabo recognized it as the same object he'd seen a copy of earlier, in Dvorak. But as he took it, he discovered this one was heavier, and warm to the touch. Not only that, he sensed a wrongness about it.

It had words written on one side, in a CAPTCHA format, the same style of obfuscated writing used in his world to prove that the reader was a person and not some kind of computer. He already knew what it said, but when he looked at the words again, he felt his anger rise once more.

He pulled in a deep breath and tried to let go of his anger as he exhaled.

"Reporting in for duty," he read. "I'm from STAG."

The card exploded into fine dust, and the world went dark.

A cacophony of voices erupted all around him. He felt himself being moved. Nicole cried out. But it was the headmistress's voice that cut through the din.

"No, you may not accompany him into the tower. You are forbidden access to the plainswalker."

As Peabo felt his body floating in a sea of darkness, the last thing he sensed was Nicole's voice in his head: *"Don't admit to being paired with me. It'll keep you safer in there."*

AUTHOR'S NOTE

Well, that's the end of *The Plainswalker*, and I sincerely hope you enjoyed it.

If this is the first book of mine you've read, I owe you a bit of an introduction. For the rest of you who have seen this before, skip to the new stuff.

I'm a lifelong science researcher who has been in the high-tech industry longer than I'd like to admit. There's nothing particularly unusual about my beginnings, but I suppose it should be noted I grew up with English as my third language, although nowadays, it is by far my strongest. As an Army brat, I traveled a lot and did what many people do: I went to school, got a job, got married, and had kids.

I grew up reading science magazines, which led me into reading science fiction, mostly the classics by Asimov, Niven, Pournelle, etc. And then I found epic fantasy, which introduced me to a whole new world, in fact many new worlds, and it was Eddings, Tolkien, and the like who set me on the path of appreciating that genre. And as I grew older, and stuffier, I grew to appreciate thrillers from Cussler, Crichton, Grisham, and others.

When I had young kids, I began to make up stories for them, which kept them entertained. After all, who wouldn't be entertained when you're hearing about dwarves, elves, dragons, and whatnot? These were the bedtime stories of their youth. And to help me keep things straight, I ended up writing these stories down, so I wouldn't have it all jumbled in my head.

Well, the kids grew up, and after writing all that stuff down to keep them entertained, it turns out I caught the bug—the writing bug. I got an itch to start writing… but not the traditional things I'd written for the kids.

Over the years I'd made friends with some rather well-known authors, and when I talked to them about maybe getting more serious about this writing thing, several of them gave me the same advice: "Write what you know."

Write what I know? I began to think about Michael Crichton. He was a non-practicing MD, who started off with a medical thriller. John Grisham was an attorney for a decade before writing a series of legal thrillers. Maybe there was something to that advice.

I began to ponder, "What do I know?" And then it hit me.

I know science. It's what I do for a living and what I enjoy. In fact, one of my hobbies is reading formal papers spanning many scientific disciplines. My interests range from particle physics, computers, the military sciences (you know, the science behind what makes stuff go boom), and medicine. I'm admittedly a bit of a nerd in that way. I've also traveled extensively during my life, and am an informal student of foreign languages and cultures.

With the advice of some *New York Times*-bestselling authors, I started my foray into writing novels.

My first book, *Primordial Threat*, became a *USA Today* bestseller, and since then I've hit that list a handful of times. With 20-20 hindsight, I'm pleased that I took the plunge and started writing.

That's enough of an intro, and I'm not a fan of talking about myself, so let me get back to where I was before I rudely interrupted myself.

This book started on a dare of sorts. I have a friend who's a rather successful author, and he claimed that writing a single book that catered to fans of thrillers *and* fans of sci-fi/fantasy couldn't work. "Too different," he said. "Not possible."

** Challenge Accepted**

Now, let's be honest. There's a reason why some things aren't seen often, and usually it's because it's a mistake. However, every once in a while, someone takes a risk that works. I suppose you, the readers, will let me know soon enough whether this is a risk that worked or failed miserably.

Admittedly, before the gauntlet was thrown by my author friend, I'd been noodling on the idea for a book that had

Tolkienesque elements within it. As a kid, and now more recently as a parent, I played Dungeons and Dragons, which for those who don't know is a role-playing game involving magic, monsters, and of course dungeons. I didn't want to write a D&D book *per se*, that was never the intent, because my typical reader today isn't one that I'd classify as being a "gamer" or strongly into fantasy.

I didn't write that kind of book, but my author friend posed what is ultimately the toughest nut to crack: how do you attract an audience to a novel whose elements may represent genres that don't have a wide overlap with the genres they already read?

Well, most of my stories revolve around a central "what if" type of question. This is a "what if" story that at its roots was a technothriller, but it puts the main character into a situation where things evolved in ways that are totally unexpected, at least for a typical technothriller.

We start with the main character, a former Special Forces soldier who finds himself with an opportunity to get back into the mix.

One of the things they teach you in many military forces around the world is to improvise, adapt, and overcome. This is especially true of the Army's Special Forces, who are masters of unconventional warfare. That being said, I intended for the main character to encounter a situation that no prior training would have prepared him for.

Let's face it, when Neil Armstrong and Buzz Aldrin strolled on the moon, they were as prepared as two people could be for an environment that no human being had ever experienced. For the scientists, it was all theoretical and equations on paper. We can only simulate low gravity on earth via buoyancy exercises in the pool and with the vomit comet in the air, neither of which is like the real thing.

Our main character was faced with the same task, but with a lot less information.

At its root, I wanted *The Plainswalker* to be a science fiction story, but with elements of both fantasy and the best part of a thriller. After all, we have a clandestine organization doing something that's very cutting-edge. We, the readers, know that everyone isn't being told everything. And even when our hapless adventurer finds himself in a new world, it's a new world that he learns is hostile to him. Someone wants him dead, and he has no idea why.

All he knows is that they're serious, and his partner is dead.

So far, we've set up a story that skates along the edge of where many a technothriller would go. Some might call it science fiction, and that's the beauty of the genre that Crichton started. He fundamentally was writing science fiction, but it was marketed as a thriller with technology.

Well, that's when the scientist in me comes in. What if a few little things were tweaked in the way physics worked in this new universe our adventurer finds himself in?

This isn't so much a story about advanced technology looking like magic, as Arthur C. Clarke stated many years ago. After all, these people seemingly had, at best, the technology levels present in what we'd know as our Middle Ages.

But as we go deeper into the story, the science fiction tale with thriller elements starts to become very recognizable to another class of readers: those who like fantasy or even LitRPG.

The story evolves when elements of epic fantasy come into play. Trees that move? Is that a play on an Ent? The ability to hear someone's thoughts? That's a ploy that's been used across all genres.

This entire story is about what if another world's laws of physics were just a *little* different than ours.

Would things have developed differently?

How would technology evolve differently if some people had the inherent ability to instantly heal a cut or a broken bone? The medical world that we know would certainly have been vastly different. What about other tweaks? You can imagine the ripple effects it would have on what "technology" looks like in that world.

Well, I'll leave some of the more science-nerdy aspects of what I've done for the addendum, because like in most of my books where I touch on scientific topics within the story, I have a section dedicated to talking about the science at a deeper level. And this time, the addendum is kind of sizable. I've definitely "scienced up" this fantasy novel.

Hopefully, if you're reading this, I've kept you entertained. Because that truly is my primary goal. I'm not here to invent new genres, or fit square pegs into round holes. I'm trying to write things that I think people will enjoy, and frankly, I think it's possible to write what in my mind is a TechnoSciFiFantasy-Thriller, which I admit doesn't roll off the tongue nicely. Maybe FantaSci? FantaThriller? Or maybe just one of those less traditional Rothman novels.

Is what I've done a new genre? I have no idea. I've mashed up elements of Thrillers, Science Fiction, and Fantasy to make what I think is something traditional publishers are scared to publish—mostly because they wouldn't know how to market it.

And I may be in the same boat. We shall see.

Update: It's a little more than a week after the release of this book in two languages and I'm very pleased at how well it's been received. I've gotten over a dozen e-mails asking the same thing, "When is the next book?" Let's just say that I'm working on *The Sage's Tower* right now and I expect to release it before the end of the year.

If I could ask anything from you, dear reader, it would be to please share your thoughts/reviews about the story on Amazon and with your friends. It's only through reviews and word of mouth that this story will find other readers, and I do hope *The Plainswalker* (and the rest of my books) find as wide an audience as possible.

Again, thank you for taking the chance on a relatively unknown author. After all, I'm no Stephen King.

It's my intent to release two to four books a year, and I'll be completely honest, I'm heavily influenced by my readership on what gets attention next. An example of that being my first book, *Primordial Threat*, a book that was not going to have a follow-on title. But when I released it, it became a hit in the US and abroad, so due to demand, I released a second in what is now known as the Exodus Series.

I should note that if you're interested in getting updates about my latest work, join my mailing list at:

https://mailinglist.michaelarothman.com/new-reader

Mike Rothman
April 8, 2021

"To learn more about LitRPG, talk to authors including myself, and just have an awesome time, please join the LitRPG Group on Facebook."

ADDENDUM

The addendum is the place where I get to roll my sleeves up and talk about the technical pieces of the story you've just read. As of the moment I'm writing this, I haven't even figured out what genre this book truly fits into: is it science fiction, thriller, fantasy, some weird mashup of all three? I had a beta reader call it FantaSci. Either way, it doesn't really matter since most of the books I write tend to have elements of history, science, or other tidbits I've borrowed from the real world.

You'd think that because many might say this story is at least adjacent to the fantasy genre, that the science I'd be describing is fairly limited.

Au contraire, mon ami. (I said "on the contrary, my friend" in French, because I think it makes me sound fancy, and I'm basically a goofball at times.)

From the moment I set pen to paper on this novel I intended to keep this story following some very specific scientific principles. I admittedly tweaked how some physics would work in this universe, but only a little. The natural ramifications of those changes follow known science almost exactly. In fact, I borrow many things from science fact to create this science fiction.

That being said, the story touches on a few things that span the gamut of scientific topics such as brane cosmology, the multiverse, time dilation, and the uncanny valley. These are all elements that I've weaved into the story, and for many people, they often wonder, "How much of this is real, and how much is made up?"

One of the most common comments I get from readers is when they tell me how they kept looking things up as they read to see whether or not something was real, and often they were surprised that it was. My goal is to make it very hard to figure out when I'm stretching science and when I'm not. And in the case of this particular novel, I'd want people to maybe even be surprised that something that they were absolutely certain was a complete fabrication is actually real.

However, just because I weave real science into my stories, that shouldn't mean you need advanced degrees to understand what is happening. All you should need is a love of good stories that contain science and technology. It is up to me, the author, to make the science portion accessible to all who would read it.

In this addendum, I'll give brief explanations of what may be very complex concepts. My intent is to only leave you with sufficient information to give a remedial understanding of the subject. However, for those who want to know more, it's also my intent to leave you with enough keywords that would allow you to initiate your own research and gain a more complete background understanding of any of these topics.

This should also give you a peek into some of the things that have influenced my writing of this story, and maybe have you start asking what all authors inevitably ask themselves, "What if?"

I'm covering the elements of the story in no particular order. However, I did pick these topics because I think they're interesting and figure people might want to know more about them or because I wanted to explain further something about the science that may otherwise be overlooked from the context of the story.

The Multiverse:

The story starts off with what may seem like a very strange premise. Our intrepid main character resides in one world, but ends up in another. I'll actually cover this in two phases: first the concept of the multiverse, and then something I referenced in the book called brane cosmology.

When Peabo's mind gets launched from our world to the next, it's not just another world, but another universe.

In this case, it's another world within a new universe, but this story could have gone a very different way. In fact, I wrote the first couple chapters both ways, and ended up choosing the one you read.

What was this other way?

Imagine that instead of being transported to another world in another universe, Peabo was transported to our world, in the multiverse.

Wait a minute, multiverse? What's that?

It's a topic that has been debated in the physics community for years. A hypothesis that there are many (possibly infinite) copies of our universe that all exist in parallel to each other. Take the sum total of all the matter, energy, time, and space in all of these universes, and you have the "multiverse."

Although the idea has long been popular in science fiction and fantasy novels, many well-regarded figures in the scientific community (e.g. Stephen Hawking and Michio Kaku) are supporters of the concept. A related theory, known as counterpart theory, hypothesizes that in multiple copies of a given world, each item or event is not necessarily identical, but a copy in which variability may exist. Taking it one step further, there is something known as "possible world semantics." This is a mechanism by which one can conceive that the actual world we live in is but one of many possible worlds. And more to the point, for each different way the world could have evolved, there is a distinct and separate world that represents that outcome.

If that seems confusing, welcome to the multiverse.

However, I opted for something that is a bit closer to science reality, although still speculative. And that's where we enter the topic of brane cosmology.

Brane Cosmology:

I'll define this twice. First I'll speak in "science" terms, all of which you'll be able to look up if you like, then I'll explain it in layman's terms and it'll be much clearer why I referenced this in the story.

The central idea behind brane cosmology is that the visible, three-dimensional universe is restricted to a brane inside a higher-dimensional space, called the "bulk" (also known as "hyperspace").

If the additional dimensions are compact, then the observed universe contains the extra dimension, and then no reference to the bulk is appropriate. In the bulk model, at least some of the extra dimensions are extensive (possibly infinite), and other branes may be moving through this bulk.

Interactions with the bulk, and possibly with other branes, can influence our brane and thus introduce effects not seen in more standard cosmological models.

This can also explain why we see the "dark" influences at the galactic level for expansion being faster than expected for the known mass in the universe—in other words, it can be the influence of another universe in one of the n-dimensions that's causing the faster than expected expansion of our universe.

Okay, most of you are probably saying, "Those were all English words, but I don't know what you're talking about."

Let me further explain:

Imagine our entire universe has three dimensions. Front to back. Side to side. Up and down. Those are all easy concepts to grasp. In the science nerd community we often refer to the fourth dimension being time, and that's where the term space-time comes from, which you may have heard of before.

Okay, now let's zoom out from our universe and imagine it's all sort of a flat pancake. A membrane of sorts (thus the term brane cosmology). The idea being described here is very complex, but at its most coarse level, imagine there are many other pancakes that exist. An infinite amount, potentially. Each of those is a universe unto itself floating around in a bigger soup the scientists call the bulk—but for this explanation, let's suffice it to say that these branes are big flat objects floating in a soup next to each other.

Now the weird thing is, these branes, our universe being one of them, may be no more than a hair's breadth apart from each other. And yet, we cannot see or touch them from within our universe.

Admittedly this is freaky science, and without going too deep, it's totally speculative at this moment, but it's real science, theoretical physicists and such are actually doing research and studying the possibilities. From such studies come breakthroughs. You never know what may come. It wouldn't be the first time today's science fiction becomes tomorrow's science fact.

You want an example?

I'm so glad you asked, because here's a nerdy example that I enjoy tossing out: everyone hopefully remembers that in *Star Trek IV*, Scotty was talking about needing transparent aluminum for building some water tanks to hold two humpback whales. No? Well, that was mentioned back then, and it sounded cool, but there was no such thing.

Fast forward to today and we have aluminum oxynitride, which is a ceramic composed of aluminum, oxygen, and nitrogen. Oh, and it's clear.

There's plenty more examples of that sort of thing, but that's the fun one that may be in some reader's pop culture arsenal that I hope would be appreciated.

Tweaks to the laws of physics:

Okay, now that we've established some of the basics with regard to landing in a new world and what that actually means in the context of the story, the natural question for Peabo to ask and seek answers for is, "Now that I'm here, what's different?"

Like I said earlier, I wrote this story to be as grounded in reality as possible, despite some likely calling it a fantasy genre novel. To do that, I needed to establish what the rules were for this world.

The basic premise is that this world is very much like ours, with a few exceptions.

We'll see some different types of animals we're not used to seeing, but that's easily explainable due to biodiversity in evolution. Realistically, even the Earth has some very weird stuff in it, from anteaters to zebras, we have lots of examples of strange things, so it isn't much of a stretch to say I could get creative with the animals without breaking anyone's mind.

Yes, even the trees. We have plant life that is carnivorous, like the pitcher plant, Venus fly trap, etc. They're examples of plants that take on characteristics of animals.

There's very little reason we couldn't imagine some animals growing to resemble what we think of as plants. In fact, we have plenty of animals that resemble sticks and vines in the snake and insect world, so why not have animals resemble entire trees? Can something like an Ent be possible? I'd assert yes, and even in our world. It doesn't require much to imagine such a thing even on Earth.

However, in this new world, let's imagine that some things are a bit different than they are here at home.

Most people are aware that when people think, there's actual activity that's going on up in the brain. It's mostly chemical and electrical, but nonetheless, the act of thinking is a process that at a certain level involves signals going from one place to another. I want to move my finger, I'm thinking about an ice cream cone, I'm intrigued by a painting I'm seeing—all of those things involve signals going back and forth from various parts of the body.

With all that electrical activity, you'd think that someone might be able to hear what's going on up there in your head. Guess what: they can.

Today we study these electrical signals via something known as an electroencephalogram (EEG). Think of it like an x-ray video machine on steroids.

With all this energy flowing through our bodies, you'd think we could do some rather neat stuff with it, wouldn't you? In fact, there are folks who are doing real work on this. For instance, a high school kid recently won a prize at a science fair for an LED flashlight powered by nothing but the heat of a person's hand. Admittedly, it may only last for ten to twenty minutes, but it uses Peltier tiles to take advantage of generating electricity from the heat difference of someone's hand and the flashlight itself. For more information, look up the Peltier effect.

In additional to the real science of leveraging people's energy in our world, there's lots of people who believe that some folks have the ability to detect or read these signals flowing through our bodies and that's the basis of ESP and various other "capabilities" that have actually been studied with mixed results.

I took some of that speculation and tweaked it.

In Peabo's new world, imagine that some people have the ability to detect these signals. It's detectable in such a way as if it were the equivalent of a radio signal. That's not too much of a stretch. In addition, let's imagine that some people have the ability to manipulate the energy in their body or even in the outside world. Some practitioners of eastern meditation have shown the ability to control body temperature and other electrical signals such as biorhythms at will. Let's imagine that ability cranked up to the nth degree.

And the way I thought of it was in two classes of manipulation: manipulating your own energies, and manipulating outside energies.

This is the "cheat" so to speak that I used in the book, inasmuch as we don't have that ability today to any great extent, aside from examples I've mentioned to do this, but imagine if you could. If you were able to do such things, you wouldn't be very far from doing what we in our world would think of as magical feats. Whether it's pulling down lightning, reading thoughts, or infusing someone with energy to heal them.

I mention this largely because the things I talk about in the book may seem fantastical… or otherwise not possible. But using these tweaks as guardrails, I try not to deviate from that one basic premise of manipulating energy in various ways. Some of the other things that look like pure "magic" you may find aren't quite as magical as they seem.

Teleportation? Not possible, right? Keep reading, I explain that and various other things as well.

Time dilation:

If you'll recall at the beginning of the story, Nolan, Peabo's partner in this journey, was sent to this new world mere seconds before Peabo was, yet it quickly became evident that many years elapsed at their destination.

The concept of time dilation, where the perception of time elapsed varies greatly from one place to another, is all relative. What I mean by that is that we on Earth see time elapsing at a normal pace, one second is one second, one minute is one minute, etc. In the world that Peabo lands in, the same can be said. Yet it seems somewhat fantastical that such a difference in time occurred between Peabo's and Nolan's arrivals at a place.

It isn't. That's real science.

Well, this really has a lot to do with the concepts of general and special relativity. These concepts are things Einstein came up with to explain various things, but in relationship to time and space, let's look at special relativity.

For special relativity, observers from different reference points will measure mass and speed differently, because space and time will expand and contract so that the speed of light in a vacuum is constant to all observers.

Sometimes these things are best explained with an example. For instance, I may turn on a flashlight and the light pouring forth will be traveling at 300,000 kilometers per second, usually denoted as the symbol *c*. If I'm on a spaceship traveling at .5c and I turned on that same flashlight, the light pouring forth is also traveling at c.

I know for some of you, you're scratching your head and asking the following question. "If you were standing on Earth and could see the light from the spaceship rushing by, wouldn't the light be going 1.5c, and if it isn't, why not?"

For the person in the spaceship, all seems to be going normally, when in reality, time and space have warped around them. Time is moving slower for them, and distances are contracted. That's what allows the person in the spaceship and the person watching the spaceship to both observe things that comply with special relativity.

I'll leave the reader to stew on that for a moment, and I offer a good-natured apology if it is confusing, it *is* a complicated topic.

Now imagine the world Peabo comes from and the one he lands in are moving through the bulk (that big soup where the pancakes aka universes are floating around). Since both locations are moving, potentially at very high speeds, it would be reasonable to presume that time may elapse at very different speeds when you compare them directly, but folks in each of the worlds would never notice the difference.

Let me give one final example that was an experiment that confirmed this phenomenon of time dilation.

I'll refer you to the US Naval Observatory experiments by

Hafele and Keating, which documented what happened when four incredibly accurate atomic clocks were synchronized and two of them were flown around the world while the other two remained stationary. When the clocks were brought back together, the time had shifted ever so slightly for the clocks which had been traveling at jet-like speeds.

Even though these numbers aren't accurate to the above experiment, this would be like if one minute had elapsed while you were flying on the jet, and one minute and one second had elapsed on the Earth. Everyone you knew had aged one second more than you had.

Now imagine if the jet had been traveling at much higher speeds. Let's say the jet was traveling at 99.99999999% of the speed of light. If you were on the jet for one minute and came back to visit Earth, 49 days would have elapsed for them, while it was only one minute for you. Add three more 9's to that speed and it would 4.5 years, and three more, 134 years, etc.

The world is sometimes stranger than it seems, but those time differences are all very real.

Daytime Sensitivity:

When I began my writing journey, I never imagined I'd write anything that included a vampire, much less attempt to explain that away… well, Lord Dvorak was most certainly a vampire, and even though I won't attempt to science up what a vampire is, I did mention a few things that warrant some explanation.

In the book, before anyone knew what Dvorak was, I mentioned that he'd only be seen at night and that one of the characters attempted to explain that away based on a rumor the man had allergies, which were less an issue at night.

Most people may not be aware of it, but for those who suffer pollen allergies, they tend to find that their suffering diminishes at night, thus supporting the rationale behind Dvorak only being seen at night.

The reason this is true is actually very simple. In almost all cases, plants go somewhat dormant at night, when the sun is down, and the pollen isn't as exposed to the open air. Yes, even the plant life on Earth tends to take a nap at night.

I'll also note another thing about vampires and where some of that fear of the sun comes from. Sure, there's arguments that say evil hides in the shadows, but in reality there were some people who are suspected to have had a genetic disorder that resembled what we "know" is the vampire trait of extreme sensitivity to sunlight.

Today, we know that disorder as xeroderma pigmentosum (XP). It's a disorder that ultimately makes it very difficult for a person's body to detect the DNA damage associated with environmental factors such as exposure to ultraviolet light. This means that someone with XP can actually get severe sunburn after only seconds of exposure to direct sunlight.

It's actually a horrible problem with no cure, but the best modern treatments are to avoid sunlight, use heavy skin and eye creams, and mostly avoid the day.

In pre-modern times, you can imagine what kind of mystery such a disease would bring, and it helped reinforce some of the myths and legends around the vampire and its aversion to sunlight.

The Uncanny Valley:

In the story, we ran into a creature known as a skinwalker. Basically a doppelgänger, something that mimics the form of another.

Even though there is really no such thing as a skinwalker, I did mention something associated with those scenes that was quite real. It's called the uncanny valley.

"What is it?"

Even though I explained what it is in the book, I do want to emphasize that it is a real concept in today's social sciences. It has everything to do with our human reaction to things that we think look like another human.

When we look at a cartoon that is clearly drawn to mimic a human, but isn't, we find the images pleasing. And when psychologists graphed the likability against the similarity, we see an upward slope that shows to us that the more similar it is to a human, the more we tend to like it.

However, there comes a time when the similarity is getting to be very close, but it isn't quite perfect, and it's been observed that the likability suddenly falls off a cliff. We get an eerie revulsion to what we're seeing. And only when the image gets to be perfect and we're fooled into thinking it's real does the likability shoot back up. That trough between the two high points is what psychologists call the uncanny valley.

Many people don't like to think of us humans as a bunch of programming up in our head, but there are some very distinct presets that we have evolved with. Recognizing fellow humans is clearly one of those. And when something isn't quite right, we get a very adverse reaction.

That's exactly what Peabo saw and felt when encountering the skinwalker.

An area of silence:

There was a spell that Brodie used that dampened all the sound in a certain radius. That certainly seems like magic, and for the most part it is, yet there's a good deal of science to it. I say that only because I'd assert we could create such an effect using technology today. Furthermore, we already use it in many of our sound-dampening headphones and various other devices.

How does that work? It's actually very simple.

Sound is really a wave with two main characteristics: its amplitude and its wavelength.

By amplitude let's simply say that it's the power behind the sound, or the volume.

The wavelength, also known as the frequency, tells you the pitch, such as high or low. Humans can hear frequencies from as low as 20 hertz (waves per second) to 20,000 hertz.

If you could visualize what a sound wave looks like, it's got a peak and a trough, and when drawn on a graph paper you'll see a line going above and below the zero line as it is drawn from left to right. The zero line is in effect silence—a straight line running horizontally across the page.

So, at any one moment, you could say that a sound has a particular value from +n to -n.

Sound dampening works on this principle that says a particular sound wave has a value at a given time, and if you have a device that emits the opposite value, they in effect cancel each other out. What happens when a sound is canceled?

Silence.

And that's what happens with the more advanced headphones that advertise "active" dampening of sound. What that means is that the headphone actually has a little microphone that's listening to what's coming toward your ear. Almost instantaneously, it determines there's a sound at -3.5, and it emits a +3.5. Thus when your ear actually receives the sound, there's nothing to hear. The sound wave has been smothered.

So, even though Brodie seems to have cast an impossible example of magic, I'd argue that if technology could achieve it, is it really magical?

I'll leave that for the reader to decide.

Explosives:

I'll be brief on this, because I don't want to be accused of giving anyone any bad ideas, but we did see Peabo create a smoke bomb as well as a grenade.

All of the principles he used in its construction are completely accurate, even the details with regard to the bat guano… that's how black powder had been made for centuries.

With a little know-how and the proper ratios and care, explosives are relatively easy to make. Admittedly, these might be crude compared to some of the more modern style of chemical explosives that exist, and we might see Peabo crack more eggs in his experimentation in the future. After all, he did get his master's in chemical engineering.

Skin coloration—the blue people of Kentucky:

This may seem like an odd topic to cover in my addendum, but I assure you it'll make sense in a second.

When arriving in the new world, Peabo had an unusual patterning to his skin, and later in the book we encounter an alchemical "remedy" of sorts which allows him to in effect fade the pattern away so that he doesn't look unique.

Granted, the alchemy involved in such a thing is fictitious, but I did want to bring up cases where people's skin color did change drastically based on blood chemistry.

In the late nineteenth and twentieth century there was a family in Kentucky known as the Fugates, I mention them so that you can read more about them; it's actually a fascinating story. There's also some video if you look hard enough.

Nonetheless, they were famous in their small rural area for literally having blue skin. And we're not talking about a weird shade of pale, we're talking Smurf blue.

Ultimately it came down to a genetic disorder that was inherited, and even though it was a recessive trait, in those parts, the genetic diversity wasn't all that great, so you did have in a small area this rather expansive family with blue people in it.

It had to do with something called methemoglobinemia, which overall affected the blood chemistry giving the blood a brown coloration instead of red. And oddly enough, that translated into these otherwise Caucasian people turning blue.

When treated with certain medicines, it was possible for the blue skin to lose its naturally blue quality, but that simply gave me the idea of the alchemist solution.

So, is the idea of drinking some sort of potion and having it affect your skin color a crazy one? Not really.

Just remember the Fugates of Kentucky if there's ever a doubt.

Communication Rings:

In this story, I introduced a pair of gold rings that people can use to communicate. When one person taps or squeezes their ring, the person carrying the matching ring will feel the tap or squeeze in their ring. The idea for this originated from within a deep dark cave in the world of particle physics. A cave called quantum entanglement. This is the same science that Einstein dubbed, "Spooky action at a distance."

Briefly explained, quantum entanglement is the idea that through a variety of methods a single item can be split into two parts where each of the parts ends up sharing an unseen link even though they may have a relatively great distance between them.

It seems like fantasy, doesn't it? But believe me, it's a real thing.

This is most easily imagined as a photon of light being split (via a special type of beam splitter) such that each corresponding half can be affected in ways that affect the other. Quantum entanglement has already been experimentally verified both at the subatomic level as well as at the macroscopic level using two small diamonds.

This is a very active area of research in academic circles today. I would greatly appreciate it if any of my readers with the proper background and wherewithal would kindly advance the concept. Because I want one of these rings.

Teleportation:

I used an example that of course seemed like utter fantasy, and frankly I thought was kind of cool: the magic mailbox.

The prelate wanted to send something to Brodie, and somehow or another, the item just appeared in Brodie's box. We've seen such things in *Star Trek* and always known them to be science fantasy.

Very much like the telegraph must have seemed like magic to those in the 1800s, the concept of moving an object from one place to another seems like magic to us. Or at least, like science fiction.

Would it surprise you to learn that the most fundamental aspects of teleportation are science fact?

Granted, the teleportations demonstrated to date have been at the atomic level, but nonetheless, real experiments have demonstrated some measure of success. For instance, particles have actually been teleported up to eighty-nine miles between two of the Canary Islands.

Suffice it to say that this is a topic that is vastly too complex for true engineering-level discussion as an addendum to this novel, but the topics one could research further if you are interested in learning more would be Quantum Entanglement and Quantum Teleportation.

Another fascinating scientific topic that demonstrates that teleportation is theoretically possible, at least on paper, is the concept of a wormhole. This is, simply put, the ability for two points in space-time to be connected together as a "shortcut" of sorts. Imagine if you were standing in Spain and wanted to travel to New Zealand on the other side of the world. If there were a direct flight, it would be approximately 12,000 miles. But if there were a wormhole between these two locations, it would only be roughly 8,000 miles. Such shortcuts are the exotic areas where science fiction meets the world of the possible. Not only could one potentially be zapped from one place to another, a thing such as a wormhole can even establish a means to travel backward in time.

Teleportation—the Divine 3D Printer version

Okay, Rothman—now you've gone completely off your rocker. A divine 3D printer? What gives?

All right, you got me—there is no such thing, but since I mentioned *Star Trek* and the teleporter, I wanted to talk just briefly about what it would actually take to do such a thing: transport someone from one place to another.

Here's a strange question for you: what does the number seven octillion represent?

Well, before we go there, let's imagine we're looking at a bitmap image of a girl.

The picture is roughly about 700K in size (assume 8-bit color depth), about 700 pixels by 1000 pixels. It's a 2D representation of her, and let's for sake of simplicity call her Vanessa.

So, even though we've captured Vanessa's image in 700,000 pieces of data, we wouldn't know much more about her other than the very basic image. What's Vanessa's blood type? Is her hair dyed? Of course we don't know that.

Yet we've transmitted Vanessa's image across the internet.

How much data would it actually be if we wanted to transmit Vanessa herself—not just her image, but every bit of information that represents her physical being? Every atom, connection, scar, brain cell, etc. If we had a magic machine (all technology we don't understand is often thought of as magic) that could transport Vanessa from where she is to wherever your computer is, how much data are we talking about?

That's where we go back to the number seven octillion.

That's roughly how many atoms someone her size is composed of.

How big is that number?

Well, think of 7 times 10 to the 27th power.

Or more easily said, 7 billion billion billion.

Or 7,000,000,000,000,000,000,000,000,000.

To put that in perspective, it is expected that in 2017, roughly 1.1 zettabytes (or 1.1 times 10^21 bytes) of information will be transmitted across the entire internet.

So—I suppose it'll be a while before we can build a transporter for human-sized things. In the meantime, we'll have to just deal with pictures.

However, it may not be that far away. I vividly remember buying in the early '80 s a 156K floppy drive for $599, and today, I can buy a 6TB drive for half that price. That's a 3,846,153,800% increase in 35 years. So in another 35 years, I should be able to buy, for roughly the same price, a 230 exabyte drive, which is roughly 0.2 zettabytes. Not quite where we need to be, but getting closer.

Maybe, just maybe, by the end of the 21st century we'll have the capacity to entertain moving people in the blink of an eye. Of course, there's lots of other complicated things that would need to be worked out, but this gives you an inkling of just how much information that is.

Where did I get the original number?

Let's start with a 70kg person is:

65% by weight O

24% by weight C

10% by weight H

(Ignoring the other 1% for simplicity)

65% of 70 is 45.5kg/16g = M

Solve for M = 2843M of O

24% of 70 is 16.8kg/12g = 1400M

10% of 70 is 7kg/1g = 7000M

7000+1400+2843 = 11243M

11243 * 6.02x10^23 = 6.768286e27

Also, I'm presuming some lossless compression to offset the necessary metadata that would be needed to maintain attributes of the atom positions, etc.

Out-of-Body Experience/Remote Viewing:

In the preview of the next book, *The Sage's Tower*, I did talk a bit about out-of-body experiences. We've heard of folks who claim to have had them, but would you believe there's been lots of studies done on such things? Often out-of-body experiences and remote viewing go hand in hand. The former is where a person feels that their consciousness is separated from their physical being and can float outside their own body. Remote viewing is where one takes that concept to an extreme and can see things in distant places.

The out-of-body experience is interesting, but as you can imagine, being able to see things that are happening far away has many practical applications—especially for the military.

It shouldn't be a big surprise that remote viewing is a field of research that's been invested in by some relatively serious organizations in various governments around the world. The Stargate Project is just one example, which set the protocols for testing of out-of-body experiences. A previously top-secret project conducted by the US government's Defense Intelligence Agency, the project's mission was to investigate psychic phenomena such as remote viewing for military applications.

We now know that remote viewing research was conducted by the CIA from 1972 through 1995, when the project was "officially" canceled and information debunking remote viewing was declassified.

Some might question why it took twenty-three years to determine that remote viewing was impossible. Conspiracy theorists might posit that there is no possible way the government would have let a project last so long if it wasn't yielding results. And if it was yielding results, does that mean the declassified statements debunking it are a mere ruse?

I'll leave that as fodder for the reader to contemplate. I, your humble reporter (author), am only noting things that stimulate my "what if" writing instinct.

ABOUT THE AUTHOR

I am an Army brat, a polyglot, and the first person in my family born in the United States. This heavily influenced my youth by instilling in me a love of reading and a burning curiosity about the world and all of the things within it. As an adult, my love of travel and adventure has driven me to explore many exotic locations, and these places sometimes creep into the stories I write.

I hope you've found this story entertaining.

- Mike Rothman

For occasional news on my latest work, join my mailing list at:
https://mailinglist.michaelarothman.com/new-reader

You can find my blog at: www.michaelarothman.com
Facebook at: www.facebook.com/MichaelARothman
And on Twitter: @MichaelARothman

Lightning Source UK Ltd.
Milton Keynes UK
UKHW011818201221
395986UK00001B/269